Dear Reader,

Are you like me? Do
times I like a story with an element of mystery in it, on other occasions I enjoy a sexy read; there are times when I love my romance novels spiced with a little humour and others when I look forward to a warm and involving family-centred story. How about you?

Each month, I work hard to provide a balanced list for you, to ensure that every ***Scarlet*** reader's taste is catered for. As you can imagine, this is quite a difficult feat, particularly as I may suddenly be offered four similar stories – four tales of romantic suspense, for example, all at one time. So far, from your letters and questionnaires, it seems that we're getting the mix just right. But do let us know, won't you, if there is anything you particularly want to see more of on *your* list. Or is there something you think is missing from the ***Scarlet*** list? In the light of the current interest in Jane Austen, would you like ***Scarlet*** to include some Regency romances?

Keep those letters and questionnaires coming, won't you?

Till next month,

Sally Cooper

SALLY COOPER,
Editor-in-Chief – ***Scarlet***

About the Author

Come Home Forever is **Jan McDaniel**'s twenty-first published romance novel. A native of Detroit, Michigan, she now makes her home in Chattanooga, Tennessee, with her husband Bruce, their two teenagers, and an assortment of dogs and cats.

Before turning to full-time fiction writing, Jan worked as a newspaper reporter and technical editor.

Jan is always delighted to hear from her readers, so please write to her, care of: East Tennessee Romance Writers, PO Box 22193, Chattanooga, Tennessee 37422–2193, USA.

*Other **Scarlet** titles available this month:*

WICKED IN SILK – Andrea Young
NEVER SAY NEVER – Tina Leonard
WOMAN OF DREAMS – Angela Drake

JAN McDANIEL

COME HOME FOREVER

SCARLET

Enquiries to:
Robinson Publishing Ltd
7 Kensington Church Court
London W8 4SP

First published in the UK by Scarlet, 1996

A copy of the British Library Cataloguing in Publication data is available from the British Library

ISBN 1-85487-717-8

Printed and bound in the EC

10 9 8 7 6 5 4 3 2 1

To my husband Bruce . . . always

CHAPTER 1

Matt Rollins looked up just in time to see an aged white Volvo creeping up the country road, its bright exterior a stark contrast against the darkening Texas sky. As the vehicle crested the horizon, his troubled blue eyes intensified to match the color of his denim shirt.

What now? he thought irritably. Hadn't he coped with enough headaches for one day? He knew this car. He'd seen it in town this morning, parked at the curb with Sierra ushering out a striking dark-haired boy on the passenger side.

She should have known better than to come here. But then, common sense had never ranked among Sierra's strong points. If it had, she never would have messed with the likes of him in the first place. Matt couldn't afford to get all tied up thinking about her right now. After banishing her from his mind for over a decade, he wasn't disposed to open his consciousness nor anything else to her.

A gust of raw wind blew over him, rustling his

hair and nearly taking his hat. After an unseasonably warm and sunny November afternoon, a 'blue norther', a blast of Arctic air that could drop the temperature as much as forty degrees within minutes, was pushing through. The threatening backdrop suited his turbulent mood.

He kept his eyes riveted on the road, hoping the car would pass without turning. Approaching the ribbon drive, it slowed. He saw the blinker flashing.

'Bad weather comin',' his sister, who was leaning against the fence alongside him, observed. Leeann was still wearing the church dress she'd put on to visit her husband in the hospital earlier. An antiseptic smell clung to her clothes.

'Go in the house,' Matt ordered distractedly, glancing around the back of the house where his niece and nephew were playing on the rusted swing seat. 'Take the kids in.'

Wrinkling her brow, Leeann followed her brother's pensive glance. As she too recognized the car, her pretty features scrunched into a scowl. 'I'll be damned!' she declared incredulously. 'She thinks she's coming here? I can't believe her nerve. She acts like she owns this town. Well, I got news for Mrs Davenport . . .'

'Go on inside, Leeann. I'll get rid of her.'

'After what she did to you, Matt? I can't see how you could bring yourself to speak to her. *You* go in. It's my fault you're here, and I won't have her botherin' you. I'll tell her you're not here.'

Matt exhaled heavily. 'This is a small town, Leeann. If I'm going to be here a while, I'm going to run into her sooner or later,' he told her. 'Might as well get it over with.'

Leeann stood her ground. 'She changed you, Matt. She chose another man without even telling you to your face she loved someone else, and now that he's dead she deserves to be alone.'

He shot her a look so reminiscent of their father that Leeann shrank back. 'No one is alone because they deserve it,' he stated. Seeing her reaction, he realized he had frightened her and softened his tone. 'Do you think, my lunatic sister, that after ten years, a marriage and a child she's come to beg to have me back?'

Leeann kicked at a stick. 'If she had a lick of sense, she would. You're too good for her, Matt, and you always were. I told you nothin' but trouble would come from mixin' with those rich folks. But no matter what she's come for, I don't want her around. Why, when I see her in town she doesn't even speak.'

'And I suppose you rush up to her all friendly-like?'

'I can't believe you're defendin' her.'

'I'm not defending her. I just want to let it go. Lord knows, if *I* can, you should be able to. It's been a long time, and none of it matters any more.

My being back here has nothing to do with her. Now go round up your children. Anything I've got to say to Sierra isn't fit for anyone else's ears. I'll be in in a minute.'

After eyeing him skeptically, Leeann slipped sullenly towards the house. 'You watch out. Don't let her get you to feelin' sorry for her.'

Behind her, Matt squared his shoulders. He had never wanted to see Sierra Ross Davenport again, never wanted to imagine Ben Davenport touching her, sowing his seed in her. But now, her car was pulling to a stop a few yards away. Why the hell had she come?

Ignoring his sudden overwhelming urge to light a cigarette, he took a deep breath and approached the car. Each step brought him closer to a past he'd thought he'd left far behind.

Sierra jerked the car to a halt, contemplating the dashboard as she debated whether she could go through with this. Damn Sam. If only he hadn't called her this afternoon. He'd meant well enough; nobody knew horses the way Matt Rollins did. And Sam had heard of her predicament. He was pretty upset at his grandson for turning away a hard-working man like Matt, especially when everyone knew Matt's brother-in-law was lying in St Anthony's Hospital with both legs crushed. But he couldn't argue with Duncan's contention that Matt was just passing through and not dependable enough to hire. Besides, Sam had pretty much turned his ranch over to Dunc, and with the business being the way it was, he'd already hired all the help he could afford.

Sam wouldn't have called her from Houston if this wasn't important to him. And considering the circumstances, he didn't need to be worrying over it. She felt compelled to help the old man keep the promise he'd made Matt. Not that she saw any choice.

For the past eight months she'd been relying on Tom Wayling to manage her stables. What a shock when Sheriff Boulder had come and arrested him last night. Her stomach was still roiling at the memory of harboring one of the most notorious con-men in the southwest, allowing him to stay on the place with her and Will there alone most of the time. Dwelling on it gave her the shudders. After the way Ben had died, she felt vulnerable enough without this.

Fortunately she'd still been in too much of a stupor from Ben's sudden death to be anything more than flattered by Tom's suave good looks and cunning charm. All she could think of was keeping the stables running and caring for her son. The last thing she wanted in her life was another man. Apparently Tom had settled for an out-of-the way place to hide. Unknown to her, he'd cajoled a string of wealthy women out of their money. The sheriff's implication that he might have intended to prey on her was a bad joke. All she owned was an empty pocketbook, a rapidly dwindling savings account, an old car, and few acres of land.

Without Tom, she was stuck with a barnful of horses who needed more tending than she could manage, riding students due tomorrow afternoon, and a distrust of strangers.

This wouldn't happen again. This time she was going to learn the business herself and never leave herself to anyone's mercy. All her life she'd depended on other people – her father, Ben, Tom – leaving herself helpless to their whims. No more. Her sole cherished asset was Will, and she was determined to provide for herself and her son.

But to do that she had to bend this one last time, and to Matt of all people. How he must despise her. She dreaded facing him. But she'd trust him quicker than she would risk having another stranger on the place. Once upon a time, she would have handed her life over to him in a heartbeat. But thinking about that now would only complicate what she had to do. Falling in love with Matt had been the biggest mistake of her life. Not because, as her father had claimed, his family was socially unacceptable. But because she'd known before she gave herself to him, in heart and spirit and body, that he'd never be hers to keep. Being young and reckless, she hadn't worried about tomorrow.

After growing up in a sterile home with her father and a string of faceless housekeepers, she'd wanted lots of children some day. When she'd described her dream to Matt, he'd countered that her imaginary big, loving family was an impossible fantasy. He told her he'd vowed never to bring a child into the world. Sierra had felt as though steel doors had closed between them. But knowing Matt wasn't likely to become her husband failed to restrain her youthful heart. She was too intrigued by his raw, male, compelling aura, the tenderness he masked in all but the most intimate moments, his bold determination and integrity. All that had mattered to her were their stolen hours together when he unraveled for her the mysteries of expressing love in exciting ways, lessons all her family's wealth couldn't have bought her.

At the point that she'd realized she couldn't envisage a future without Matt, she'd begun praying that, once he'd opened his heart to her, he'd realize how much love he was capable of sharing. But all too soon she'd run out of time and everything else had got in the way. Maybe they'd been destined from the outset to be apart.

Now, snapping her neck up, she watched Matt approach. His expression was grim, but the sight of him triggered a wave of warring emotions she'd believed herself immune to. Despite her apprehension, her body warmed as if possessing a memory of its own.

The change in his appearance shocked her. If she hadn't recognized him by his straight, steady stride, and the way he held his head high, she might have mistaken him for a vagrant. A scraggly beard shadowed his handsome face, its sharp features enhanced by maturity. His shirt and jeans were faded and frayed. The light she remembered had vanished from his eyes.

As he neared the car, she sensed his power and his masculinity. Nothing could diminish or mask that. Matt Rollins carried something fine and proud inside him that few people looked close enough to see. She'd never been able to escape it. Nor had she understood why he wanted that nobility to end with him.

Her stomach churning, she suddenly could not sit still and await this confrontation. Pushing open the door, she emerged from her car.

In spite of her resolve, she was trembling as Matt halted mere inches before her. His familiar scent, a hint of musk and leather now tainted by stale tobacco, made her dizzy. She felt the heat of him in the rapidly chilling air, and she saw contempt in eyes clear as spring water, eyes that had once looked upon her with sleepy contentment and proud adoration.

Her skin heated. She knew she deserved every ounce of scorn he could dish out. She cared only about getting past it.

'Sierra,' he greeted her non-committally, his voice husky and solemn. He did not tip the weather-beaten Stetson sitting at an angle atop the headful of wavy, coffee-colored hair that jutted over his collar.

She set one hand on her churning stomach as his eyes raked over her.

The wind kicked up suddenly. 'Hello, Matt,' she replied, reminding herself why she had come here. After all these years, another lifetime as Ben Davenport's wife, she shouldn't be feeling anything. But she supposed something about a first love remained a part of you forever, no matter how badly it had turned out. She attributed her reaction to nostalgia, something akin to hearing an old song on the radio. Regardless of how much she wanted to, she couldn't stand before him and pretend he'd never touched her.

Matt studied the woman with the delicate bone-structure, curves sloping as subtly as the nearby hills, alert brown eyes fringed by long dark lashes peering at him from a pretty oval face, lips the color of cranberries puckered in perplexity. Her thick black hair with a brownish cast no longer cascaded down her back but was stylishly cut to feather her face and fall across the nape of her neck. She resembled a little girl playing grown-up in her black pumps, gray skirt, and a silver-blue silk blouse too thin to protect her from the cooling air. A tiny circle pendant set with diamond chips hung from a gold chain around her neck, dangling over her breastbone at the open collar of her blouse. He caught the scent of jasmine and ginger wafting from her skin.

A searing pull in his loins told him he wanted her physically as much as ever. God, she was as addictive and as poisonous as nicotine.

But he had standards and pride. And, as he'd told Leeann, Widow Davenport certainly hadn't driven all the way out here looking for a good time.

'You look classy,' he noted without enthusiasm.

Sierra folded her arms across her chest to ward off the cold. Her nipples tightened, and she wasn't sure the plummeting temperature was totally to blame.

She cast him a hard, appraising look. 'You look like a scruffy old prospector who's been on the trail a few months too long.'

A tiny gleam flickered in his eyes, the corners of his mouth curling slightly. Raising one hand, he rubbed his grizzled jaw. She'd always been straightforward with a wicked sense of humor.

But he wasn't playing games today. 'You didn't come here to discuss my grooming,' he countered.

When he met her glance, he knew something about her had changed, aside from the new hairstyle and the sophisticated clothing that made her look older than she was. She'd always been quick to laugh, open and loving and as high-spirited and impulsive as a wild mustang. Now, she was as subdued and distant as a whipped colt.

'No, I didn't,' she admitted. 'Sam Burke told me you were looking for a job.'

He raised his chin defensively. 'Sam's not even in town.'

'Dunc called and told him you'd come around today. Sam phoned me from Houston.'

Matt shrugged. 'So?' He didn't need to be reminded he'd failed at something he'd counted on as a sure thing. Hadn't Sam promised if he ever came back, if he ever needed a job, there'd be one here for him? Sam was the only person – well, one of two people – who'd ever promised him anything, and he sure wasn't the first to let him down. Sam had been the only one left he'd thought he could count on. Matt figured he should have been cured long ago of taking people at their word.

'So. I have one.' She shivered.

He gaped incredulously. 'You're kidding.'

'We've had some trouble, and my manager is gone. I need someone to run my stables. You know horses better than anyone.'

His expression tightened. 'No, Sierra, I mean you're kidding if you think I'm going to come be your hired hand. The last thing I'll ever need is your charity or Davenport money. And I'll be damned if I'll ease your conscience by working for you. My coming back here is about helping my sister's family, not giving you a chance to make amends for the past. Once I'm sure Leeann and the kids are OK, I'm out of here. Don't insult me this way. Or yourself. Now go home. Leeann doesn't want you here.'

Sierra didn't budge. She hadn't expected this meeting to be cordial. 'Matt, now that you've made your speech, please, hear me out. I know what you must think of me. I wouldn't have come here if I could see any way around it. I'm in no position to hand out charity. Ben didn't leave us with much. I've already had to sell two of the horses. I don't want to sell any more. Things are different for me now. I have a son to support. Don't you understand, I'm asking out of desperation and not on a whim? Do you think I enjoy standing here and having you glowering at me the way you are? This isn't any easier for me than it is for you.'

A blue cast tinted her skin. Let her stand here and freeze if she's determined to, Matt told himself. Cold air seldom bothered him. He doubted she could be as hard-up as she claimed when she had access to both her father's and the Davenports' money.

Nevertheless, he softened his harsh gaze. 'Why don't you ask your family for help?'

Sighing impatiently, she shifted her stance. 'I'm on my own here. I'm not asking anyone to bail me out.'

Matt knew well what that was like. He'd been standing alone most of his life.

'Why?'

'It's a long story, and it's personal.'

'Why don't you check with the employment commission?'

'Because I won't allow just anyone to stay on the ranch with us. Will is at an impressionable age. And because I want someone with enough patience to teach me how to run the place. I can't afford to hire the wrong person this time.'

Matt watched the pulse beating at the base of her throat. He knew she was telling the truth or she wouldn't have sacrificed her dignity to plead with him. And he couldn't help thinking of the young boy who'd recently lost his father. Still, he wasn't about to let a moment of sentimentality dim his principles. Not that he still cared about her one way or the other, of course. Over the years, he'd enjoyed plenty of other women. He'd told some of them he loved them without meaning it because they'd wanted that, and he never bedded a woman he didn't feel affection towards. But Sierra was the only one he'd said that to and meant it. And he suspected, no matter how far he pushed her from his mind, she lingered there, souring him against really risking love for any woman. Allowing himself to love her had been like falling down a ravine, and he been badly bruised when he'd hit bottom. Maybe because he'd been naïve enough for a while to believe her when she'd professed to love him. Yeah, he'd been young, and he'd believed anything was possible. Almost as stupid as his ma and her tea-leaves. In his book, there were mistakes and there were sins: a sin was making the same mistake the second time. And he sure didn't need to be looking at her every day, remembering how she'd deceived him, remembering emotions flowing as rampantly as his hormones.

No, he couldn't work for someone he distrusted. The safest distance for him was too far away to see those full breasts straining under that skimpy fabric, too far away to have his reason clouded by the fragrance of tropical spices, too far to trace the outline of her lips with his eyes and remember their taste.

'I hope you find someone,' he said, tipping his smudged Stetson and spinning on one heel. 'But it's not going to be me.'

'Matt, please,' she urged, running after him. Matt stopped. He didn't need Sierra chasing him into the house where Leeann would have at her. At the moment his baby sister was like a caged lioness, seeking a target on which to spring her pent-up tension. Leeann was sick with worry over managing her home and family until her husband recovered. Leeann's anxiety had nothing to do with Sierra, and he wasn't going to give his sister the chance to vent it on her.

Sierra's hand fell lightly on his sleeve. He gazed down at it with the same look of calculating annoyance he might have given a tarantula crawling up his arm. She withdrew her hand.

Looking down on the face of an angel, he felt his armor chipping. But he heeded his sister's warning.

'I can appreciate your situation. But for one thing, I need to be here and help my sister with the kids so she can be with her husband. For another, considering our past, I don't think the two of us camped out at your place alone is a good idea.'

Sierra maintained her calm demeanor, but color bloomed in her cheeks. 'If that's what you're worried about, the manager's quarters are in a building separate from the house. As long as the horses are cared for and everyone gets their riding lessons, you can come and go as you please. The students don't arrive until after lunch, and there aren't many. I have two hands and a part-time stable boy who'll be working under your supervision.'

'Are you sure it's just not a little too lonely out there by yourself?' he asked wickedly. 'Got some cold nights coming?'

As utter horror seized her expression, he immediately regretted his heartless barb. He wasn't as callous as his comment implied. The frustration of having loved her long after he had lost her had finally caught up with him. She must have loved Ben to have married him, must still be grieving for him. The truth was, even with Ben dead, Matt's blood boiled at the thought of his having possessed rights Matt had once come to think of as his.

She drew her hand back, and in the nick of time he realized she was about to slap him. He caught her wrist in mid-air.

'I'm sorry, Sierra,' he said quickly, still holding her slim wrist. Pain flashed in her dark eyes, but he knew he wasn't hurting her physically. God knew he didn't want to become that kind of monster, lashing out in self-defense at everyone who hurt him. He wouldn't be like his father, the master of verbal torture.

She wrenched at her arm. He released her, but she continued meeting his gaze. 'I expected you'd have a poor opinion of me. You never forget, and you sure don't forgive. But you were never cruel. You're not the same man I used to know, and I was wrong to have come here,' she excused herself quickly. 'I thought we could manage to be friends again. I know how things must have looked to you, but I intended to tell you about Ben. His mother rushed to put the engagement announcement in the paper without telling me.'

'If you had such fine intentions, why marry Ben at all?' he asked.

Sierra balled her hands into fists. She couldn't

tell him it was because she hoped that by some miracle she wouldn't have to. She could never explain.

'I loved my husband,' she proclaimed, meeting his defiant stare. 'Since his death, I haven't looked at another man, and I don't intend to. You needn't fear I'm trying to seduce you. I've more important things on my mind.'

'Fear? Hardly. I'm merely sparing you the trouble.'

'If I were looking for a man to keep my bed warm, I assure you I wouldn't have to look far to find one less arrogant. In all this time, hasn't it occurred to you that I wasn't the only one at fault?'

Matt shrugged. 'So you expect me to step in and rescue you from a mess you've gotten yourself into and just pretend we're casual acquaintances?'

'Yes. Look, I don't want to argue. And I don't think you want this any more than I do. We've both made mistakes. I'm offering you employment. I have no intention of harassing you sexually or otherwise. I know you're trying to help your sister, and I don't know of a single rancher who's hiring this time of year.'

Matt leaned to one side and adjusted his hat. 'Suppose I were to consider your proposition. My mind might clear a tad if you were to come clean about a few things. It's damn hard to forget things I keep wondering about.'

She drew in a deep breath, forcing herself to meet his gaze. She swallowed hard. 'Such as?'

'That last night you met me by the creek was the night before that wedding announcement came out in the paper. You were making love with me like the world was about to end when you had already promised Ben Davenport you'd marry him. That's what always got to me, Sierra. Doesn't that strike you as being a mite two-faced? I've always wondered whether you'd just come from being with him, or whether you went to him later.'

Sierra's eyes burned but remained dry. His reference to the abandonment she'd known in his arms pricked her nerves. She didn't need to hear his reminder of it. Now, she knew what she'd feared all these years was true. He'd left town believing her a whore.

But she refused to show how deeply that troubled her. She'd shed all her tears for Matt and for herself years ago. She'd done what she had to.

'It wasn't like that. I wasn't sleeping with him.'

'I guess you might as well have been. You'd already made up your mind to marry him. Was it some kind of game I didn't know the rules to? You and Ben moved with a fast crowd. Was it a dare, the thrill of venturing into forbidden territory?'

'I was never that flighty, and you know it.'

'Well, whatever I did, I took it serious. If you were just looking for entertainment, you should have been straight with me. Hell, I would have accommodated you.'

'Seriously enough to make it clear you were passing time until you saved enough money to leave town? If you proposed, I didn't hear it. Stop this, Matt. I'm not going to apologize for the choice I made. Vindictiveness doesn't become you, and I've taken all the humiliation I'm going to tolerate. I've only withstood this much because I regret how everything must have appeared to you. I hadn't intended to handle the situation that way. But letting you carry it this far was a mistake. You think I was a spoiled rich princess, always taking anything I wanted and getting my own way. Maybe I did take life as lightly as you took it seriously. And I have paid for that. But I swear, things weren't the way they looked to you. Other forces were involved; my father . . .'

'You were twenty years old. If your father or someone else was pressing you to marry Ben, you could have refused. I would have helped you. I would have moved Jupiter for you.'

Sierra chewed back a reflective bittersweet smile. If she remembered correctly, many times he had. But God, she didn't need to dwell on that now.

Honesty was part of her nature. But at this point she'd become entangled in the never-ending web of topping one lie with another to safeguard the original one. Matt deserved the truth, but she couldn't tell him everything, even now. 'I truly cared for you, Matt. But marrying Ben was my decision. I didn't come here seeking forgiveness. I came only to offer a business proposition. Sam hasn't forgotten he once promised you work whenever you needed it. But you've been away so long, he's not in a position to undermine his grandson's authority. I suppose he'd hoped I could help him keep his word. I'm sorry to have intruded. Please apologize to your sister for me and express my regrets over her husband's accident. I'd tell her myself, but I know she doesn't like me. And, despite your hostility, it is good to see you again.'

Matt shot a glance at the white frame house nearby. Sierra had betrayed him, and if he were the only one concerned here he'd never set foot on her property or accept one cent of her money. But he thought of the tired lines in his sister's face and the two round-eyed little kids who kept asking where their Daddy was. Damn, but if he didn't need a quick pay-check. She was right about nobody hiring. This time of year folks got too carried away with goodwill towards men to care about a fella needing work.

And damn if she didn't look small and lost standing out her in the merciless wind. He couldn't stop those old protective feelings kicking in. They could dance around it all day, but the fact was, he'd come from the wrong part of town for her ever to have really been his. He'd known it in his gut from that very first day.

She wouldn't have come here, subjected herself to his lingering bitterness, unless she was desperate.

She turned to go.

'Wait, Sierra.'

'Hmm?'

His expression grew impassive. Sierra had found his outright contempt less alarming.

'You're right. No reason the past should keep me from accepting honest work. As long as we understand I'm doing this for my sister, not for you, I might help you for a couple of days until you can find a real manager. But I want cash at the end of each day.'

Her face brightened. 'Of course. Thank you, Matt. I'll see you in the morning, then?'

'I said maybe. I'll have to think it over. I've got serious reservations about working for you. I'm not sure I can even if I want to.'

Her countenance darkened as though he'd intentionally tricked her. If it weren't for the thought of Will flashing through her mind, she would have told him to forget it. Instead, she opened the car door and reached inside to retrieve her pocketbook. Extracting a scrap of paper and a pen, she jotted something on it and handed it to him.

'I promise you, you'll be in charge. Call me later and let me know. As soon as possible, please. I've got to make some arrangements.'

His hand brushed hers as he accepted the paper, sending a disconcerting gradual warmth up her arm. She avoided his eyes. Her body was responding to him as if it were independent of her brain, oblivious to the heartache he'd inflicted. She shook off the feeling. Reviving her old attraction to him was an indulgence she couldn't afford; she'd paid heavily for succumbing to it once. And she would spit nails before his accusation that she was trying to lure him into her bed was proved true. But in the light of her lack of interest, why couldn't she stop thinking of it?

His eyes lingering on her, he nodded. 'I'll let you know tonight, either way. I just need a while. It won't take long.'

'Thank you.'

'I am sorry about your loss. What I said . . .'

'I expected you to be angry. Forget it. My skin's tougher than it used to be.'

He watched her get inside the car and start the engine, warming her palms over the heater vents before she shifted to back up.

Needing a minute before facing Leeann, he crossed the yard back to the white wooden fence that separated the Wiltons' property from a vast open pasture. Across the distance, he watched cows grazing under the threatening blue-gray sky.

Damn, it was hard to look at that woman without hankering for another taste of her. Getting anywhere near her was like playing catch with a hot iron. After he'd all but called her a whore, she'd probably rather wrestle a grizzly bear than come within ten feet of him. One thing was for sure: if she'd come here to amuse herself, she wouldn't have stayed long enough to endure his rough talk. She must really need him. As he recalled, she'd barely known one end of a horse from the other.

Besides, she'd been adamant about having loved Ben. Why should he doubt that? He realized he'd always been hoping there'd be some other explanation for her marriage. Just to salvage his damaged pride.

Even under his barrage of accusations, she'd held on to her dignity. He couldn't help admiring her grit. Still, he couldn't imagine himself watching her all day long and staving off his reckless yearning to touch her one more time. Why the devil had Sam called her? Sam didn't know about them – almost nobody did. Matt supposed Sam believed he'd found a clever way to make good his promise. If he turned her down, his old friend was going to take it personally.

Matt picked a rumpled cigarette pack from his pocket, extracted a cigarette and lit it with a match.

Until now, he hadn't allowed himself to think about what being back here meant. Digging his boot heels into Texas soil again reawakened images of the long-forgotten dream that had once kept him alive. The kinship he felt with this land got him to thinking about wanting a piece of it to call his own. Along the way, Sierra had been drawn into that dream, and when everything went sour he'd abandoned it.

He'd learned long ago how dangerous his visions could be and accepted the wisdom of denying them. Maybe Daddy had been right to call him a fool. Too much pain lingered here.

He could hear the old man's voice. 'The trouble with you, boy, is your ma has turned your head with a bunch of nonsense, makin' you think you're something better than a workin' man's son. You'll see where all your grand dreams get ya. The sooner you understand where you fit in and resign yourself to stayin' there, the easier life will go for ya.'

But he'd always had a fire inside him that wouldn't allow him to give up or stay where he was supposed to. Daddy had despised him for it.

Until a few days ago, he'd believed nothing would have brought him home. At the moment, he was wondering whether coming hadn't been a mistake. He'd figured giving Leeann and the kids a hand would be easy.

What had he expected? Life here had gone on without him. Folks weren't going to stop and turn things around just because he was back. Could he hold Sam to such an ancient promise?

Leaning against the fence, he scanned the expanse of sloping hills.

Turning to one side, he studied the flat, rectangular white frame house nestled amid a grove of maples and live oaks. Lace curtain panels hung over the windows, and the front porch boasted two rockers and an assortment of potted plants. Unlike him, Leeann had got everything she wanted. She expected little enough. Now, with two young children to care for, no money coming in and medical bills to pay, the fragile foundation of the life she and Jerry had made was crumbling.

Guiltily he puffed on the half-finished cigarette he held between long, work-toughened fingers. Over the past three years he'd managed only to half-quit, tapering down to two or three cancer sticks on a good day. Right now, his addiction demanded soothing. But, since arriving, he indulged his habit only when he was outside alone, out of his niece and nephew's sight.

At the slam of the screen door, he stiffened.

Turning, he watched Leeann approach. She'd changed clothes and was wearing jeans, running shoes and one of her husband's flannel shirts. With her short, straight brown-blonde hair tied back in a floral-print scarf, she more closely resembled the seventeen-year-old kid he remembered last seeing her as than a mother only a few years short of thirty.

Coming up beside him, she fell half a foot shy of his six-foot two-inch height. Although she had the Rollins tapered nose and defiantly tilted chin, the harsh features were offset by her wide, even smile and dimpled cheeks.

Nothing softened the severe angles of Matt's features. He cringed each time he looked in a mirror and saw a face that more closely favored his father's each day. Ma used to say the Rollins kids wore chips on their chins instead of their shoulders. Leeann reminded him of her – soft-spoken and thoughtful, with the inner stamina of a bull. Coming back here had hammered home Ma's absence. She'd been dead several years, but the loss was real to him now, her absence triggering an emptiness he hadn't felt before.

Leeann's voice interrupted his thoughts. 'She stayed long enough.' Wiping her hands on a dishtowel, Leeann sniffed the air. Her aqua eyes leveled on the cigarette in his hand.

'This is bad for you,' she scolded, wresting the butt from between his fingers, helping herself to a long drag, then handing it back.

Matt dropped the butt and pulverized it with his boot heel. 'My last,' he informed her. 'Just like the one before it. You buy a pack and the damn things own you.'

'Must have been wicked if she drove you to smokin'.'

Matt studied his sister's face. Dark half-moons underscored her eyes, and worry creased her forehead. Despite their long separation, the bond was still there, an undying camaraderie akin to that shared by war veterans. Together, they'd survived the battle of growing up in the Rollins family, and they'd never forget, no matter how much each one wanted to. He'd always looked out for her, knowing all too well how easily the Rollins kids got lost in the shuffle – whether they were up against their own past or the entire world.

'I'm afraid I was too hard on her,' he admitted.

Leeann's eyes rounded. 'Hard on her? Are you kidding?' She turned to look at him, narrowing her gaze. 'She did get to you. You're still in love with your rich girlfriend, aren't you?' she accused. 'Even after all this time and everything she did.'

Matt laughed. 'Respect and love go hand-in-hand. No, I'm not still in love with her. But I don't understand why you're gettin' so riled.'

'Because I saw how she hurt you before. Your comin' back here again is like a miracle, and I'm scared she's goin' to do it all over again, drive you away again.'

Matt's face settled into a firm mask, his blue eyes freezing. In bringing up old confidences, Leeann was sparring below the belt-buckle. She was the only human being he'd told that he loved Sierra Ross, that he was going to buy his own ranch and marry her one day.

Even back then, as young as Leeann was, she'd told him he was full of cow chips. She'd yanked him outside behind the ramshackle house Daddy'd built for them and pointed out the moon in the night sky, telling him that the distance to it from where they stood was maybe half the difference between being a Ross and a Rollins in Winter, Texas.

'She's pretty,' Leeann had admitted then. 'But even perfect roses have thorns that stab you and make you bleed. Her only interest in you is defyin' her strict father, samplin' life among the lowly townsfolk just like she goes to art museums and inspects paintings. You fall for her and when she's through with you, she'll grind your heart into prairie dust.'

Bolstered by youthful confidence and idealism, Matt wouldn't have listened if Leeann had told him Sierra was Satan's mistress. Because Leeann didn't know Sierra, and he'd believed he did. Ultimately, he'd been the one who was wrong. He hadn't known her at all.

But he wasn't inclined to discuss that now. Only by pushing Sierra out of his mind had he been able to come this far.

'I have no intention of staying on. Sierra has nothing to do with that. This doesn't feel like home any more. OK?'

Leeann managed a regretful smile. 'I'm sorry, Matt. It's unfair to bring her up. But every time I see her, I get angry at how she deceived you. While you're off in faraway places alone, she prances around town like she's royalty.'

'If you're thinking I'm going to start packing my bags just because she showed up, forget it. I told you I was staying until Jerry gets back on his feet, and I mean it.'

Emotion clouded Leeann's eyes, but she blinked it back. 'If he ever is.'

He whipped around to face her, eyes blazing. He set a bracing hand on her shoulder. 'He will be. I didn't have a chance to ask you, how was he feeling today?'

'Ornery as a bear. He detests feelin' helpless.'

Matt nodded solemnly. Watching his youngest sister age this quick wasn't easy. As soon as he'd heard about her husband's car accident, he'd rushed to the town he'd successfully avoided most of his adult life to see what he could do. He'd been watching out for Leeann since she was a baby and he was in kindergarten. With precious little of their family intact, his sense of obligation had overriden his desire to stay away. He'd pushed caution out of his mind as he'd left little behind in Wyoming except a one-bedroom furnished apartment and a job as a trail guide, a job that had suited him just fine aside from the chore of accommodating whiny, wealthy greenhorn vacationers.

Leeann shook her head, gnawing her lower lip as another thought occurred to her. 'The business manager at the hospital asked me this afternoon if I can pay something on Jerry's bill. Doesn't that hang all? With a husband flat on his back and two kids to feed, they chase me down the halls and act like I should be walking around with a wad of bills in my purse. Now the doctors are talking about months of physical therapy before Jerry might walk again.'

A slow-burning anger kindled inside Matt as he listened. 'You know I'll be here as long as it takes. Don't worry so much or you won't be worth anything to Jerry, the kids or yourself.'

Leeann fell silent for a long moment. 'I'm sorry. I'm just so scared, and I can't let the kids see it. I still can't believe you're really here. I didn't know who else to call, but I didn't think you'd come. After you missed Mama's funeral, I thought I'd never see you again.'

'I wouldn't have come for anyone else. And you know why I missed Ma's funeral.'

Leeann stared at a blade of grass. 'Daddy didn't show either. Thank God – it's the last thing Mama would have wanted. I was relieved when he finally left us.'

'Ma held us together. No matter how broke she was or how long Daddy stayed away, she kept believing in things working out for the best. She placed as much faith in her tarot cards and horoscopes as she did in the Lord, and she refused to understand that embracing it all defied logic. I would have chanced coming to see Ma, if I'd known she was sick.'

His mother had repeatedly told him he was special, destined for a fine future because he'd been born at sunrise. He could almost hear her describing the funny feeling that had gripped her at the moment he entered the world, blocking out all her pain. Although she was inside a windowless delivery room, she'd checked the almanac later and discovered the sun had come up at that exact moment. For a woman who'd lived most of her life bordering on poverty, she'd entertained grand delusions.

'Nobody knew. When she was feelin' bad, she kept it to herself, just like she always did. She was pourin' coffee down at the diner when she collapsed. Isn't it strange to come from such a big family and feel so alone?'

Matt looked down at her. He'd been alone ever since their elder brother Dylan had left home a year and a half before he did. For him, it felt more normal than strange. 'You have Jerry and the kids, and his family.'

'Jerry's folks are great, but they're not part of who I really am or where I come from. I know I'm bein' selfish, but I don't want you to go when this is over.'

Matt diverted his glance skyward. 'Maybe the Rollinses shouldn't be remembering too much. I stayed on as long as I could. And it wasn't only because of Sierra that I left.'

'I know. Matt, why did Daddy hate you so much? He was always hardest on you.'

Matt's broad shoulders heaved slightly. 'Because I wasn't Dylan, I guess. Hey, don't worry about it. We survived.'

'Don't you get tired of movin' around?' Her eyes brightened as she spoke. 'Now that you're back anyway, you don't have to leave. This is your home too, Matt. Don't you ever want something to call your own? It used to be all you talked about. Stay and get yourself a place.'

Regret speared his chest. He sure hadn't come back to revive his grand youthful dreams, although they spoke to him here, whispering seductively on the breeze as though they'd been waiting for him.

'Talk comes cheap when you don't understand how the world is. I always thought there had to be something better, but I haven't found it yet.'

'Then stop looking and stay. Sally and Tanner adore their Uncle Matt. And I miss you.'

'This is your life, Leeann, not mine.'

'You could make one here as well as anyplace else. Daddy's not coming back.'

'I'm not worried about him any more. I don't believe we'll ever see him again either. But he's not the only reason I left. This place reeks of bad memories. I needed to start someplace new.'

Leeann set her hands to hips only slightly thickened by having carried two children. As she raised her chin, her thin eyebrows slanted.

'You said that ten years ago, and I've worn out two pages in my address book keepin' up with you. Do I have to beg? I need you here. Not just now when my family is in trouble. Maybe we could find Dylan and the others . . .'

'Dylan doesn't want to be found. You're too rational, Turtle, to be imagining the Rollins clan cozying up to the fire together, munching fried chicken and potato salad.'

She ignored his reference to her by her baby nickname. 'We can't always keep blaming each other for the way we grew up. But that's not it with you, is it? Livin' this close to Sierra does bother you. What did she want anyway?'

'She offered me a job.'

Leeann gave him a blank look. 'But you're going to work for Sam, aren't you?'

'Sam's pretty old now. His grandson's doing most of the hiring, and he's scaled down the operation. Dunc says he's got all the help he needs right now, but he'll let me know if something opens up.'

'You turned her down, didn't you?'

'I told her I might take it temporarily, until she can find someone else.'

'Don't, Matt. She's always been trouble for you. There's an older couple in town looking for a housekeeper a few days a week. I could do that while you keep looking.'

His dark eyebrows arched. 'No.'

'I can't dump everything on you.'

'You need to spend your time with Jerry and the kids. As it is, you're splitting yourself in two.'

'Try another ranch. A few days more or less won't mean the world . . .'

'I'm not a kid any more. I'm not awed by her stunning looks or impressed by where she comes from. Have some faith in me, Leeann. We need the money. I made up my mind to leave as quick as possible before I even got here, and maybe going back and proving to myself she's out of my system forever is the best thing I could do.'

'I wish you wouldn't,' Leeann warned anxiously.

'Well, it looks like I am.'

'Let's go in, it's colder than the North Pole out here. The kids are watching the cartoon video Jerry's ma gave 'em, and dinner's in the oven. I'll be going back to the hospital, if you're OK with watching the kids. I hate taking them back to Jerry's folks after his ma has kept them all day.'

'I'll look after them,' he assured her.

Later, after his niece and nephew were tucked in their beds and the house was quiet, he swallowed his fierce pride as Sierra had sacrificed hers this afternoon and dialed the number she'd left him. She had a son to look after; he had Leeann's family.

He thought he'd steeled himself, but the sound of her voice rippled through his detached façade. She gave him directions to her place, and he said he'd be there around ten after he ran an errand in town for Leeann. His only personal request was that she keep the boy out of his and harm's way. He didn't tell her he had more than the boy's safety on his mind. For all his claims that he was immune to her, he couldn't tolerate the thought of constantly facing concrete evidence of Sierra's happy union with Ben – the son they'd made together.

Nothing, he vowed, was going to let her slink under his skin again. As his Daddy had always professed, the rich stuck together and seldom strayed beyond their own circles, nor did they admit outsiders into them. Matt could almost hear Lester Rollins' scratchy voice warning, 'You stay clear of those hills, boy. There's folks up there'll skin you alive.' But Matt had never given much credence to Daddy's backwoods philosophy. Like almost everything else, he'd had to learn it the hard way.

He went to bed that night with the prospect of dealing with Sierra tomorrow weighing on his mind. When he stretched out and closed his eyes, in place of sleep, the memories came . . .

CHAPTER 2

Matt whistled as he drove down the dirt road leading to Sam Burke's place. The windows rolled down on both sides provided his pickup's only air-conditioning. Wind tousled his longish hair, and the air smelled of wild mint and grass, cleansed after a summer thunderstorm. The sun had come back out now, burning off the moisture and leaving the air hot and sticky. He'd just gotten out of his community college class and was headed to work. Absently, he raked his hair back with one hand. For once in his life, he was feeling pretty good about things. Daddy was still guffawing over his plan to become a veterinarian, but the old man came home with increasing infrequency now that Dylan was gone. Matt had long ago numbed himself to his father's contempt, which had intensified without Dylan around. As if the old man blamed him for driving Dylan away.

But he could put everything at home aside for a while whenever he thought about Sierra. Lately, she stuck in his mind. In a few more hours he'd be meeting her at the creek again. She was the oddest young woman he'd ever met. One rainy afternoon, he'd given her a jump-start when her battery died and left her stranded on the roadside. She'd befriended him despite his attempts to drive her away.

'I remember you from high school,' she'd said, leaning over his shoulder as he ducked his head under her hood and attached the cables to her battery posts. 'You probably didn't notice me. You were a senior and I was a lowly sophomore.'

Matt had wished she'd move back, although her closeness was more distraction than physical obstacle. She smelled all clean and powdery, like a garden after the rain.

'I remember seeing you in the halls,' he'd admitted casually. Her striking beauty was impossible to ignore. But she was always surrounded by rich, preppy snobs, and he'd never considered approaching her. 'How come I never saw you any other year?'

'My father sent me back to boarding school. He'd never wanted to let me attend public school in the first place.'

He'd looked up at her with narrowed eyes. 'But you wanted to?'

'I wanted to make friends here. I've lived in Winter all my life and I hardly know anyone. Father means well, but sometimes he makes me feel like a china doll shut inside a glass case.'

'Maybe you're lucky to be protected that way,' he'd suggested, finding it difficult to believe that anyone who lived in a mansion could be too unhappy.

'It's different now that I'm in college. I don't feel as if I'm being watched all the time.'

'You're off for the summer?'

'Yes. You have books in your truck.'

'I'm taking summer classes. I'm going to be a veterinarian.' He hadn't meant to tell her that. It was a pretty ambitious dream for someone still attending a two-year college.

'You have nice hands. You'll be good at it.'

'Maybe.'

'You usually accomplish whatever you set your mind on, don't you?' she asked.

'Sometimes. Can't depend on anybody if you don't do for yourself.'

'What do you do after school?'

He shrugged. 'Work.'

'And after work?'

'Sometimes I go to the library or fishing. When my old man's off on a long haul, I help out at home.'

'What about tonight?'

'I'll probably go fishing down at the lake.'

'Would it bother you if I tagged along?'

Turning, he took a hard look at her. He liked being alone because ever since he could remember there'd been a little brother or sister waiting to follow him everywhere he went. Sierra was pretty and cheerful, and, while she had his blood pumping, he wasn't out to get his life tangled up with anyone else's. Rich girls were off-limits. And Sierra was just the kind who'd be probing into his background, asking questions about the family he'd long ago been ashamed to learn wasn't like anyone else's.

'Why do you want to do that?' he asked finally.

'Because no one ever taught me how to fish, and I like you.'

Matt didn't know what to say.

'Don't worry,' she added. 'I'm not going to chatter and drive the fish away. I know you're not supposed to do that.'

'You'll have to touch worms,' he warned.

'I said my father treats me like a china doll, not that I am one. I'm not afraid of a few nasty worms.' Even as she denied it, he saw the revulsion in her eyes.

'Suit yourself, then. Follow the old Alamo Road out to Spring Lake around eight-thirty. But I'd get this battery checked first.'

'Thanks. I will.'

He'd never believed she'd show. But to his astonishment, she was waiting on the beach when he arrived. When he tried to bait a hook for her, she protested that he was violating their agreement. She'd said she'd do it herself, and she would. Watching her hold the squirming bait at arm's length, her expression one of obvious distaste, he could scarcely keep from laughing. But he couldn't help admiring her spunk. Was she enduring this to impress him?

When the worm suddenly writhed wildly, she screamed and flung it in the lake.

Matt burst into laughter, unable to hold back any longer. He thought she'd be angry, but after scowling briefly, she broke into laughter too. Neither of them was able to stop, and Sierra smothered her chuckles in his shirtfront as naturally as a treetop bows in the wind, unaware of the effect her casual gesture had on him.

As the sun was going down, striping the sky with pink and orange, he showed her how to cast. He stood behind her, his arms encircling her slim, rounded body as he guided her hands. Suddenly, a wave of longing so fierce stabbed him that he had to move away or he would have ensnared her more tightly and kissed that sunny smile.

Now, they met almost every night by the creek because it was closer and more private. They'd long abandoned any pretense of fishing but shared long philosophical discussions and watched for the first stars to appear in the sky as night fell.

One clear night, she spotted the first light in the sky and made a wish.

'So what did you wish for?' he asked.

She was lying back against the blanket on the

slanted creek-bank, her hair fanned around her head and her hands tucked under it. She looked relaxed and happy, her eyes sparkling. Matt was sitting up beside her. His glance traced the length of her sleek body, and he resisted his feverish urge to touch her.

'For this summer never to end,' she said. 'I'm enjoying being lazy.'

'I thought you liked college.'

'I like being there on my own. Studying art is interesting, but I don't like listening to long, boring lectures. And I'm not learning anything I'll ever need in life.'

'You're spoiled,' he noted.

Fire exploded in her eyes. 'I'm not. I just know what's important to me.'

'Calm down, Sierra. I wasn't criticizing you. It's just that things that come the hardest are what you appreciate the most.'

She raised herself up and looked him in the eyes so intently that he felt as though the breath had been knocked out of him. To his astonishment, she dived down, cradling her head in his lap.

His loins clamped miserably, and he froze like a granite statue.

'Hold me, Matt,' she murmured.

He dropped an arm over the back of her shoulders. She snuggled closer, resting her cheek against the leg of his jeans. He stroked her hair, entwining his fingers in the deep, silky mass. He grazed his thumb against the side of her face.

'You're right,' she said. 'The good things don't come easy, do they?'

'It doesn't matter. Wishes on stars or anything else are just superstition. What would you do with yourself, if you weren't in college?'

'I'd go to Mexico and find the place where my mother was born. I'm half Mexican, you know.'

A smile curled his lips. 'Sierra, anyone can look at you and tell that.'

'Good, because I'm proud of it. But I was just a baby when my mother died, and growing up with my father, I never got to know anything about her family or my heritage. I mean, I must have scads of aunts and uncles and cousins south of the border.'

'So why aren't you there now, *amada*?'

She raised her head. 'You speak Spanish?'

'I've picked up a word here and there from some of Sam's hands. Cuss words, mostly.'

'That one's not. Sam's hands teach you that one?'

'You know Spanish too?'

'Sure, I took it in school. How else am I going to talk to all my new-found relatives?'

'But you haven't gone.'

'My father says it's too dangerous to travel so deep into the interior of Mexico. But I think it really disturbs him to bring up memories of my mother. He seldom talks about her. She was so young when she died, I don't think he ever got over her. I'm all the family he has left, and I don't want to hurt him by defying his wishes on such a delicate matter.' Her voice wavered. 'It's just that he sent her home to be buried. I would like to put flowers on her grave.'

Matt rubbed her shoulderblade. In his family, there were no delicate matters.

'So, you never knew her?

'Not to remember. I've seen her photograph. She was quite beautiful.'

'You must favour her, then.'

'Thank you. My father says I act like her sometimes as well. I'll have to take his word for it. I'm glad. I love my father, but he can be grim and somber.'

'Well, since you can't go to Mexico, you might as well be in college.'

'No, I want to make a home for myself, with kids running down the hallways and playing and arguing together. I want a noisy house. Everyone in my father's house speaks in hushed, reverent tones, as if they were in church.'

'How many kids?'

'Two or three of my own. Then I'd adopt orphans until the house was full.'

'You'd change your mind if you ever lived in a house with wall-to-wall people, always sharing a room, lying in bed at night and listening to your parents screaming at each other.' He clamped off his thoughts. Ashamed and embarrassed, he hadn't meant to reveal so much about his family. He didn't want her sympathy.

'But there must be good times too,' she countered.

He shook his head, 'This is the good time, Sierra. I always get by.'

She lit into one of her generously embellished tales describing her father's pompous behavior, making Matt laugh, and laughing with her felt good. He'd almost begun to believe that one day he'd be able to laugh at his own father. Almost. When he was with her, the rest stopped mattering so much.

Especially when he kissed her. She felt so warm and tiny in his arms, her heart fluttering beneath his hands like a captured bird. Tasting her lips was like biting into one of the fancy chocolates Ma's customers gave her at Christmastime, sweet edges caving into a burst of softer, tangier flavors inside. But each time they were together, saying goodnight got harder. Once he started kissing her, he didn't want to stop.

The hours he spent away from her stretched out as endlessly as the Texas sky. But today, when he pulled up in Sam's drive and the bow-legged gray-haired man rushed out to greet him, he knew immediately that something was dreadfully wrong. Walking towards the house, Matt caught and clutched the apple he'd been tossing in the air.

'Howdy, Matt,' Sam began in a stilted tone. The older man stood much shorter than Matt, but his small body was all powerful compressed muscle.

'What's happened?' Matt asked.

Sam studied his boots before answering. 'It's Star. I know you've taken a liking to the mare, but she was struck by lightning this afternoon. One of those freak accidents.'

'Lightning? Where is she?'

'It killed her instantly. She didn't suffer much.'

'Oh,' Matt said, dropping the apple. He wouldn't be feeding it to her now.

Sam looped his thumbs in the pockets of his jeans. 'I watch you talk to them horses, and I've never seen a man who could communicate with critters the way you do. But all they are is critters, Matt, and you've got to be careful about getting too attached.'

Matt nodded dully.

Sam reached up to set a hand on Matt's shoulder. 'Go on home this afternoon. I'll clean the stables myself.'

Matt glanced over Sam's shoulder towards the paddock.

'You don't want to go back there, son,' the rancher cautioned. 'There's nothing you can do for her now. We're gonna have to bulldoze a hole to bury her.'

'I've got to see her.'

With a resigned jerk of his head, Sam stepped back and motioned for Matt to pass.

Out in the field, Matt knelt on the grass beside the lifeless animal, wishing he'd heeded Sam's advice. One last time, he brushed her mane and pressed his fingertips to the white starburst marking on her forehead. Her flesh felt icy. The mare's spirit and grace and beauty he'd loved had been ripped from this poor empty body.

'Goodbye, girl,' he whispered, giving her neck a final pat.

He left quickly, ashamed of the misery in his face, the tears stinging his eyelids. He'd grown accustomed to Star's quiet company when he worked in the stables. When he rode her, they understood each other. She'd always known where to turn before he pulled the reins. For some mysterious reason she'd become his favorite. Animals had personalities, feelings and souls, he believed.

He drove to the house, but as he approached, he spotted his father's rig parked out front and, without stopping, he made a U-turn.

He headed straight for the creek and parked the old truck off the roadside where no one would see it. He and Sierra never discussed why they never met in town. They both knew.

As he made his way blindly down the winding path through the woods, he remembered that

Sierra, the one human he dared hold close, would be going back to college at the summer's end. He was destined to lose her too. Nothing was ever his to keep. He had to stop believing it could be. And he nearly left without waiting for her, but he had no place else to go.

He spread the tattered wool blanket he kept in the pickup over the wet grass. Listening to the rippling water, birds chirping overhead, he sprawled on his back and watched sunlight filter through the tree-tops. He wasn't sure how long he lay there before he drifted into an uneasy sleep.

When he awoke, the sun had slipped lower in the sky, and Sierra was standing over him.

'How long have you been here?' he asked, propping himself on his forearms.

'Only a few minutes. I liked watching you sleep. You looked peaceful. When you're awake, you never look so happy. But how long have *you* been here?

She sat Indian-fashion beside him as he related what had happened at Sam's, told her he couldn't go home because his father was there.

'You hate your father that much?' she asked. Her hair was pulled back in a long braid. She tossed the end of it over her shoulder and began undoing it.

'No. My brother Dylan was his favorite, and he blames me because Dylan left home. Something about me sets him off. He's different with the other kids, more tolerant. Ma always says I should try to understand him, but I don't think I ever will. Sometimes I don't think I want to. Personally, I don't think he cares what I do as long as it doesn't inconvenience him. He hates his own life, and he's got to blame someone else for it.'

Sierra sighed as she continued unweaving her hair. 'Where is your brother?'

'We haven't heard from him.'

'Your father's probably worried.'

'No. He says he'd never let Dylan back in the house. Dylan can take care of himself. Actually, I envy him being out on his own.'

'But you can't run away from who you really are. It's hard to imagine wanting to. My father wants to know everything I do. I suppose he's overprotective because I'm an only child. He was past forty when he married my mother, and I guess it's unlikely he'll ever have another child. Sometimes being loved too much can be as oppressive as indifference.'

His eyes locked on hers. 'I don't think it's possible to love too much. It doesn't come in degrees,' he professed, but in the back of his mind he thought of Star.

Sierra raised her head, and her scent blended with the smell of damp leaves and moss. 'You're not afraid, then, to be loved?'

'Maybe love is like wishing on stars, something people imagine to make themselves feel better.'

She arched one dark eyebrow. 'You don't believe there's a magical chemistry drawing two people together? That if they're meant to be together, they will be, no matter how unlikely?'

He smiled up at her. 'You're naïve. What's that you're doing with your hair? It's downright distracting. You said it was too hot to wear it that way.'

She shook her head, dark hair tumbling across her shoulders. 'But don't you like it better down?'

'Yes.'

'You're a good man and you deserve to be happy, Matt. I know it's hard for you to take anything from anybody.'

'I don't want you to be uncomfortable because of me,' he qualified. 'Knowing you're sweating doesn't exactly bring joy to my heart.'

Her eyes danced. She reached out and ran one hand across the muscles of his chest. His body burned as though he'd struck a match to it. Too late he tried to steel himself to the passion rising inside him.

'What would?' she asked, dropping down to lie beside him.

He groaned inwardly. 'Maybe you should consider backing off before you ask me that,' he suggested.

But she pressed closer, moving across his chest. With a start, he felt warm flesh against him and realized she wore no bra beneath her loose cotton shirt.

'Sierra?' he asked, peering inquisitively into her eyes.

'Yes, I am trying to seduce you.'

'Oh, God. You don't know how much I want to make love to you. But I don't think we should.'

'I'm not attractive enough for you?'

'You know you are.'

'Then you have no feelings for me?'

'Sierra, you mean more to me than anybody in my life ever has. But we go home every night to two different planets. No sense complicating things.'

'Ha! I thought you were the kind of man who wouldn't put a woman under a glass case. When you feel something, you act on it. That's nature's way. Don't you care about what I want? I want to see how you look when you're awake and happy.'

'Your father wouldn't approve.'

'He would if he knew you. I'm a woman, not a puppet, and I know what I want. I want the two of us to make something beautiful that no one can take away. I want to give you something that's yours to keep forever.'

'Good God, honey, you're tearing me apart. There is no forever.'

'Haven't we both known for weeks now this was bound to happen? Let me prove how much I believe in you.'

Overcome with tenderness, a need to hold on to her and never let go, he rolled over her, bowing to kiss her upraised lips. His loins throbbed achingly, straining at his jeans. He'd had willing women before during a few experimental encounters, and in his wallet he was carrying the square package Dylan had once advised him never to leave home without. But he hadn't been able to get over thinking that this woman who lived in a house with an electric fence around it was out of bounds. He'd known desire before, but never mingled with this exquisite tenderness.

'I want to be good to you.' He brushed her hair with his hand.

'I know. I know you will be.'

'Sierra, I want to make love to you.'

'Good.'

'Are you sure?'

'I feel it in my heart. Here.' She captured his hand in hers and set it over the base of her breast. He hesitated as though he were holding a priceless porcelain figurine.

'Not here,' he protested, his voice hoarse and strained. 'Not like kids hiding out in the woods. Let me take you someplace nice.'

'No. You'll change your mind. This is our place.'

Already, he was beyond stopping. He'd adored this dark-haired angel from the moment he'd set eyes on her.

Gliding over her, he slid his hand under the hem of her loose shirt, skirting it slowly over the trembling skin of her belly. slowly raising it to her tight midriff.

He watched her face, her lips curling in pleasure, colors swirling in the depths of her dark eyes. Heat rose from her silky, perfumed skin. He inhaled sultry air rich with her alluring feminine scent.

Then he captured her round, firm breast, curving his hand to cup it, watching her face slacken, her eyes flutter shut and her lips part slightly. She arched her back, her hair spread around her like black velvet. His fingertip lit on the mound's peak. He drew circles and felt it stiffen.

Leaning down, he pressed his lips over her parted ones, sliding his tongue through the small opening, giddy with her sweet taste. He felt the moisture on her skin, smelled her arousal. His own need spearing him, he fumbled with her shirt buttons.

Her hands reached up to help him, slim, delicate fingers brushing against his rough ones. The texture of her skin was so exotic, he couldn't fill his head with enough of it. He wanted to explore every part of her.

With the buttons unfastened, she let her hands fall to her sides without moving the blouse. Matt brushed the cloth flaps aside, staring down appreciatively at the pink, ruby-tipped mounds.

She moved her arms up to cover her chest.

'No,' he protested, puzzled by her sudden modesty. 'You're so beautiful, Sierra. Let me look at you.'

She hesitated before withdrawing her arms, but her sudden shyness gave him an uneasy feeling. She'd been away to college – she'd been to Europe. He'd just assumed a woman as appealing as she was . . .

He pulled back, sitting up, and stared down at her accusingly.

'You have done this before, haven't you, darling?' he asked.

'Don't be angry. Did I do something wrong?'

'No, of course not. But you should have told me.' He wanted to accept what she was offering, but he wasn't prepared to take this much, more than anyone had ever given him.

'It was hard enough to persuade you to make love to me without more problems. I didn't want you to like it less.'

'That's not the point. You must have waited this long for a reason.'

'I was waiting for a man I felt safe with. And now I've found him.'

He caressed her stomach. 'The first time isn't always so wonderful.'

'I've heard that.'

'Sierra, you're seeing too much in me. I've got nothing to promise you.'

'Why can't you believe I simply want to do this? My heart's telling me it's the right thing. Can't you listen to yours?'

'I have one request.'

'A blindfold?'

'Not on your life.'

'What?'

'No matter what happens this first time, there will be a second.'

'I was counting on that.' She brushed a hand over the inside of his jeans, licking fire across his loins.

He dived down, holding her close and kissing her until he thought his heart would explode. Trailing kisses across her throat and neck, he buried his face between her breasts, kissing and nibbling. Her hands tightened over his shoulderblades.

Raising up, he kissed her quivering belly. His hands traced the length of her, and he pushed down the elastic band of her shorts, exposing lace-trimmed white satin panties to the steamy air. Leisurely, he rubbed her belly in a downward spiral, sneaking his fingertips beneath the sheer fabric until they reached the thick cashmere patch below, every bit as lush and supple as she was.

A soft moan fell from her lips, and he felt her tense.

'Oh, *amada*,' he whispered, moving up to kiss her lips, each of her eyelids until she relaxed once again in his arms. 'I've found the sweetest part of you.'

And gently he probed deeper, until he discovered the moist, molten centre of her need. She stiffened and gasped. He stopped to tear his clothes off and find the condom.

She smiled up at him. Carefully, he climbed between her legs. He stroked her slowly, crooning to her and caressing her heaving breast with his other hand, coaxing her to open her herself like a blooming flower. He watched her face change as her pleasure heightened.

Ignoring his own throbbing need, he continued probing, teasing, stoking her passion.

Suddenly, she cried out, writhing and clinging to him as spasms racked her.

Matt held her until she was quiet and still. When she opened her eyes, surprise and delight shone in them. She smiled into his face. Matt smiled back and slipped inside her.

Drawing in a long, sharp breath, she tensed, but her smile never dropped. A puff of air escaped her lips.

Burning need engulfed him, pulling him, but he didn't move until he felt her muscles slacken beneath him. Slowly, he began rocking to the silent rhythm of the creek's current. She moved in sync with him, drawing him deeper into a place from which he'd never return. Nothing had ever felt more right. It was though they had fallen in step with the cycles of nature, of the universe, quickening, spiraling, crashing. Finally, he surrendered, losing himself to it, to her.

All thought escaped him as his desire crested with the force of a falling meteor.

When he opened his eyes, he looked down on the face of the woman who had just given him the greatest gift he'd ever received. For the first time in his life, he'd found love, something that was his alone.

She was staring up at him. 'Did I hurt you?' she asked.

He grinned. 'No, smart-ass.' His expression grew solemn. 'Are you all right?'

'I chose wisely. You look happy now, and it becomes you,' she said. 'Are you happy?'

He kissed her mouth. 'As a turtle in the sun.'

'You're patient and kind. You see why I couldn't help falling in love with you.'

'Sierra, I felt it.'

'Felt what? You have to say it.'

'The magic. This would never have happened if I didn't love you.'

'I know. But I'm glad you said it.'

'Sierra?'

'Hmm?'

'Thank you.'

She nestled against his chest, and he held her to him, sinking one hand in her tresses. His heart swelled in a way it never had before. She had indeed given him something no one could ever take away. And for the first time in his life he wanted to believe that if something was good enough and pure enough, it would indeed last forever . . .

With a start, Matt awoke, blinking in the darkness and confused to find himself sprawled across a narrow bed in a room with plastic trucks and teddy bears lining the shelves. Blue curtains billowed over the partially opened window like a pair of icy ghosts.

Clasping a hand to his forehead, he remembered that he was in his nephew's room. Tossing the quilt back, he swung his long legs over the side of the bed, setting bare feet on the wooden floor. In nothing but a pair of briefs, he padded across the room, rubbing his stiff neck.

He eased the window pane shut. When he'd turned in, the air had been cold but still. The wind must have sprung up in the night.

He lingered before the window, staring across the moonlit fields. Groggily, he wondered whether it was the wind that had awakened him, or his dream about Sierra. He couldn't get her out of his blood any more than he could this land. All that had ended long ago, and he didn't want to recall what had passed between them.

All his life, he'd moved aside to accommodate other people – his father, Sierra, Ben Davenport. And no matter where he went or how long he lived in one place, he always felt like a nomad passing through. Maybe Leeann was right. Maybe it was time to say to hell with everybody and make something out of the place that had once been home.

But he didn't see how. Not here. Aside from Leeann and her family, there was no more for him here than anywhere else. And there wasn't room enough even here to escape seeing Sierra and her son. Just their brief and none-too-friendly reunion this afternoon had triggered too many reminders of what he'd once felt for her.

But maybe that would wear off. He'd deaden himself to her just as he'd shut himself off to his father's torments. Tomorrow would tell. Leeann needed the money too much for him to back out of a chance for an honest day's work. No matter how disturbing the source.

As he moved to draw the curtains, a shooting star split the sky in a trail of light.

His ma would have said it was a sign. But he was damned if he knew what it might mean. And he'd long abandoned any inclination to believe in destiny. His ma had been wrong about it, and so had Sierra. You took what life handed you and did the best you could with it. Wanting too much made a man dangerous.

Turning away from the window, he was startled to find a small figure hovering in the doorway, staring at him. Peering closely through the darkness, he recognized his pyjama-clad nephew.

'Howdy, Tanner. What are you doing up?' Matt asked quietly.

'I'm thirsty,' the boy replied. 'Why are you up? Did you have a bad dream?'

Matt chuckled softly. 'Sort of. Maybe we should both go to the kitchen and get some water. Let's let your ma sleep, OK? She's real tired.'

The boy nodded his solemn approval.

Matt grabbed his jeans off the chair and stepped into them.

'Don't you have jammers?' Tanner asked, watching him.

'No.'

'Why?'

'Don't like to carry too much around.'

'You're supposed to leave 'em at home, in your dresser.'

'Well, I don't have a house either, not like you do.'

'Is that why you're using ours?'

'You sure are talkative for a dude who's supposed to be sleeping.'

The boy's eyes were open wide, and it occurred to Matt he was probably worried about his dad being gone.

'When I see Santa, I'll tell him you need jammers and a house.'

It knocked Matt out, the way the kid was so trusting. He couldn't remember ever believing in

Santa. But he had believed in schemes nearly as far-fetched. 'Well, I'd sure appreciate that. Now let's go get that drink before we wake everybody up with all this yakking.'

As he moved toward the doorway, little Tanner reached up a chubby hand to his uncle. Matt took it and led him to the kitchen. Whatever it took, Matt promised himself, he wasn't going to let this kid down.

The next morning, Matt marched down the hospital corridor, the smells and fluorescent lights reminding him of the times Ma had corralled her five kids and taken them to the health department for shots. Leeann and Gage always used to wail and scream until it was over, while he and Dylan and Darcy accepted the ordeal with stoic resignation.

He kept a watchful eye ahead of him. He didn't want to risk bumping into Leeann here today. She was already furious about his decision to work for Sierra. They'd argued about it again after supper last night. She'd accused him of being stubborn as a donkey.

Determinedly, he followed the signs pointing towards, the business office. A sullen-faced blonde woman was shuffling papers behind a glass window.

'Can I help you?' she asked in a monotone. When she raised her head, he saw she was younger than her navy blue suit and severe upswept hairstyle indicated.

'Where's the manager's office?'

She pointed to a door behind her, a charm bracelet jangling on her wrist.

'Thanks,' Matt said, starting around the partition.

'You can't go in there,' she ordered with annoyance.

Without stopping, Matt gave her a cold stare and proceeded to push open the door.

A wavy-haired man in a brown suit, white shirt and hideous tan and purple mottled tie was seated at a desk, sipping a mugful of coffee and scanning the pages of the morning paper. His thick-rimmed glasses had slid halfway down the bridge of his nose.

The woman from out front ran in after Matt.

The man looked up from his desk.

'Mr Hathaway, I'm sorry . . .'

Matt took his hat off. 'Pardon me, but I see you're not busy, and this won't take long.' He dropped into one of two leather chairs in front of the man's desk.

Mr Hathaway eyed him uneasily.

Matt leaned back in the chair, stretching out his long legs. 'I wanted to clear up my sister's bill. You're the person to see about that, aren't you, Mr Hathaway?'

After studying Matt intently, the man nodded. 'It's all right, Maggie,' he told the clerk poised in the doorway.

She walked away but left the door open. The man

pushed up his glasses with one finger, peering through them at Matt.

'Now,' the man said. 'Whose bill is it you've come to pay?'

Matt laughed. 'I didn't say I'd come to pay it. I just wanted to make it clear that it will be paid.'

'That goes without saying. I'm not running a loan company here.'

The blue of Matt's eyes deepened. 'My sister's husband is lying in this place with casts on both his legs. Kinda hard for him to make it in to work that way. She's worried sick and running herself ragged, trying to make him feel better while she's taking care of two small children and trying to make ends meet without a pay-check.'

'We understand it's difficult for anyone when a family member is hospitalized . . .'

'I'm not talking about *anyone*. I'm talking about my sister. Now, if she's going to owe you money after what the insurance pays, you're going to get it. But you're not going to get it any sooner by making things worse for her and hounding her when she comes to see her husband.'

'Mr . . .'

'Rollins.'

'Mr Rollins, we're not asking her to pay all of it now . . .'

'Her husband is here instead of working. She has bills to pay, children to feed.'

'Maybe social services . . .'

'She doesn't need charity. That's why I'm here. I'll see to it you get your money. But don't let me hear again about you harassing her or her husband. They have enough to worry about without being bullied.'

'It's natural she'd be hypersensitive. We merely enquired . . .'

'Well, stop enquiring. I'm giving you your answer. Leave them alone and just send the bill. Maybe you've never had a chance to lie flat on your back and worry about things you're helpless to do anything about.'

The man's pasty face registered his comprehension of Matt's implied threat.

He cleared his throat as though he were about to choke. 'You've had your say, Mr Rollins. Now, I'm going to call Security.'

'Don't bother. I'm through.'

He took a peppermint out of the basket on the desk on his way out.

'Appreciate it,' he said, waving the wrapped candy as he went out the door.

CHAPTER 3

Will sat slumped over the long wooden kitchen table, skimming the remainder of his milk and cereal with the tip of the spoon, his chin propped on one elbow as he stared into the bowl.

'Don't dawdle or you'll miss the school bus,' Sierra chided her son as she opened the refrigerator door and searched for the jam.

'I'm ready,' he announced, bounding up and reaching for the jacket looped over one corner of the straight-backed chair. A magnificent child with his slim height, dark hair, olive complexion and almond-shaped green eyes fringed by long, dark lashes, he often possessed an aura of maturity beyond his years. Witnessing it saddened her. The true pain of childbirth, she'd learned, came not in the quickly forgotten physical agony of delivery, but in giving him up by inches with each passing day.

A sunbeam slanting through the window haloed his dark hair as he stuffed his arm into the canvas jacket.

'You didn't eat much,' she observed.

'Why do you buy the same kind of cereal all the time?'

'I thought this was your favorite.'

'Naw. It used to be. I don't like it any more.'

She sighed. 'I'll get something else, then. Next time I go into town.'

'Are you going today?'

'No, I have too much to do around here. The new stable manager's coming.'

'Is it OK if Luke comes home with me after school?'

She tousled his dark hair, noticing that he shirked away from her. 'Don't mess my hair up, Mom.'

'Sorry.'

'What about Luke?'

'If it's all right with his parents.'

Actually, she was relieved by his request. With a friend visiting, her son was less likely to take interest in the new, albeit temporary stable manager.

'Thanks.'

'Let me get my jacket. I'll walk with you.'

'The bus stop is just outside the gate. I can go by myself, Mom.'

She knew he could. He could wait for the bus without ever being out of sight of the ranch hands who were already grooming the horses and cleaning the stables. Not wanting to smother him any more than she wanted to lose him, she stretched her palms in the air. 'OK. So go. Bye.'

'Bye.'

'I love you.'

'I love you too,' came his muffled reply just before the door closed.

Her heart clenched. He'd had to deal with so much in the past year. Ben's death, moving here, doing without the expensive clothes and toys she could no longer buy him, accepting the unexplained absence of his grandparents. She knew he was strong like his father, but how much could a little boy take? Why did she feel sometimes as if he blamed her for all of it?

Maybe he sensed her failings and resented her for them. Her inability to love Ben as a wife should certainly had contributed to habits that had led to his death. That responsibility pressed heavily on her conscience.

Alone in the house, Sierra watched through the window until she saw her son, with that straight, proud walk of his, board the yellow school bus. Will's dog, Thunder, who had been sitting inside the gate, got up, turned, and lumbered towards the house. The medium-sized brown and white mutt had shown up as a stray one Saturday, just as a thunderstorm was breaking. Keeping a dog in the house was where Ben had drawn the line at indulging the boy. It had become the sole point of contention between father and son. But Will had immediately taken a shine to the half-starved creature, so, hoping a new pet would ease the pain Will locked inside himself, she'd bathed the beast and taken him on an astonishingly expensive trip to the vet. She hadn't regretted it a moment. When Will was in the yard he was seldom beyond Thunder's watchful eye.

As the bus roared down the road, Sierra busied herself cleaning the kitchen, then folding laundry in the utility room. From outside, she heard the hands calling to each other, talking to the horses as they led them out of their stalls for morning exercise. Her usual routine was to make rounds once Will had left for school, visiting the animals and maybe brushing a mane or two before she returned to her household tasks and bookwork. Today, she was avoiding the stables. She couldn't tolerate the disdain in Matt's eyes when he looked at her.

She'd had to tell him she'd loved Ben. Wasn't it best to get that out in the open and have it done with? She was protecting herself and Will the best way she knew how. Still, the raging truth in her heart condemned her. She'd never loved any man as she'd once loved Matt. But she'd pledged herself to Ben, and God help her, she'd tried to fulfil her vows. But there was always that one tough place in her heart that refused to yield to him. She couldn't help it. Matt Rollins had claimed that part of her, taken it for his own so it was no longer hers to give.

Was she ever so young? She'd loved him freely, eagerly, unaware that circumstances wouldn't always allow her to do so. That part of her life was over now. She'd never be loved that way again, and thinking about it was useless.

Now, as she inspected a pair of Will's well-worn jeans that were free of holes but getting too short for him, she reflected on the irony of once having assumed she'd never have to work for a living except to sit on the board of her father's oil company one day. She'd fancied herself an artist, traveling to tropical beaches and capturing the variations of sunlight on sand and water.

Well, she could blame neither her father nor herself, nor Ben and his family. She'd done this to herself. And never again would she innocently trust that someone else would always take care of her. Nor would she entrust her son's welfare to anyone else. He was her responsibility – hers alone.

People turned away for reasons she didn't understand. Her father, who had believed Ben was the perfect match for her, had washed his hands of her when Ben hadn't lived up to his expectations and yet she'd stood by him. That was what marriage was about, wasn't it? For better or worse . . . Ben had never been abusive, he'd just stopped caring. About her, anyway. He and Will had been close since the day the child was born and, despite his indifference towards her, Ben had never stopped being a good father.

Ben's parents had always treated her with cool reserve. Since the funeral, she had neither seen nor heard from them. Their distancing themselves not only from her but from their only grandchild deepened the wound of that rejection. She couldn't imagine what she or Will could have done to alienate them.

Or maybe, with Ben gone, she and Will just weren't important to them any more.

Deeply ashamed, she wondered if they simply guessed the truth, knowing their son would be alive today if she'd repaid all she owed him. Still, she failed to understand how anyone could freely give love, then one day yank it away. She knew Matt must think her guilty of doing exactly that.

She had to stop thinking about Matt.

But she found herself going to the window, parting the curtains to see if he'd arrived yet. She couldn't blame him if he broke his word and didn't show. She wasn't worthy of his consideration. Maybe his sister had talked him out of coming. She could understand Leeann's attitude towards her. When it came to the way she'd treated Matt, she didn't approve of her own actions. But she couldn't undo any of it.

She let the curtain drop. If he didn't come by eleven, she'd have to call the students and cancel the riding lessons. The hands worked well with the horses, but she wasn't sure she could trust them with people.

She could tolerate being alone, although she missed having someone to be close to. She'd always been quick to display her emotions, whether they were loving or less generous. Having Will gave her the strength to go on each day. He was all she had left. But now, he was drifting farther away from her in a way she didn't understand.

Restlessly, she pulled the vacuum out of the cupboard and ran it over the rugs. In the kitchen, she put away the clean dishes and wiped the counters clean. Finally, she made herself a cup of tea, laced it with milk and sugar, and sat at the table to drink it.

Sun slanted through the windows.

It warmed her skin as the hot tea trickled down her throat.

When, she wondered, had she become so cold and dull inside? The fire that once burned inside her had died away without a whisper.

Christmas was approaching, and she dreaded it this year. The festive season that had once shot rippling excitement and awe at being alive through her filled her now with dread. For Will, she'd have to go through the motions – put up a tree, wrap gifts, bake cookies. But these traditions loomed as nothing more than additions to her long list of chores.

'Yee-ha!' The call rang out from the yard like a cannon-shot.

Leaping out of her chair, nearly knocking over the remnants of her tea, she recognized the voice and raced to the window, pulled back the curtain, and grinned as she watched Matt's familiar tall, fine form race across the pasture atop Wildfire, the orneriest of her five remaining quarterhorses. The filly strutted magnificently, as though she'd always been his. As though she'd been waiting for him to come and take command of her.

Two of a kind, she thought. Tears rimmed the corners of her eyes. If Matt hadn't kept his word, she would have had nothing left to believe in. Everything he touched, he owned, and he didn't even know it.

First thing this morning, Sierra had instructed the hands to show Matt around, introduce him to the horses and let him know which were theirs and which were boarding, but she'd made it clear he was in charge. She hoped if she stayed in the background, away from Matt, he might be willing to stay on more than a few days. Finding a permanent replacement would take her longer than that, and she couldn't see any way around taking a chance on another stranger. Unless Matt stayed. Damn it. She needed him, and he needed the job. Maybe after a few days his initial anger at seeing her again, the revival of the old hurt, would fade. Maybe he'd finally accept the decision she'd made so long ago and listen to reason.

For the rest of the morning, she holed up inside, attending to paperwork and endless domestic tasks, peering through the curtains periodically to make sure all was well.

When the sheriff's car came rolling through the gate, she dropped the potato she'd been peeling, grabbed her jacket and rushed out of the door.

Sheriff Boulder and his deputy had already found Matt by the time she arrived.

'What's going on here?' she demanded breathlessly, avoiding Matt's eyes by facing the sheriff.

'Matt here says he's working for you. Is that true?

Her dark gaze narrowed. 'Yes, he is.'

'There was some trouble at the hospital this morning. The business manager says Matt stormed in and threatened him.'

Shifting her eyes to Matt, she saw the slow anger rising inside him. She knew he had to be pushed far to get angry, but once he was, it took him a long while to get over it.

She straightened the black velveteen collar on her cropped denim jacket, rubbed damp palms against her jeans. 'He must have misunderstood. Matt and I went to high school together, and I've never known him to hurt anybody.'

'Look . . .' Matt broke in.

Sierra cringed. She'd been hoping Matt wouldn't say anything, because she knew he must have gone to the hospital this morning and done something threatening, and he wouldn't lie about it. If he just didn't say anything, she was sure she could persuade the sheriff to go away.

'I just told him to get off my sister's back. She has a right to visit her husband without being dogged about money. Besides, the insurance company's paying most of the bill anyway. I mean, does he bother everyone like that, or just people who look to him like they can't pay?'

'He says you threatened to put him in a hospital bed.'

'That's a doggone lie. I only asked him to imagine how he'd feel in my brother-in-law's situation. If he read something else into it, that's his problem.'

Sierra rolled her eyes. She could well imagine how Matt might have phrased his description of this hypothetical scenario. 'Is Matt under arrest?'

'No, not as long as you're vouching for him, Mrs Davenport, but he's to stay away from the hospital.'

'Glad to oblige that,' Matt said.

Sierra's dark eyes swung from her new employee to the sheriff. 'Perhaps the business manager could be reminded to approach his job with a touch of compassion so things won't get blown out of proportion. I should think he'd act professionally enough to respect the Wiltons' privacy.'

'I'll mention it, Mrs Davenport.'

'You might also remind Eric that my mother-in-law sits on the hospital board. Would you and your deputy care to come in for coffee?'

'No, thanks, ma'am.'

'Well, if you don't mind, then, we have work to finish here. Good day, sheriff.'

She felt Matt's eyes on her as the lawmen walked away.

'Thank you for coming to my rescue, Mrs Davenport but I believe I could have handled that on my own.'

She lifted her chin, raising her eyes to meet his, then shocked by the tremor he sparked inside her. Over six feet of lean, raw muscle topped by hair the color of evening sunlight and deep blue eyes, finely carved features. Even sweaty and boasting that scruffy beard, he would have triggered a physical reaction from most women, she reasoned. Any woman who hadn't shut herself off to feeling anything for any man.

'I couldn't afford to have you escorted off to jail one of the few days you promised to work for me,' she retorted, unwilling to admit she was ashamed at resorting to tactics akin to those frequently employed by her father. While she hadn't lied about the elder Mrs Davenport's sitting on the board, she'd failed to mention her mother-in-law wasn't likely to speak up on her behalf, let alone Matt's.

'I was beginning to wonder if you weren't going to invite them to stay for dinner?'

'They were just doing their jobs, Matt. There's no point in not being civil to them. You might try it. Maybe if you stopped running around looking as if your face belonged on a cough-drop box and smiled at people instead of scowling as if you hate their guts, things would go a little better for you in this town.'

'I reckon I should listen to you. You always have known how to get what you want from folks.'

Her face blistered. But she quickly dismissed her anger.

'You wouldn't be able to help Leeann much from a jail cell.'

'I thought you believed I didn't do anything.'

'I do. But life isn't always fair. Be careful, Matt. I know you're on edge.'

'Well, at least the sheriff accomplished one thing. He got you out here. I was beginning to wonder if you were ever going to make an appearance.'

'I left instructions for the hands . . .'

'You said you wanted to learn the business.'

'Well, yes, I do . . .'

'You're not going to learn anything looking out from behind closed curtains. Come on in the stable, I want to show you how your horses have been neglected.'

'Neglected?'

'Cracks in their hooves.'

'So what do I do?'

'Come on, I'll show you how to file them.'

With a heavy sigh, she followed.

A load of feed in the back of his pickup, a sleeker, more recent model than the old tin can he'd used to drive around as a kid, Matt slowed to a crawl along the dusty road, watching the two boys perched on a fence up ahead. Running into town was an errand either of the hands could have done, but after a couple of hours of riding lessons and smiling at the students while Sierra watched as though she were about to be stabbed with a thousand needles, he needed some space.

He leaned closer to get a look at the kids, who were doing something peculiar. The dark-haired, taller one he immediately recognized as Sierra's boy. The other was about a head shorter, as fair-haired as his companion was dark.

It was the Davenport boy acting like a fool. He was dangling his legs inside the fence, waving a jagged stick about three feet long in the air at a black animal standing no more than fifteen feet away.

'You stupid cow!' the boy taunted the huge, motionless beast. He dropped off the fence into the pen.

'Moo!' his friend bellowed, laughing, but Matt noticed he hadn't hopped the fence.

Matt took another look at the animal, his eyes rounding as he realized the boy's mistake. Was this kid nuts? Stepping on the gas, he brought the truck up alongside them.

The blond boy glanced backwards. Matt ignored him. 'Get out of there!' he commanded Sierra's son.

The boy looked up, his expression narrowing into annoyance and indignation. He stared defiantly through the fence.

'This your cow, mister?' he asked with the air of a rich, spoiled child addressing one of his parents' servants.

Matt cleared his throat, rubbed his whiskers. 'Suit yourself, kid,' he called with a shrug of his shoulders. 'But when that bull attacks you, I'm not going to pull you out of there.'

The boy's face went chalk-white as he took a last, horrified look at the penned animal. The stick flew out of his hand as he propelled himself over the fence, racing down the road behind his friend. Neither boy looked back.

Matt shook his head. He pulled the pickup alongside the running boys. 'Y'all need a lift?' he asked.

They just kept running, so he sped off without them.

When he got back, his first impulse was to tell Sierra her boy needed to learn a few things if he was going to survive country living. Instead, he went to the stables and started unloading the feed. The kid had got enough of a scare that he wasn't likely to be goading any more bulls. So if he told her, she'd probably have a heart attack, then resent him for telling her her business. Without reason to think the boy would do it again, there wasn't any need to report the incident. When he had a chance, he'd say something to the kid himself.

He let the episode drift from his mind as he worked with the hands to get the horses fed and bedded for the night. The sun was already dipping down in the late afternoon sky.

He'd just got Wildfire in her stall when he felt eyes on him. Turning, he found the boy watching him. A brown and white dog sat at his heels.

'You like to ride?' Matt asked, not stopping his work.

'I used to, with my dad. Mom won't let me ride alone.'

'Maybe she'll let you ride with me tomorrow. You reckon?'

'Are you going to tell her, about the bull?'

'I guess not. No sense in worrying her about something that's over and done with.'

'Really?'

'Not unless I catch you doing some fool-headed thing like that again. In the first place, you could have been badly hurt. In the second, you had no call to be tormenting an animal that wasn't bothering you.'

'It was just a joke.'

Matt gave him a caustic glance. 'Ya gotta show some respect for what's around you. And don't be talking to people like they're your servants. I'm not taking you riding unless we come to some kind of understanding right off.'

The boy's face reddened. 'Uhh, yes, sir. What's your name?'

'Matt. What's yours?'

'Will. William really. I'm named after my great grandfather and my grandfather. My great-grandfather came to Texas and discovered oil. Who are you named after?'

'St Matthew, I guess.'

'What did he do?'

'I'm not sure.'

Matt paused and extended a hand to the boy. 'Pleasure to meet you, Will,' he said.

Round-eyed, the boy tentatively accepted his handshake, enjoying the gesture normally reserved for adults. His chest swelled and he stood taller, but the grasp of his small hand reminded Matt oddly of little Tanner reaching out to him last night.

'What are you doing out here, Will?' Sierra's voice broke through the encroaching darkness. 'I told you not to disturb Mr Rollins while he's working.'

'He's not bothering me,' Matt insisted calmly. 'We were just discussing going riding tomorrow.'

Matt saw her hand ball into a fist.

'Can I, Mom?' Will pleaded. 'I wasn't begging. It was Matt's idea.'

Matt nodded to confirm this.

'We'll see,' she said. 'Why don't you go inside and get washed for dinner?' Reluctantly, he marched off. It had been a long time since she'd seen his eyes shine about anything.

'He's a nice kid, Sierra,' Matt noted. 'I'd like to take him riding.'

'I don't want him to impose on you,' she said stiffly. She held her neck up high, and Matt traced his glance down the length of her. 'Children can be quite demanding.'

'No bother,' he said.

She nodded gravely. 'As long as he understands it's a one-time thing and you're only here for a few days. He's still grieving for Ben, and I don't want him getting too attached to someone who's not going to be around long. I know you mean well, but he needs a man to look up to and he could easily read too much into a casual act of friendship.'

'Why don't you ride with him?'

'This place was always one of Ben's toys, like his airplane and his speedboat. I've never been around horses until Will and I moved out here, and I never learned how to ride.'

'You're kidding!'

'I wish I were.'

'Why don't you take lessons, seeing as how you've hired yourself an instructor for the time being?'

She folded her arms across her chest. 'I'm too busy,' she insisted.

'No you're not. You're afraid of the critters, aren't you, Sierra? I suspected it when I watched you with them earlier. You don't even like 'em much. Damn, I didn't think anything scared you.'

'People change.'

He shrugged. 'Well, I'll teach you if you change your mind. Seems like it would be a good way to keep up with the boy. Besides, how are you going to run your own business if you're skittish around the horses? They can smell the fear on you quicker than a hound-dog.'

She stared down at the ground, and Matt couldn't keep his eyes off the deep V centring her embroidered white blouse, the delicate patch of skin. Even now, he remembered how she'd rippled like velvet in his arms. The scent of her perfume in the cold air against the smell of clean, sweet hay evoked memories of the taste of her skin on a summer day. She looked tired, he observed, but no less beautiful than he remembered.

He yearned to reach out and raise her chin, force her to meet his glance the way she'd once willingly lifted her face to him of her own accord.

The animal inside him still wanted her in the most basic way, wanted to shove his pride aside and have her right then and there, prompt his name from her lips, show her how damn wrong she'd been to think she'd ever loved Ben Davenport.

But he knew better than to touch her.

'Sierra, if it comes down to your not trusting me with the boy . . .'

She shook her head before he could finish. 'No. That's not it.'

'I like your son, Sierra. A boy can't help who his father is, and I'm not holding his being Ben's son against him. And what happened between us has nothing to do with him. The fact is, he reminds me a little of myself at that age.'

'I know,' she said quietly, letting her arms fall to her sides. Then she turned and disappeared into the house. The dog, who'd remained by her side watching Matt, trotted behind her.

The next day dawned as one of those golden November gems reminiscent of summer – sunny and clear beneath a glassy sky. The bare spiky branches on the trees served as the only reminder that today wasn't a summer day out of season. Matt had arrived early. After seeing his pickup roll into the yard and hearing his voice echoing across the fields, Sierra busied herself with her morning chores, then pulled out the cookbook she'd once purchased during a PTO fund-raiser at Will's school and found the recipe she'd been looking for.

Painstakingly, she mixed batter for apple and cinnamon cake, carefully pouring batter into the greased pan, arranging the apples and topping, then popping it into the preheated oven. Satisfied with her effort, she set the timer and put a fresh pot of coffee on to brew.

Although she'd promised herself not to, when she heard the familiar cowboy whoop, she peered out the window. Matt was riding Wildfire again. He was in his shirt-sleeves, wearing a white T-shirt that hugged his chest muscles. He looked good, she thought. Very good. His jeans-clad hips swayed in time to Wildfire's movements. She'd seen him through the window, but she'd been careful not to draw the curtain back. Yesterday he'd noticed her watching him, and she didn't want him getting the wrong idea about why she was doing it. Absently, she sighed. A long time had passed since she'd known a man's touch. And because of her long abstinence, it was hard not to recall the shivery delight Matt once sparked in her. He'd had a way about him, treating her as though she were a fiberglass angel requiring careful handling.

A smile curled the corners of her lips. Realizing her glance was lingering overlong and her thoughts were headed in a dangerous direction, she moved away from the window. Watching him this way seemed terribly adolescent, especially for a widow and a mother. The man didn't even want to work for her. He probably regretted every moment they'd spent together. She wished he had stayed in town long enough for her to explain things to him. She'd fully intended to talk to him before he'd learned of her engagement. How was she to know that her mother-in-law to be would be in a such a rush to make it public? Mrs Davenport was a stickler for appearances.

But the truth of it was, if the newspaper announcement hadn't appeared prematurely, if Matt hadn't left town without saying goodbye, she would have had to lie to him anyway.

She had to push out of her mind what he once was to her. Her idle fantasies would only distract her. She had to persuade him to stay for a while. At least until after the holidays. His sister would require his help at least that long, and having him here would ease her mind.

Over coffee and cake, she was going to appeal to him to stay on. The house smelled pleasantly of apples and cinnamon and fresh coffee. Everything was ready, and she watched him walk Wildfire back to the stable, then allowed time for him to brush her down.

Just as she was stepping outside to request his presence in the house, a familiar red convertible turned into the driveway. She hadn't been expecting company this morning.

Alison. On any other day, Sierra would have been

happy to see her. Typically, her old friend had remarkably bad timing. Sierra glanced back towards Matt, who, seemingly unaware of her, was shouting instructions to the hands. Turning, she watched the approaching car, forced a smile and waved.

CHAPTER 4

'Cake and coffee – you shouldn't have,' Alison declared as she sat in Sierra's living room stirring her coffee. 'I can see I timed my arrival perfectly. But baking, SiSi? When did you get so domestic?'

'Just a whim,' Sierra lied. She'd been doing an alarming amount of that lately.

Alison sampled a bite of the still-warm cake. 'Lucky I came. Be a shame if you ended up feeding this to the ranch hands.'

Sierra felt her cheeks warming.

Alison swept her glance across the spacious room with the exposed rafters and stone fireplace at one end. It looked more like a hunting lodge than the elegant homes they were both accustomed to. But Sierra hadn't had any choice about her living quarters. When Ben had bought this place he'd had no intention of moving his family here.

'This place does have a certain rustic charm.'

'Alison, why are you here?'

Her friend shrugged. 'Someone's got to look out for you.'

'Will and I are fine, Alison, but it is good to see you.'

Alison swung her neatly coiffed auburn hair over her shoulder. A pair of long silver and turquoise earrings, the turquoise matching her eyes, dangled from her earlobes. Although she had aristocratic features – straight nose, high cheekbones, a long forehead – she wasn't an especially pretty woman, but she carried herself in a manner that created the illusion that she was. Her parents lived next door, if half a mile away could be considered next door, to Sierra's father.

As girls, Sierra and Alison had been best friends, and Alison was the one person from her old life who'd stuck by her through Ben's gambling, his death, all of it. Alison's presence reminded Sierra of the privileged world she'd left behind, a world she was no longer part of.

'Sierra, was that Matt Rollins I saw working your stables? I'd heard he was out here, but I didn't believe it.'

So, that was what had prompted her friend's unexpected visit. 'Yes, it's Matt. So what?'

Alison's eyes sparkled. 'Come on, SiSi, you may be a widow, but you're still a young woman. You were wild for him once, and to tell you the truth, he doesn't look any the worse for wear. Rough around the edges maybe, but not hard on the eye at all.'

Sierra shook her head. After two failed marriages, Alison had gone back to college to study for a master's degree and taken a full-time job she didn't need directing a local charity. Despite her past experience, she'd remained friends with both her former husbands and still believed she'd find her Prince Charming one day. She was an incurable, reckless romantic.

'His sister's husband is in the hospital. They have two small children and, from what I understand, the family's pretty badly off. Matt needs a job, and I need a stable manager. That's all there is to it. If you're wondering whether we picked up where we left off – no.'

'Come on SiSi, you don't find him attractive? All that rugged muscle.'

'Too much has happened between us. I'm looking for neither a husband nor a lover, Alison. All I'm concerned about now that Ben is gone is raising my son.'

'You have a long time left, then, to live alone. And you always wanted more children. I mean, I suppose with modern technology you can bypass the lover, but how incredibly boring.'

Sierra sighed heavily. Once Alison got hold of a notion, she wouldn't let go. 'I know life can be lonely growing up as an only child. That's not what I wanted for Will. But it looks as if it's the best I can do. The big family I dreamed of having wasn't meant to be.'

Alison dropped her tongue-in-cheek tone. 'Your childbearing years are far from over, honey.'

'I've no intention of ever marrying again. I always pictured a big, loving family. M . . . someone told me once there was no such thing. I didn't believe him back then, but now I'm starting to.'

'My family wasn't so big, but my mom and dad and my brother and I always got along fine. I know Matt's family had a lot of problems, but he was young and cynical. I'm sure in his maturity he's gotten over it.'

Sierra shook her head. 'Matt's father was an ignorant, selfish man. He couldn't deal with having a son who was better than he was, so he took his problems out on Matt, tried to make him feel worthless. Sam Burke gave Matt a chance to do work he was good at, and in Sam Matt found someone he could look up to. Still, you know we're all afraid we'll turn into our parents. When Matt's brother, his dad's favorite, left home, Matt's dad looked him in the eye and told him he wished he had never been born. Matt swore he'd never bring a child into the world and subject it to the Rollins legacy.'

'But that was before he fell in love with you.'

'No. Even after. At first, I thought as long as I was with him right then and there, nothing else mattered. Then I realized I wanted to spend the rest of my life with him, even if it meant giving up my dream. I thought if I loved him enough, made him feel comfortable with it, he'd see he was more of a man than his father ever was, change his mind. But there wasn't time. I was pregnant, and demanding anything of him would be like sending him straight to hell. I loved him too much to do that to him.'

'Does Matt suspect he's Will's father?'

Sierra nearly spat out her coffee.

'No, and he's never going to.'

'Not even with Ben dead?'

'Ben was the only father Will ever knew. To tell him the truth now would destroy him. And Matt's not back to stay.'

'Honey, I can look at Will and see Matt. Don't you think your cowboy's going to start adding things up and figure it out? I'm amazed it's not the first thing that came into his mind when he got a look at the boy.'

Sierra shook her head. 'We might have been young, but Matt took his responsibilities seriously. We never made love without using birth control. He never considered that those precautions might have failed us.'

'But they did, of course.'

'I'm sure he realized nothing is foolproof. But since I never got a chance to tell him . . . Will is destiny's child. He was meant to be, and nothing

Matt or I could have done would have prevented it. No matter what's happened, I'm thankful I have him.'

'Wouldn't Matt be too, if he knew?' Alison's voice was barely a whisper.

'No.'

Alison gave her a long, hard look.

'I remember that summer when we were both home from college, and you came over glowing like a Christmas tree and told me you'd been seeing Matt Rollins.'

'You said I'd lost my mind.'

'I thought you were doing it to defy your father – forbidden fruit and all that.'

'You warned me to walk away before I was in too deep.'

'But being bullheaded as you are, you didn't.'

'I couldn't. I didn't want to.'

'I was considering everything you'd be giving up if your father found out. I think I was jealous because you dared to follow where your heart was leading you, even if it was to the wrong side of town. Yes, I know it's snobbery, but face it, Sierra, we were both brought up that way. I was wrong. I should have told you to go for it.'

'Alison, I can't tell Matt now. He thinks little enough of me for having married Ben so quickly, but all things considered, it was the only choice I had. Had Matt known the truth he would have stood by us, borne his responsibilities, and resented me for chaining him to a life he never wanted.'

'You two were so young. Maybe Matt's changed.'

'I really don't know him now. And I can't take the chance. Telling him would add to the risk of Will finding out. And I'm afraid Matt would be too angry to continue working for me. I had a hard enough time convincing him as it was.'

'He has a right to know.'

Sierra held her head high and shook her head. 'Ben accepted Will as his son and never treated him as anything less. Regardless of Ben's failings, the rest is just biology.'

Alison eyed her friend critically. 'I can't imagine his conception resulted from a science project. Honestly, you talk as though the heart has been cut right out of you. Is this the evidence of Ben's caring, that he couldn't even provide for his wife and son?'

Sierra leaned forward, setting down her coffee cup. 'Shouldn't you be in your office?'

'This time of year, I'm keeping crazy hours. Everyone's opening their hearts and pocketbooks to the disadvantaged, and I'm on call to accept donations. Which reminds me, the Winter Hoedown is coming up in a couple of weeks. It's for a good cause, and a good time will be had by all.'

'A dance? No, not for me. I'll buy a ticket, though.'

Alison held up her palms. 'I'm not hitting you up for a donation. The fact is, I bought several extra tickets and I thought you might use one. Isn't it time you got back out among people again? It's been nearly a year, a generously respectable period of mourning.'

'I can't leave Will here alone.'

'My mom would be delighted to watch him.'

'No, Alison, I don't think so.'

'You'll make yourself old before your time if you don't get out, SiSi. No one's asking you to fall in love or get married again. Even us working women need some kind of social life. Of course, I don't blame you for staying in with the view you have out your back window. Is that what's keeping you here?'

Sierra glanced out of the window and saw Matt in the pasture, his back to them. He was leaning over, inspecting one of the horse's hooves. 'Alison!' she chided her friend, blushing like a schoolgirl. 'You have a dirty mind.'

'In the past you would have been the first to notice. I think you let Ben make you lose sight of who you are. No, a man like that, he'd leave his brand on a woman. Is he as good as he looks?'

Sierra's face blazed crimson. 'You're making me wish I'd never told you. Do you want some more coffee?'

'No. I do have to get back to the office. I wanted to tell you, I saw your father a few days ago.'

A cool silence filtered through the air. 'How is he?'

'Miserable, but he'd never admit it. He did ask about you and Will.'

Sierra swallowed hard. Coming from William Ross, even that was a major concession. 'I'm not responsible for his misery. It's self-imposed.'

'Hey, I know. But it's almost Christmas, and he's all alone. You know how stubborn he is, and I'm sure he's sorry he got so angry over Ben.'

Sierra straightened her narrow shoulders. 'If he's sorry, he can say so. He knows where to find us.'

Alison stood, straightened the skirt of her caramel-colored suit. 'I never realized before that you're as stubborn as he is. I didn't think you had it in you to be cold and vindictive.'

'I've never stopped loving my father, Alison. God knows I want him in our lives; Will should have a chance to know his grandfather. But my father uses his anger to control people. For a long time, I went along with his wishes. But I couldn't leave Ben just because he wanted me to. I owed Ben more than that, despite his problems. I keep thinking maybe if I'd been a better wife to Ben he could have handled his responsibilities better. My father has to accept that I'm making my own decisions now – with or without his approval.'

'Stop taking the blame for everything. Ben Davenport's parents babied him all his life. He never had to work, never had to make a decision. He never grew up, and he wasn't capable of taking care of you or Will. I'm amazed you stuck it out with him.'

'He married me knowing I was having another man's baby. And he never threw that in my face. Even over all the rest, I was grateful. And I'd promised to be faithful.'

'No one takes marriage vows literally these days.'

'I guess I'm like a dinosaur, then.'

'You know your father will welcome you back if you go to him.'

'That's just it. Don't you think I've tried to talk to him? He's willing to make up, as long as it's on his terms, which don't include Will and me living here on our own. I can't do it. I can't give in to him on this, or he'll start trying to run my life again.'

Alison sighed, giving her hair a final pat. 'Do what you have to, but have you stopped to consider your dad could give Will advantages you can't afford – private schools, summer camps, social contacts?'

Sierra's dark eyes narrowed. 'All the benefits I had, you mean? Is all that worth so much?'

'He's your son, I suppose it's your choice.'

Alison turned, taking a last long look out the window.

Then she swung to face Sierra again. 'So, what do I tell your father if I should see him again?'

'Tell him Will and I are fine and we love him, but I'm not going to pretend to regret standing by my husband.'

'I'll just tell him you send your love.'

'You've been placed in an awkward situation. I'm sorry, Alison. This must make you awfully uncomfortable.'

'I just hate to see you and Will struggling like this when it doesn't have to be this way. But I have to admit, I admire you for not taking the easy way out.' She peered intently through the curtains. 'Does Matt know about Sam?'

'I don't think so. Sam made it clear he didn't want anybody telling him.'

'Well, since you've lost interest in Matt, Sierra, you won't mind if I invite him to have dinner with me, would you?'

Dumbfounded, Sierra gaped at her friend. Fire sizzled in her eyes.

To her astonishment, Alison smiled triumphantly. 'Exactly what I thought. Don't look so distressed, I doubt he'd give me or anyone else a second look with you within a hundred-mile vicinity.'

'That was blatantly unfair,' Sierra accused her friend.

'And very telling. You're not as disinterested as you profess to be. Shame on you, Sierra.'

After Alison left, Sierra picked up the dishes and napkins in the living room and carried them into the kitchen. Just as she started water running to rinse the cups, the doorbell rang.

'What now?' she muttered, still reeling over her reaction to Alison's ribbing. Wiping her hands on a dishtowel, she went to answer it. She opened the door to find Neal Adamson smiling at her. With a pang of disappointment, she realized she'd been hoping it was Matt.

'Gorgeous day, isn't it?' he asked. The young paediatrician came from somewhere up north – Ohio, she thought – and his speech was flat and quick. He had a smooth, roundish face with dark eyebrows, eyes the deep yellow of ale, and a quick, even smile that couldn't have failed to put his tiny patients at ease. His thick, wavy brown hair was parted on the side and neatly combed in place.

'Hello, Dr Adamson,' she greeted him. 'It is a magnificent day.'

'Sorry to barge in on you unannounced, but I've got the morning off and came to ride White Fang. I decided while I'm here I might as well catch up on her boarding bill.'

'That's no problem. I can have Fang saddled up for you while you're writing your check.'

'Fine. Here, I'll walk over to the stable with you.'

She'd planned to have an intercom installed between the stables and the house, but that was one item on a long list of improvements that would have to wait until they started making a profit.

'Is November always like this here?' he asked as he accompanied her to the barn.

Sierra laughed. 'No. Our weather's so unstable, it could snow tomorrow.'

'Oh.' He sounded disappointed.

'I'm exaggerating, Dr Adamson. We've had a few inches of snow occasionally, but it's extremely rare.'

'Neal, please.'

'Neal,' She shot him a sidelong smile.

He removed one of the hands he had stuffed in the pockets of his trousers and rubbed his neck.

'What's this I hear about your manager being arrested?'

'Oh, he's been replaced. The horses are being well cared for, as you'll see for yourself.'

'Well, good. Fang's a fine animal, and I'm pretty particular where he's concerned. I was afraid I might have to move him to another stable.'

'Totally unnecessary.'

As she approached the stable, she looked up and saw Matt leading Fancy to the pasture. He was staring at her and not looking happy. The intensity in his eyes distracted her so much that she tripped on a clod of earth, pitching forward. Dr Adamson caught her by the arm.

'Careful,' he said. 'Are you all right, Mrs Davenport?'

'Yes. Thank you,' she replied, cheeks flaming with embarrassment. Even without looking at

Matt, she felt the heat of his eyes on her. At first she was puzzled, wondering what she had done to prompt such a tough glance from him. Then she realized he must think Dr Adamson was someone other than a client.

How dared he look at her like that? Her life was her concern. And she realized Alison had been right. Shutting herself off from the rest of the world could only push her towards Matt. Maybe she did harbor some underlying hunger, some nostalgic affection for him. Maybe she simply needed sex. She couldn't allow it to lead her to make yet another mistake in her life.

Neal's hands lingered on her slender forearm, bared because she'd rolled up her shirtsleeves in the kitchen. The contact reminded her only of how Matt's hands had once played over her, and she felt her midsection softening as she thought of him.

Regaining both her balance and her dignity, she flashed Neal a smile. 'Please, call me Sierra.'

She approached Matt, trying to ignore how his T-shirt stretched over strapping muscle. Strange how a man who exuded such power could be so infinitely gentle. She had to stop remembering.

'Matt, could you saddle up White Fang for Dr Adamson? He'll be riding him this morning.'

'Yes, ma'am,' he said, mockingly. His face was a tight mask. She heard him telling one of the hands to saddle the horse.

Returning to Neal's side, she headed back towards the house. 'Would you like some coffee?' she asked. She thought she heard Matt groan, but she couldn't swear to it. If Neal heard anything, he ignored it.

'Great idea. Thank you,' he said. 'I could use a caffeine jolt this morning. I got in late last night, driving back from Houston.'

'Business trip?'

'No, strictly pleasure. A new art gallery opened, and I was trying to find some pieces for my house. All those bare walls are a little stark.'

'Something in particular you're looking for?'

He shrugged. 'I'll know it when I see it; my tastes vary. I appreciate art, but frequently I don't understand it.'

'It's not unusual to feel overwhelmed. Often it's best to trust your instincts.'

'In any case, I didn't buy anything. Do you know anything about art, Sierra?'

'I studied art history in college.'

'If I'd known, I would have asked you to come along and advise me.'

'I seldom get that far from the ranch these days.'

'Yes, I see you have plenty to keep you busy. Do you do any original artwork?'

'I used to do some painting. Nothing serious. I gave it up a long time ago.'

'It's a shame, isn't it, how we grow up and

abandon the pursuits we love? In any event, maybe you could help me out with something else.'

'What's that?'

'I bought a couple of tickets to this Winter Hoedown, and I've heard it's fun – line-dancing and fiddling and the like. I was wondering if you'd like to go. Of course, you probably already have plans.'

'No, as a matter of fact I don't.' Neal was friendly and attractive, and she did need to get out, so she'd stop dwelling on her old attraction to Matt. 'I'd enjoy going with you. Of course, I'll have to find a sitter.'

'My office keeps a list of people who complete the babysitting seminar the hospital offers.'

'I don't want to leave him with a stranger. He's had enough upheavals losing his father.'

'He seems like a tough kid. He's certainly a healthy one, anyway. You know, Sierra, sometimes children can cope beyond what we give them credit for.'

'I know someone who might stay with him.'

'Good. I'll check back with you towards the end of next week to make sure. Now, about that coffee . . .'

Sierra grinned. 'And about that check . . .'

'Don't let her forget you're there,' Matt instructed the sober-face young boy on the horse trotting alongside his. 'Ease up on those reins.'

Will complied.

'That's better. Nice 'n' easy.'

Will grinned proudly.

This afternoon, Matt had left Wildfire in her stall and opted to ride slower, more dependable Fancy instead. The sun warmed his skin, and ahead lay nothing but an expanse of open field. 'Nothin' better in this life than going riding,' he said. Well, almost. Reaching out, he patted Fancy's mane. 'Best exercise you can give your horse is a good long ride.'

'How come you know so much about horses?' the boy asked.

'Grew up around them. If you treat a horse right, it's going to respect you back. I wasn't much older than you when I started shovelling out stalls to earn spending money.'

'I could shovel out stalls, but my mom won't let me.'

'She watches over you pretty close, huh?'

Will nodded. 'All the time. I know she needs me to take care of her, because my dad died.'

Matt whistled. 'That's a pile of responsibility.'

'She never wants to have fun any more. She used to take me places.'

'She's got a lot of work now, a lot on her mind.'

'You mean things will be like this forever?'

'I reckon not. She's probably got to get over missing your dad too.'

'Will I stop missing him?'

'I don't know.'

'Will you show me how to make the horse jump?'

'Not today.'

'If you show me how to take care of the horses, Mom won't have to worry so much.'

'She worries a lot, does she?'

'Uh-huh. Are you sure you were named after St Matthew?'

'No. I don't think I was really named after anybody. Why?'

'Matthew means a gift from God.'

Matt chuckled. 'I'll be hanged. Where'd you learn that, Sunday school?'

'No, I was looking up Matthew on my computer encyclopaedia.'

'Damn.'

'Excuse me?'

'Nothing. You have your own computer?'

'My dad got it for me. Mom said we could keep it, but we can't get it upgraded like Dad said we would.'

'You're pretty smart when it comes to finding things out.'

Will dropped his head. 'I guess not when it comes to animals.'

'Some things you can't learn off a computer.'

'I'm going to be in a play at school.'

The way the kid flitted from one subject to the

next was making Matt dizzy. 'A Christmas pageant?'

'No. *A Christmas Carol.* I'm Scrooge.' He puffed his chest and deepened his voice. 'Bah! Humbug!'

'That's a good part. Makes you the star.'

'I get two tickets. Free. One's for Mom, and I want you to have the other one.'

'Me?'

'You'll come, won't you?'

'I don't know, Will. Maybe you should give it to one of your grandparents.'

'None of them would come. They don't come and see us any more.'

'None of them?'

'No.'

'Well, I'd sure like to see that play. But I don't know how long I'll be here. I'm just kind of visiting.'

'You can stay. My mom doesn't know anything about horses and our old manager got arrested. She's been happier since you came, I can tell.'

'Arrested?'

'The police took him away.'

'Will, are you making this up?'

'No, sir.'

Sierra hadn't been stretching the truth when she'd claimed she and Will were on their own. For reasons Matt couldn't fathom, everyone in her life had abandoned her. He intended to find out why. And he wasn't leaving her and the kid until he was confident she could handle both the horses and the business. He'd feel better about leaving once he knew that. Maybe she'd made her own life, but the kid deserved better. And so did these animals. He couldn't leave knowing she'd take her next manager at his word if he claimed he was tending the horses properly. He wanted to know she'd check and make sure.

The boy's enthusiasm about his acting debut reminded Matt of the first rodeo he'd competed in. He'd bought his parents passes out of his earnings working at Sam's ranch and proudly presented them at the dinner table one night. Daddy'd chewed him out for squandering his money. Of course, the night of the rodeo, they didn't show. When Daddy was home, Mama couldn't go anywhere without his approval.

He remembered how his pride had eroded into emptiness, and he'd accepted then that nothing he could ever do would win his daddy's approval. But Sam had been in the stands cheering him on. He'd often wished he'd had someone more like the weathered rancher for a father.

Thank God for Sam. Matt needed to go and see him, let him know he didn't hold a grudge about his grandson not giving him a job.

And now here was this poor kid with his dad dead and cold-fish grandparents who apparently didn't give a damn about him, a mama who treated him like he was still a baby, and no one to explain life's subtleties, such as the distinct differences between a bull and a cow. Matt supposed it wouldn't kill him to be Sam for the kid, for one night anyway.

'This is a front-row seat, right?' he asked.

'You'll have to come early if you want a good spot.'

'I'll be there.'

It was almost dark, and Sierra didn't see Will or Thunder around anywhere.

With the sun down, the air had a slight chill to it, and she tossed a cardigan over her shoulders before setting out to look for him. Everything was still and silent, except for the occasional braying of horses.

She passed the stables and went round to the back, surprised to hear the soft twang of old-timey country music coming from the darkened apartment in the square white outbuilding.

'What in the world . . .?' she muttered, moving closer to the door. She knew Matt had declined to move in here. Had Will broken in somehow? He knew better, but lately, she didn't know what to expect from him.

Stepping up to the wooden door, she rapped lightly. 'Hello?' she called.

When no answer came, she tried the door and found it wasn't locked. Hesitantly, she eased it open.

'Hello?' she called again. No answer came. The room was empty.

She flipped on the overhead light. The miniature front room/dining room contained nothing that hadn't been there when she'd scrubbed the place down after Tom's departure. She crossed the living room, glancing into the kitchen, then scanned the single bedroom. The apartment was dingy and needed paint, the furniture was secondhand cast-offs. But she'd brought over some of her nicer linens from the house and curtains she'd saved from the house on Dallas Avenue. She'd accessorized with potted silk plants and framed prints to make the small, drab rooms more cheerful.

The radio sat in the bedroom on the nightstand. Sierra stepped inside to turn it off, wondering if some kind of power surge had activated it.

Just as she pressed the switch, a tall shadow filled the doorframe.

She jumped.

'Don't care for my choice of music?' Matt asked.

She clasped a hand to her chest. Her heart was galloping.

'I'm sorry,' she replied. 'I thought you'd gone home.'

'I was just looking the place over and stepped outside for a smoke. I didn't think you'd appreciate the smell of tobacco in your frilly curtains.'

'Thank you. I didn't see you outside. I wouldn't have come in if I'd known . . .'

'Sierra, no harm done. You gave me a key, so I didn't think to say anything about coming in here.'

'No, you didn't need to. I thought – I understood you'd decided not to move in.'

Her knees felt shaky, but she resisted sitting down, since the only place to sit was on the bed.

He rubbed his whiskers. In the past few days, she'd come to hate that gesture. He was so handsome clean-shaven; why did he insist on hiding behind a tangle of fuzz that detracted from his appearance? She wanted to see his face. As it was, she felt as though she were peering over a hedge to glimpse his eyes.

'I was thinking I might keep a few things over here so I could stay the night if there was a problem with one of the horses, or being around Leeann and the kids got too stifling. Place still comes with the job, doesn't it?'

'Yes.' She studied the fine lines of his face, ignoring the tightening in her chest. 'Does that mean you're staying on?' she asked incredulously.

'For a while. Nothing permanent. I'll be leaving Winter as soon as Leeann and Jerry get things squared away. If you still want me to, I'll work for you as long as I'm here. Does that suit you?'

'Of course it does. Thank you, Matt.'

He stepped closer, still clad in nothing heavier than his jeans and T-shirt. She smelled musk, sweat and horse ointment on him. Without the gas heater on, the room was cold, but Sierra had a sudden feverish urge to open a window. The room was so small, she was cornered in a rectangular slot between the bed and two walls. The only way out was past him.

He levelled his blue eyes on her. 'And if you meant it when you said you want to learn the business, I'll teach you. But you're going to have to stop acting as if I'm the bogeyman and be out there working with the horses every morning.'

'I was only trying to stay out of your way.'

'You're going to have to learn to ride, Sierra.'

She sighed heavily. 'All right.'

'And you're going to have to be straight with me.'

She tensed.

'What makes you think I haven't?'

'Tell me why your father and Ben's parents have left you to scratch out a living at something you don't know beans about while they have more money than they can light fires with. What happened, Sierra? What did you do that they banished you?'

Sierra's shoulders sagged. Suddenly, she felt tired of trying to be strong.

Matt loomed over her. His breath fell in hot wisps across her face. She felt heat rising from his skin. She was suffocating, her breasts straining painfully against the confines of her bra.

She closed her eyes and tried to shut out the

memory of Ben's face as he prolonged his love-making until it became gruelling, determined to take her somewhere she refused to go. He'd caught on to her act, and she couldn't blame him for being hurt and angry. 'When was it?' he'd asked cruelly, giving up in defeat. 'That you stopped liking sex?' She'd believed he was right, that she'd grown so accustomed to pretending, she'd lost the drives of a normal woman.

But now, Matt wasn't even touching her, and there was a telltale moistness in her jeans.

'Ben got heavily into debt, gambling. When my father realized what was happening, he wanted me to leave Ben. He wanted Will and me to move in with him.'

'And you couldn't leave Ben, even then?'

He was leaning over her, and she looked up into those compelling eyes.

Slowly, she shook her head. 'No.'

'But now, surely, he's had a change of heart.'

'Matt, you don't know my father. His heart is forever unchanging. I'm managing without him. I'll survive.'

'What about Ben's parents?'

'I was never very close to them. They shut us out after Ben died.'

'Why?'

She shrugged. 'I don't know.' She read in his eyes that he didn't believe her. 'Mrs Davenport says it's hard for her to be around Will and me. We remind her too much of the son she lost.'

'Bull! All the more reason to hold on . . .' he speculated, his voice dropping.

For a fleeting, dangerous second she felt lost and helpless. He was standing so close, and she needed something to lean on. Oh, she needed so much more. Over the years apart, they'd become near-strangers. Now she felt the lingering thread of closeness between them. So long ago, she'd yielded to him with total abandon and intimacy. Nothing, she realized, could ever erase that bond. This afternoon she'd flirted with a man who didn't interest her to keep herself from flirting with Matt. Her traitorous body, independent of her rational good sense and caution, was instinctively readying itself for him.

He caught hold of her hand, raising it for his inspection. He brushed calloused fingers over a palm once smooth as down, now chapped and cracked. Starbursts formed around the corners of his eyes as he lifted them to hers enquiringly.

Embarrassed, she tried to yank her hand away, but he held fast, bowing low and pressing his lips to her skin. Electric currents coiled up the length of her arm.

When he opened his arms and folded her against his chest, she willingly fell into them. Closing her eyes, she nestled her head against his firm, strong chest. She inhaled his masculine scent.

Just for a moment, she wanted some kind of reassurance.

The tingling in her belly alarmed her. Wouldn't it be easy to tumble into bed with him? God knew she needed him in more ways than one. She ached for the feel of his tough, leathery skin against her body. Her poor heart was thumping like a woodpecker's beak. The woman inside her was reawakening, craving the kind of lovemaking only he could give her. After all the years, after everything, she craved him. She almost wished she were still capable of showing a man love.

But she knew the time in her life when she could do the easy thing had passed. Matt wasn't some stud horse she could borrow for the evening. God knew she'd hurt him too much already. She could no longer leave her fate to anyone but herself.

She drew back.

'You really are trying to make this place work, aren't you? You're still the most beautiful woman I know,' he said, his eyes sweeping over her. 'And you've always been strong. You just never knew it because your old man was stronger.'

She laughed lightly. 'I could just imagine what he'd do if he heard himself being referred to as my "old man".'

Matt shrugged. 'Even if he was the devil himself, you probably miss him.'

'I do. I've missed you sometimes too.' She was

lying again. She'd missed him all the time. She shifted her eyes down to the floor.

Matt eyed her uneasily, then swung his glance around the room. 'So is this a doll house or what?'

'It used to be servants' quarters.'

'It'll do. I'll keep the door locked so you can't break in again.'

'Matt, what changed your mind about staying?'

'Will.'

Sierra recoiled as though she'd been stabbed in the heart. She'd feared hearing that. Will favored her more than he did his father, but if Matt spent too much time around him, he was going to notice how the stature, the mannerisms mocked his own.

She nodded. 'You're not as wrong about me as I might have argued you were,' she told him. 'I'm glad you're staying, but you're wise to keep your distance from me. I've never done right by you or anyone else.'

'Sierra . . .'

'Will!' she exclaimed, remembering what had brought her outside in the first place. 'Have you seen him? I was looking for him when I heard the radio.'

'No, but he can't be far away. He's probably playing in the woods.'

'He knows he's supposed to come in by sundown.'

'Boys his age don't always pay attention to the time.'

'And you're an expert on raising children?'

'I just remember I was a boy once. I reckon my memory is longer than yours.'

After fifteen minutes, they found Will. He had come into the house and was in his room doing his homework. When Sierra frantically burst in, he asked calmly when supper would be ready. Matt shook his head and told them both goodnight.

CHAPTER 5

Will emitted a loud sputtering sound as his horse broke into a gallop.

'No!' Matt called out to him. 'Bring it up out of your lungs. Like a real cowboy.'

'Yee-ha!' the boy yelled, tentatively waving one fist in the air.

Sierra, perched on the fence, laughed as she watched the two. Matt had been here over a week now, and Will, fascinated with his new hero, spent most of the daylight hours after school trailing after Matt. Matt had cheerfully allowed the boy to clean the stalls, never mind that Will had come in to dinner one night smelling like horse manure.

He'd informed her she might as well give the stable boy his notice. Her son no longer resembled a sullen little man. Color now tinted his cheeks and cheer shone in his eyes. Sierra had to admit that Matt's presence had been the best thing to happen to her and her son in a long time. In odd moments, she forgot her past struggles and worries about the future. But when she was alone, her problems never failed to hammer in her brain, making her edgy.

To her relief, at least Matt wasn't questioning Will's parentage. If he guessed the truth and confronted her, she'd have no choice but to acknowledge it.

All she wanted was a fresh start for herself and her son, a new beginning free of the entanglements of the past. If only her heart didn't start fluttering like a leaf in a whirlwind whenever Matt was around. In high school, she'd harbored a crush on him. At twenty, she'd dared to fall in love with him. Trying to hold back the rush of emotion he churned in her would have been like damming a waterfall. And time hadn't drained its force. So far, since their encounter in his apartment, she'd been careful to avoid being alone with him, avoid being too close. Collapsing into those strong arms was far too easy.

Now Matt, pivoting, spotted her watching them and waved, breaking into a slow grin. He stood tall and proud against the open expanse of pasture. She wished he knew what a fine man he truly was. If he could see himself through the eyes of his son . . . No. He could never know how she'd deceived him. How many times had she imagined a scene such as this, the two of them together with their son? That only she knew the truth was breaking her heart, but it was a secret she must keep forever. He'd never forgive her for withholding it all this time.

Smiling, she waved back, then patted her gloved

hands together. A real winter chill had settled into the brittle air, and the overcast sky had been threatening rain all day.

'That's enough for today,' Matt called to Will, walking towards Sierra. He glanced up at the darkening sky. 'It's time to bring the horses in.'

She had her head tossed back, laughing. 'You're teaching him to whoop 'n' holler?' she asked. 'What's next? Guzzling longneck beers?'

Will raced up beside her. 'Can I, Mom?'

Her eyes blazed. 'Sure – about ten or eleven years from now!'

Will turned to Matt. 'Can I take Fancy back to the stable, Matt?'

'No, hold up. Since your Ma's in such a good mood, I think it's her turn to ride.'

She blinked incredulously at Matt. 'Not now. It's about to start raining.'

'There's time,' he insisted, taking hold of the lead rope.'

'Come on, Mom,' Will coaxed. 'It's easy.'

Sierra glanced at her son, then back at Matt. She shrugged in resignation. 'All right.'

Matt smiled and playfully boosted the bottom of her chin with the side of his fist. Sierra tingled at the contact, a shudder slamming through her as her eyes met Matt's and she saw them darken to match the sky.

Quickly, he lowered his hand and shifted his attention to the horse. 'Once you're on, you'll wonder what all the fuss was about. Fancy's about as gentle as they come.'

He eased Sierra to the left side of the horse.

'Put your left foot up here in the stirrup, then throw your other leg over,' he instructed.

'Excuse me?'

With firm hands, he grasped her waist and tossed her over. His hands fitted snugly around her and lingered, pressing lightly against the swell of her belly. Sierra, heat rippling through her, looked down, met his infinite blue gaze, and recognized the fire of desire in his eyes.

A surge of warring emotions washed through her. She'd thought the prospect of ever touching her again would repel him. But he handled her with an intimacy she couldn't deny. As if she'd always been his and still was. Discovering that his desire might mirror her own shot an involuntary thrill of excitement through her. She couldn't afford to give in to it. She was so astonished, she nearly forgot she was sitting on a horse.

Until Fancy moved. Panic seized her, then she heard Matt crooning in the low, soothing voice he reserved for speaking to horses and – other occasions. What a time to think of that. To tell the truth, she had a difficult time not thinking about it. Matt wasn't the type of man who would go long without a woman. Did he have one now? Most nights, he left the ranch. Did he meet someone in town? She hoped he stayed too busy helping Leeann. Tough as it was to admit, she loathed the idea of his making love to another woman, although she'd abdicated any claim to him long ago.

Even when she'd been his lover, she realized, she'd never had access to his life, never met his friends. What a strange affair theirs had been – a feverish combination of attraction and a need to rebel. No wonder it had ended so badly.

'Relax, Sierra. You're too stiff. Let your hips move.'

Sierra's face reddened as she complied, allowing her body to sway with the horse's movements.

Matt was guiding the horse around by the lead rope, and she felt like a kid on a pony ride.

'It's raining,' she protested as the first droplets peppered her face. She peered down at him through the mist.

'All right,' he concluded with a nod. 'We'll finish this later.'

Happy for the reprieve, she moved to dismount. Matt caught her by the waist and swung her to the ground. For a split-second she stood nose-to-nose with him, her heart pounding. A thrill raced through her, and she told herself she was reading too much into small gestures. She remembered her son was watching.

Then Matt straightened, releasing her.

'Will you make hot cocoa, Mom?' Will asked.

'Sure.' She looked up at Matt. Why was she so afraid of him? No, never of him. Just those lingering, gnawing feelings she entertained. She couldn't blame him for that. His behavior towards her had been torturously polite. 'You're invited too, Matt.'

He glanced at her, then looked down at Will. 'OK,' he agreed, and began walking Fancy towards the stable. 'I'll be in shortly.' Thunder followed them.

'I'm going with Matt,' Will blurted, tearing after him before she could answer. She shook her head and headed towards the house. 'You still have to pack!' she called to her son.

As Will came up beside Matt, Matt handed him the rope. 'You going on a trip, Will?' he asked.

'No, I'm supposed to spend the night with Luke. He's my friend. You sort of met him.'

'The other cow-chaser?'

'Yeah.'

'You say you're "supposed" to go. Sounds like you haven't made up your mind.'

They entered the stable. Will led Fancy into her stall.

'I want to, and Mom says she wants me to go, but I don't like leavin' her here alone.'

'Will, your Ma's a grown-up lady. I reckon she could look after herself for one night.'

Will shook his head. 'It makes her nervous. Ever since my dad was killed.'

Matt studied the boy's face and believed he was telling the truth. He hadn't bothered to ask how Ben died. Figured if it was his business, somebody would have told him. But Ben was only a few years older than he was. Matt hadn't stopped to hear anyone use the term 'killed' before.

Matt stooped so he was eye-level with the boy. Will had a girls' eyelashes and his mother's Hispanic coloring, so everyone's first impression was that he favored Sierra. Now, Matt noticed the boy really didn't look much like her at all.

'It's probably hard for her to get used to his being gone.'

'No. He wasn't home much anyway. She's scared because a burglar came into our house and shot him.'

Matt didn't know what to say, so he didn't say anything.

'It wasn't this house. We moved.'

'You know, Will, I'll be right nearby in my apartment over yonder tonight, so you won't have to worry about your Ma. Does that set your mind at ease?'

'You won't leave her here by herself?'

'No. I won't.'

Matt was caught off-guard as the kid hugged him around the neck. 'Thanks, Matt,' he said.

'Yeah, sure thing,' he muttered, awkwardly easing himself free of Will's grasp. What kind of a damn world was it where kids were troubled over about senseless violence, even out here? One more reason he was glad he'd never had kids. Worrying over them could sure make a person skittish. He felt a surge of admiration for Sierra and her determination to raise her son alone. She didn't have anyone to help her look out for the kid. Matt was glad now that he hadn't told her about Will chasing the bull. Lucky thing he'd come along when he did. Lucky thing he was here?

Matt straightened, towering over Will. 'I reckon we'd better take care of this horse so we can get some of that cocoa.'

He watched as Will began unsaddling the horse.

'Does it scare you, what happened to your Pa?' Matt asked.

Will shrugged his slim shoulders. 'I'm not scared of anything,' he declared without looking up.

Matt studied the boy. Funny, he thought, how dang much Ben Davenport's son reminded him of himself at that age. The kid was only nine and he already knew how to shut out the worst feelings so they couldn't hurt you.

In the end, Matt would have rather had a cold beer, but sitting in Sierra's brightly lit kitchen with his long legs stretched out under the table, watching her easy, efficient movements as she pulled mugs from the cabinets and poured hot water from a kettle on the stove, was pleasurable enough. She was wearing jeans and a white-lace-trimmed sweater, and he appreciated the symmetry of her curves as she stretched to reach the top shelves. With Will around, she let her guard down as she never did on the rare occasions the two of them were alone.

'Nice place you got,' Matt commented, sweeping his glance across the pine-paneled room. Green gingham curtains hung over the windows, and a copper pot brimming with ivy was suspended from the ceiling by a chain. Matt had tossed his hat on the empty chair beside him. 'Real homey.'

'This is nothin'!' Will countered as he scooped marshmallows off the top of his cocoa. 'We used to have a good house with stained glass windows and a balcony. My dad wouldn't have liked us living in a dump like this.'

'Will!' Sierra reprimanded him.

'Well, he wouldn't have let us live here, and you know it!'

Matt lowered his glance. 'Do you know, Will, there's some folks lucky to have a sleeping bag to curl up in on a cold night like this.'

'Sure – bums. If people are poor, it's because they're lazy and don't work.'

Matt rubbed his beard. 'So if I told you my brother-in-law wasn't working, you'd say not having any money was his own fault?'

'Well, yeah . . .'

'But see, you don't know it's because he's got two broken legs. You really don't know enough about him to say. You can't make assumptions about people you don't even know.'

'That's different. And that was cheating, not telling he was crippled.'

Sierra intervened. 'Will, go get your clothes together. Luke and his mom will be here for you any minute.' Sierra's tone left no room for argument, and Will offered no resistance. But as he was leaving the room, he shot Matt a sharp parting glance.

'You'll have to forgive him, Matt. I honestly don't know what's gotten into him. He's been exposed to Ben's elitist philosophies, and Ben's views usually fell short of compassion.'

Matt kept his voice low. 'I think I know what's wrong. He was talking about how his father died. Must have been harder on the kid than he'll admit.'

'Will's suffered a lot of trauma.'

'Maybe he needs to talk about it more, get it out of his system.'

'When he's ready, I'm sure he will.'

'Maybe he's not sophisticated enough to know when he's ready. The way I figure, when a kid's hurting he locks it inside because he doesn't think anybody much gives a damn about listening.'

Sierra whirled to face him, pressing her palms against the counter behind her. 'You think it's that simple, do you? Raising kids is more complicated than riding horses around in the pasture for a few hours. And not that it's any of your business, but Will has seen a counselor.'

'You made him talk to a doctor?'

'A professional who understands what Will is going through and how he interprets it.'

'Well, not that it's any of my business, but what does this professional say?'

'He says Will needs lots of stability. And that's exactly what I'm trying to give him.' She leveled her dark eyes on him. 'He looks up to you, Matt. Please don't promise him anything you can't come through on. Kids aren't like horses. You can't just pacify them with an apple or a sugar cube.'

Matt's face darkened as fiercely as the sky outside. 'I believe I know the difference between kids and horses. Have you ever known me to make promises I didn't keep?'

Her voice fell. She knew that in his estimation she was the welsher. 'No. You never made me any promises.'

That wasn't entirely true, but at this point she wasn't inclined to remind him he'd once professed he'd spend the rest of his life loving her. Her decision to marry Ben by all rights absolved him from that vow.

'You're the boss. If you want me to stay away from him, I will.'

'No, you've been good for him. Really. It's good to see him enjoying himself. I'm grateful for that, Matt.'

'But you're uneasy about his getting too attached to someone beneath his social class.'

Sierra's mouth dropped open. She tilted her chin. 'You know that's never made a difference to me.'

His eyes narrowed, burning through her faded designer jeans and fraying hand-knit sweater. 'Doesn't it all boil down to that between us? One night I'm holding a warm, loving woman in my arms, and the next morning I read, *read*, mind you, that she's marrying someone from a fine upstanding family. You say it's because you loved him, and I'm still trying to make head or tail out of that. Not that you couldn't have, but then what the hell were you and I doing at the creek all summer?'

'Matt, I thought I explained . . .'

'You spend an awful lot of time explaining things, Sierra, and it still doesn't make them right. I started saving every penny I earned, putting it in the bank where my old man couldn't get at it, dreaming about the day I'd buy some land and a house for the two of us. You were the morning star, making my life worth living. Oh, I had plans. Then you pulled it all out from under me. Were you just toying with my dreams, Sierra? That's something I really need to know.'

She chewed her lip. 'If your plans included me, you might have let me in on them. Ben asked me to marry him. You never did.'

'How could I? What kind of life could I offer you? I had nothing. Big visions, but nothing to back them up. Maybe I could have brought you home for

Sunday dinner at the Rollins house, with Daddy strutting around in his underwear, swilling Pearl beer and spitting tobacco juice.'

Sierra dug teeth into her bottom lip so hard she winced with pain. 'I always knew who you were and where you came from, maybe better than you knew yourself.' She tossed her hair back. 'I guess I was too young and optimistic to see how impossible our being together was. I never intended to hurt anyone.'

Matt smiled faintly. 'Improbable – not impossible.'

She looked up, cocking her head. 'Excuse me?'

'Nothing is impossible. Unless you convince yourself it is.'

She busied herself clearing away dishes. 'I don't think we should talk about this.'

'Maybe we should have talked about it a long time back. God, we acted as if we were in some fairy-tale, neither one of us paying any attention to where the other one came from. As though it didn't matter, but as it turned out, our backgrounds were all that mattered. Here we stand, you and I, in our places in the world, as we really are. You think you're having hard times, but you have a business, a home, an expensive car. To people like me, poor is pulling carrots up out of the dirt and making a meal out of them because Daddy hasn't come home with his pay-check in a couple o' months. If my sister were in your shoes right now, she'd think she'd died and gone to heaven.'

'You can't know how someone else's shoes fit until you've tried them on. I've been running this place on money from Ben's insurance policy, and there's precious little left. I'm not that much better off than Leeann. At least she has Jerry. At least she has you.'

She reddened at her last admission. Self-pity, she knew, was neither becoming nor productive. She seldom allowed herself to lapse into it and was embarrassed at having done so in front of Matt. Sometimes, she felt so alone.

The blare of a car horn from out front made her jump.

She clutched her stomach. 'Will, Luke's here for you,' she called to her son.

Will emerged from the bedroom, duffel bag in hand, and Sierra raced to usher him to the door with obvious relief at having an excuse to get away.

At the door, she bent and kissed her son.

He squirmed. 'Mom, they'll see.'

'Have a good time. Did you pack your toothbrush?'

'Yeah.' He started out the door, then stopped and looked up at her. 'And don't be afraid while I'm gone, because Matt's staying here all night.'

She turned, her eyes boring into Matt's as Will slammed the door shut. Shoulders stiff, she walked back to the kitchen. 'You're staying on the ranch tonight?' she asked quietly.

'Tomorrow's Sunday. I'd have to drive back first thing in the morning anyway and get the horses out in the pasture . . .'

He knew if he told her that Will had revealed she was afraid, she'd deny it and insist he go back to Leeann's.

'Do you want some more cocoa?' His cup was still half full.

He shook his head. 'I'd rather have a beer,' he said.

'I have wine.'

'No, thanks. I'd better be getting back to the apartment.'

'It's not insulated very well. Let me give you some extra blankets.'

'I don't need 'em. The cold doesn't bother me.'

'I'm going to see what I can scrape up for dinner.'

'Suit yourself.'

She reached for his cup, and he caught hold of her hand. Sierra drew in a startled breath. The heat of his grasp flared up her arm like wildfire.

He raised his eyes to meet hers.

'I'm sorry about what I said. You work hard for what you have. Will should be proud.'

'He's just a boy. He doesn't understand about giving things up . . .' She tore her glance free of his.

Finally giving her hand back, he reached for his hat and put it on as he rose.

'He's going to have to learn it somewhere along the line. Sometimes you have to give one thing to gain something else. Might as well get it over with now,' he said.

Sierra walked with him to the front door. As she opened it, cold air blasted in. A drizzly rain was falling.

'Matt, I wish you'd take some more blankets,' she insisted, her heart hammering.

'I don't feel the cold much.' He tipped his hat to her. 'Appreciate the cocoa. If you need anything, you know where to find me.'

He was gone before she had a chance to ask him what he meant by that.

Sierra sat alone in the darkened living room, her brow knit in a solemn expression. She didn't know how long she'd been here on the sofa – ever since the power went off. Overhead, sleet pelted the shingles.

She thought of Matt in his cold, cramped apartment. He was probably cursing her for causing him to stay here tonight. Well, she certainly hadn't asked him to hang around. Still, she suspected he'd stayed on her account.

Guilt plagued her. If he'd gone back to Leeann's, he'd probably be eating dinner right now. And he was right, damn it. She owed him an explanation that made sense.

Resolutely, she got up from the sofa. Inching her way to the mantel, she found the hurricane lamp intended as a decoration and lit it with a fireplace match. Carrying it to the kitchen, she opened the refrigerator and constructed two thick ham sandwiches. After packing them in plastic bags, she took the lantern with her to the linen closet and extracted two heavy blankets. In a drawer, she found the half-burned candle leftover from Will's Hallowe'en jack-o'-lantern.

Packing her gear together in a plastic shopping bag, she found her jacket, threw it over her head like a veil, then opened the door and sprinted out into the wintry night.

By the time she reached the door of Matt's apartment, she was soaking wet and shivering. A sudden inclination told her to turn tail and run back to the house. But she'd come this far, and leaving these supplies would only take a second.

She rapped on the door and heard Matt mutter, 'What the hell . . .?'

After a few seconds of standing on the doorstep listening to rattling and clanging from inside, the door flew open, and she felt his eyes on her in the darkness.

With no overhang to protect her, she stood in a shower of icy rain. 'I just brought . . .' she began.

Gaping at him, she realized he was standing before her in his underwear. Modesty rose in her as though she'd never seen a man undressed before. Her eyes traced the firm, fine-toned muscles of a man who worked with his body, trailing down to the tip of the V ending the sprinkling of brownish hairs across his chest, like an arrowhead pointing to the bulge in the briefs below it.

She felt his warm hand cover on her shoulder, pulling her inside.

'Jeez, Sierra. Give me a break. It's freezing.'

He slammed the door shut behind her.

'I didn't expect you to answer the door naked.'

He glanced down as if realizing for the first time his state of undress.

'Sorry. I wasn't prepared for company. When I heard the knock, I thought there was an emergency.'

She stood facing him, feeling heat radiating from him in the darkness. She smelled fresh soap and shampoo mingled with beer. Raising her eyes to meet his, she realized he'd caught her staring.

'Aren't you cold walking around like that?'

'Not unless somebody opens a door and lets a blizzard in.'

'Oh,' she said, stepping back and finding little room between her and the door. 'Did I wake you?'

'No. I had just gotten out of the shower and was trying to read when the lights went out.'

She heard the sound of the radio from the bedroom, country music again, but more contemporary selections than last time. Hank Williams Junior, she thought.

She smiled softly. 'Your radio is working.'

'Runs on batteries. Your lips are blue, darlin', and your teeth are chattering. What the blazes are you doing out in this mess?'

She held out the bag. 'The power probably won't be back on again before morning. I brought you some candies and sandwiches and blankets. Obviously the blankets were unnecessary.'

Matt glanced down again. 'Look, I can't stand here talking to you like this. Make yourself at home. I'll go get my jeans.'

'Don't bother. I'll just leave this and go.'

'You're drenched, Sierra. You can't go back outside. And you won't be much good to Will if you have pneumonia.'

Throwing Will's welfare in her face was unfair. 'I have dry clothes back at the house.'

'I'll get you something dry.'

Before she could protest, he disappeared around the corner, reappearing seconds later in jeans. He handed her a dry shirt.

'Besides,' he said, 'I wouldn't mind having company for a spell. Nothing to do here in the dark but sit and talk to myself. Pretty boring.'

She laughed lightly. 'It's pretty boring back at the house too,' she admitted.

'I didn't think anything less than the house being on fire would have brought you over here. I'm glad you came, Sierra. Here, hand me that candle. I'll light it and you can carry it into the bathroom with you.'

'I really should go back.'

'You can wait until this sleet lets up. At least here there's music to listen to.'

Sierra held the fat orange candle in shaking hands as Matt lit it with a match. He cupped one hand around the side to steady hers, and she felt sparks lighting the darkness.

Leaning forward, she met his gaze across the flickering candlelight, and her heart lurched. She'd been foolish to come here, and yet she couldn't make herself stay away.

'I'll go change,' she said quickly. 'There are him sandwiches in that bag. Help yourself, if you're hungry. I know you must be.'

Holding the candle in front of her, she made her way into the bathroom, where she set it down on the sink. Peeling off her wet sweater and bra, she hung them and her jacket on the towel rack. As she put the shirt on and buttoned it, she inhaled the same soapy fragrance she'd detected on Matt a few minutes ago.

The cotton shirt was endlessly big on her, but at least it was dry. The stiff fabric smelled faintly of laundry detergent and of Matt, a scent that made her light-headed.

She shed her wet shoes and socks, leaving on her damp jeans, then used the candle to make her way to the living room. Matt was sitting on the floor, his back against the sofa, munching a sandwich.

'You were hungry,' she noted, placing the candle on the coffee table and slipping down beside him.

'A little,' he admitted. 'You make a good sandwich.' Reaching for the candle, he rose. 'Be right back,' he said. Disappearing around the corner, he was back shortly with two uncapped beer bottles. He set one in front of her.

'Thanks,' she said, unable to remember the last time she'd drunk beer. Lifting the bottle, she took a long swig of the cold, bitter liquid, enjoying the feel of it as it slid down her throat.

'You didn't have to stay here tonight, Matt.'

'I promised the boy.'

'He was wrong to extract such a promise from you. I'm not nervous about staying alone. Ben's killer got what he was after. I doubt he'll be back.'

'What did he steal?'

'Nothing. Will believes Ben was killed by a thief because he's not old enough to understand the kind of trouble Ben got himself into. Ben was gambling, running up a lot of debt. He'd turned our lives into chaos. Phone calls in the middle of the night. Sometimes he'd go out right away and not come back until morning. It got to where he'd be gone for days sometimes. Strangers came to the house looking for him. He got mixed up with an evil crowd.'

'You think someone killed him because he owed them money?'

'It's the only explanation I have. Whoever did it set the whole thing up to make it look as though Ben had surprised a prowler. Thank God Will and I had gone to Taos with my father that weekend.'

Matt put down the rest of his sandwich. 'You must have loved him, to let him drag you and the boy through all that.'

Sierra sighed heavily. 'It's over now. I paid Ben's debts after he died. That's why I had to sell the house and some other things we'd owned. I used to think our future was secure, that we'd always have our home and each other and enough money to get by. That was enough for me. Now, I see security's a cruel joke. You can't depend on anything except the ability to provide for yourself. I suppose you've always known that. I always envied how strong you were inside.'

'The whipped horse has the toughest hide.'

Sierra took a long gulp of beer. She liked the warm, sudsy feeling it made inside her. 'You expect me to feel sorry for you? You've always been able to take care of yourself.'

'No, I don't want sympathy from you. Never.'

'Good, because I don't. I wish I had half your gumption. I envy your freedom.'

'You've never been short on gumption, Sierra. You just never had any call to know you had it, any direction to channel it in. You were pretty brave to risk going against your father. Few men in this town would dare to do that.'

'Not nearly brave enough.'

His fingers skimmed lightly over her hair, sending hot shivers down her neck. She leaned towards him, listening to the steady rhythm of sleet beating against the roof.

'I came here because I do owe you an explanation, Matt.'

'No, you don't. You don't have to account to me or anybody else for the choices you made. I think in the back of my mind, I always knew I'd lose you sooner or later. Sooner just came faster than anything I was ready for.'

His firm, steady hand massaged her shoulder. Heat spread through her weary muscles. 'I know how it must have looked to you. I didn't tell you I was still dating Ben. I would have told you, if it had meant anything.'

'Sierra, what I think doesn't mean anything now. It's water under the dam. Besides, how could it have not meant anything? You married him, didn't you?'

'I want you to understand. I don't want to minimize what you and I shared once. How much it meant to me. When I came home that summer, I'd been dating Ben before I met you. My father was constantly watching me. Even when he wasn't around, the housekeeper reported my every move to him. I had to continue going out with Ben, or my dad would have suspected I was seeing someone else and investigated to find out who.'

Matt's eyes seared intently into hers. Highlighted by orange candlelight, his handsome features were constricted with remembered resentment. His beard shadowed his face, breaking up the lines so it appeared almost as a projector image. He set his hands on her shoulders.

'Stop it, Sierra,' he demanded. 'Don't you get it? I don't want to hear about you and Ben.'

She blinked back stinging tears.

'It's not what you think. Ben and I attended parties together. It wasn't . . . like you and I were. I didn't even think of him that way.'

'If it was all so innocent, why didn't you tell me you were seeing him?'

'You wouldn't have understood.'

'No, but then maybe in the end I wouldn't have felt as though I'd been kicked by a mule. What happened? You decided as long as you two were getting out so much, why not have a wedding?'

'Of course not. Ben proposed, and when my father learned I'd turned him down, he was furious.'

Matt eyed her skeptically. 'You turned him down?'

'Yes. Father demanded a reason, so I told him. I told him about us, Matt.'

Silence covered the room like a velvet cloak as Matt stared at her incredulously. 'Your father knew?'

'I thought once he knew you, he'd accept it, but

everything blew up. He insisted I marry Ben immediately, and I caved in.'

'You sold out to the highest bidder.'

'No. My father was angry, and I was upset. You've got to understand, Matt, all my life he's been my whole family. He's a harsh man, and I often resented how he dominated me. But he's also a very intelligent, competent man, and I respected his reasoning and his judgement. As young and . . . confused as I was, I allowed him to persuade me that I was doing the right thing.'

'You can talk until you're blue in the face, honey, and it's still never going to make a lick of sense to me.'

'My father and I didn't have the same kind of relationship you had with yours. Defying him wasn't something I could do easily.'

'I had a world of respect for my ma, and I wouldn't have let her tell me who to marry, not that she would have.'

'But if she had, you would have thought about it, known she had a good reason to suggest it for you.'

'Maybe. I still would have done what I knew was right.'

'But you'd probably been making decisions for yourself since you were Will's age or younger. Matt, all my life Father told me where to go to school, what stores to shop at, what parties to go to. He raised me to be too weak to function on my own. I was too afraid to break away from a force I'd always depended on to guide me.'

'I would have taken care of you, somehow.'

'And I would have become a backpack that's a little too heavy. I didn't want to hold you back, Matt. I never wanted to diminish your view of me. That's a laugh, isn't it?'

'The other day, you said you loved Ben.'

'I cared about him in many ways. He tried to be a good father if not always the ideal husband. There are aspects of our marriage Will doesn't know about, and as far as I'm concerned he'll never suspect Ben and I weren't a picture of domestic bliss.'

Matt shook his head. 'I guess people inside big, fancy houses live by different rules than us ordinary folks. You did what you believed you had to do, Sierra. I couldn't have lived with myself if I'd made you give up everything.'

'But you gave up everything. Why did you leave, Matt?'

'I didn't want to stick around and have to watch you and Ben together. But that wasn't all that drove me away. In fact, if it weren't for you and Sam, and school, I probably would have taken off sooner. Daddy and I had practically come to blows several times, and it had come to a point where we weren't going to tolerate each other much longer. I think he hated me more with each passing day.'

Sierra reached for her beer, like a lost hiker grabbing for a canteen, but Matt laid a hand on her arm to restrain her.

'Getting high's not going to change anything,' he warned. 'You don't drink beer much, do you?'

She shook her head.

'What exactly are you trying to tank up for?'

When she didn't answer, he looked at her hard.

Matt bowed over her, leaning down to kiss the hollow of her throat, exposed between the open lapels of his shirt. Her breath caught at the brush of his lips against her skin, and hot syrup poured through her chest. Her breasts strained as he pressed closer, the clean male smell of him flooding her nostrils.

She leaned back against the base of the sofa as his mouth moved up to capture hers, and, closing her eyes, she threaded her fingers into a handful of his thick hair, savoring the salty taste of his lips.

From deep within, a long yearning inside her broke free. For so long she'd denied her need for the comfort of a man's arms. For so long, she'd tried to forget that Matt could make her feel like the most beautiful, most desirable woman on earth. God help her, she wanted a connection with him tonight. She wanted to soar again.

She knew now what she had really come here for.

CHAPTER 6

Matt was raining kisses across the soft base of her throat, nibbling at the underside of her chin. His hard chest was crushed against her, and she arched against him, her breasts aching like fireballs. His hands were planted firmly on her ribcage. His beard grazed her skin like fleece, not the scratchy steel wool she had anticipated.

She let herself drift with the tidal wave of sweet sensation she couldn't shut out. Every nerve in her body was coming to life, thrilling to his touch.

Then he drew back, propping her chin in his hand, forcing her to meet his gaze. She opened her eyes, reading tenderness, longing and uncertainty in his expression. He'll never forgive me, she thought fleetingly. As his glance probed her face, she felt her skin heating.

He stroked the smooth curve of her cheek with the inside of his thumb.

He smiled into her eyes.

Her heart snapped like an overwound guitar

string as her lips curled into a smile of their own.

'You know where this is leading us,' he warned her.

She gave a slight nod. 'Is that so terrible?' she asked. Her need for him overwhelmed her, pushing aside all else.

'Not if you don't think so. I don't want you saying later it was the beer,' he said, his voice low and husky. 'I wouldn't make love to a woman who wasn't aware of what was happening to her.

Silently, he awaited an answer.

'You know differently. Besides, you wouldn't let me finish one bottle.' Reaching out, she combed her fingers through his hair. 'I never thought the day would come when I could touch you again. After everything, I was afraid you wouldn't want to.'

He flashed an endearing grin. 'Are you sure, Sierra? I don't even know how long it's been since . . .'

She crossed his lips with two fingers. 'Nothing outside this room exists right now. This is just us, here and now, as you said before.'

He kissed her fingers, then moved them away from his face.

'You never answered my question,' he reminded her.

'Which one?'

'Did you love Ben? I'm not talking about those last days. When you first married him, did you love him?'

'I tried to be good to him, Matt. I had nothing else.'

Matt nodded. 'Was it the way it was with us?'

'Nothing ever was.'

With one powerful swoop of his arm, he pushed the coffee table against the wall.

'Matt,' she broached, her heart pounding, her body aching with need.

'Hmm . . .?' He was unbuttoning the top of her shirt.

'I don't want you to be disappointed.'

He paused, setting his arms on her shoulders. 'The only way I would be disappointed is if you changed your mind.'

'No, please, don't joke about this.'

'About what, darlin'?' He ran his hand over her belly, and she felt her middle going warm and soft and damp.

'It can't be like it was before.'

His breath caressed her earlobe, and electricity shot down her spine as his lips and his tongue followed.

'Meaning what?' he asked.

If he would stop touching her for a minute, she'd be able to think straight.

'Something happened to me, Matt. I'm not the same as I was.'

'You feel the same, taste just as sweet. Sweeter, I think. Like peppermint.'

She took his face in both hands and pinned his head back. He cast her a bewildered look.

'There's something inside me that doesn't work right.'

Now, he leaned back, folding his arms across his chest.

'I reckon you'd better be more specific.'

She shot him a tentative look, then dropped her eyes.

He reached for her hand, knit his big fingers through her slender ones. 'What is it? Did something happen when you had Will?'

'No. I'm not sure when this happened. I can make love with you, Matt, I want to make love to you. But whatever happens I don't want you to think it's your fault. There's nothing physically wrong. It's in my head, some cold, hardened part of me.'

When she looked up, she saw anger in his eyes. 'What did he do to you?'

She knew to whom he was referring. 'Nothing. It's me, not anybody else.'

'Why do you assume the failing was yours and not your husband's?'

She diverted her eyes. 'Ben was an expert lover. My problem didn't stem from his lack of trying.'

Matt's gaze narrowed. 'So why do this if you won't feel anything?'

She clenched her hand into a fist. 'It's not a

matter of feeling nothing. Just not as much as I should. It feels good when you hold me.'

'And the rest is for my sake? You're offering yourself to me like some kind of long-suffering martyr?'

'I care about you, Matt.'

'For old times' sake. Is that what this is all about? You don't owe me anything.'

'No. It's about now.'

He eyed her reluctantly, and she feared he was going to leave the room. Instead, he folded her into his arms and cradled her head against his chest. 'Don't worry about it,' he murmured, rocking her. She snuggled against him, closing her eyes and inhaling his scent.

'It's still hard for you to take, isn't it?' she asked. 'You were always so stubborn that way. The only reason I'm telling you is because I know that. I don't want you to feel cheated.'

She gasped as she felt his hand massaging her breast, kneading the tip of it until it grew hard as a pinpoint.

'I make it a practice never to let anyone cheat me,' Matt countered. He watched Sierra's dark head fall back against the sofa cushion, traced the lines of her silhouette in the darkness. He couldn't deny wanting her – desire had been jabbing him like a burr stuck in his boot since he'd first laid eyes on her again a week ago.

God, just the scent of her was driving him crazy. He loved the feel of her, the way he felt her heart beating beneath his hand. Over the years, he'd learned that life was short and the trail was long. You grabbed what you could along the way and enjoyed the hell out of it. It wasn't in him to turn down an attractive woman's invitation to bed. Yet with this particular one, he hadn't anticipated this becoming a problem.

To him, she was a rare delicacy he'd once sampled and never stopped craving. So what if her reasons for marrying Ben didn't square with him? This time around, he knew better than to get all caught up with her. He wasn't some starry-eyed kid who was going to start dreaming about settling down, houses in the country. No, he knew where he stood. She'd chosen money and a pampered lifestyle over him once. He wasn't giving her the chance to do it again. He was just a hired hand, sticking around until Jerry was able to take care of his family again.

But nothing restrained him from wanting her. The throbbing in his loins was tight and painful. She was soft and smooth and sweet as marshmallow. He wanted to take her far beyond herself and the murdered husband who haunted her and these flimsy four walls.

He refused to believe this warm, loving woman had closed herself off to feeling the kind of pleasure he wanted to give her. He wasn't sure what he would do if she opened herself to him only halfway.

Holding her in his arms, he eased her down to the hardwood floor. Reaching up with one hand, he grabbed a throw pillow and tucked it under her head.

'You said not to worry about the past, yet you've brought it in here with you,' he told her, rolling over her, spreading his body over hers. His thighs crushed against her narrow hips and already he imagined himself inside her. She looked up at him with wide eyes, and he read the worry in them. 'How can I make love to a woman who's thinking of another man?' he asked.

She raked splayed hands against his chest, delighting in the feel of sinewy muscle. 'It's not Ben I'm thinking about,' she insisted.

'Then don't worry about whatever happened with him. Don't you know I despise the thought of his ever having touched you? I require your complete attention.'

She gave him a grateful smile.

'I think you pretty much have it.'

He took hold of both sides of her shirt front and startled her by ripping it open, spraying buttons across the floor. His eyes widened as he gazed down appreciatively on the rigid quivering mounds before him.

'Oh, darlin'!' he exclaimed. Bending slowly, he

pressed his lips to the satiny, copper-colored flesh, savoring her taste. A low growl emitted from his throat as he caught the hard pink peak in his mouth. He felt her stiffen beneath him, then soften, sinking back as he suckled and massaged her.

He curled his fingers around the cushion of her chest, then buried his head there.

'Let it go easy,' he crooned, as he unsnapped her still-damp jeans, sliding his hand down the centre, gliding it along her flat belly. Pushing down farther, he groaned as his probing fingers hit upon the honeycomb he'd been seeking. The intimate core of her womanhood. Slowly, he caressed the silky hidden cache, gently kneading until it was moist and slick. At discovering her readiness for him, his loins clamped painfully.

'Oh, Sierra,' he whispered, abandoning his treasure long enough to work her jeans over her hips. Stubbornly, the damp denim clung to her skin. Finally, eager for more of his touch, she pulled the pants off, kicking them away, then her hands flew in turn to his jeans, her fingers unworking the buttons.

Within seconds, both pairs of discarded jeans had been thrown against the wall, and Matt removed the remnants of the shirt, tossing those aside as well. Climbing over her, again he savored the sensation of wrapping his body over hers, skin-to-skin.

Stroking her feathery hair, he pressed his bearded

cheek against her smooth soft one, drinking in her flowery scent, heightened now by the tang of her desire.

Her arms wound around him. Her hands stroked his round buttocks, and he shuddered as fire raced through him.

His hardness mashed against her belly, trailing to the doughy, womanly part of her.

The heat of him spearing her, Sierra reached down and captured him in her small hand. With satisfaction she felt him stiffen, heard him groan with pleasure. She hadn't imagined her need for him would consume her so. A fire raged at her core, a flame never extinguished, constantly reminding her that she'd been alone for a long, long time. She kissed him.

He drew back, parting her legs, kneeling and wedging himself between them. His gaze centred on her most private, vulnerable core, lingering there. Watching him, seeing his eyes darken, she realized he was the only man she'd ever trusted. Even now, she trusted him with her life, her soul, her body. At this moment, she hid nothing from him, could hide nothing.

Yet, still she felt she had not enough to give. She was feverish with wanting him, lathered in sweat and burning in that spot he had opened. The ache was so intense, she feared she would explode if he didn't touch her.

His eyes rose to her face, and he smiled. A calmness settled into her heart. He'd always had that way about him, getting her all wet and wild like some untamed beast and making her feel it was the most natural thing in the world.

'You are the most spectacular woman I've ever seen,' he whispered, his voice husky. 'I could never get tired of seeing you, all mellow and moist. Don't be ashamed to let me see you.'

He seemed not to notice or care that her hips had thickened slightly from having carried Will, a fact Ben had never failed to comment on. A hot tear sprang into the corner of one eye, blurring her view of him. Only a fool would have ever let this man go. A surge of deep affection mingled with hot, maddening desire.

He leaned forward. As his touch fell upon her, she cried out, waves of pleasure rolling through her as he kissed and probed. He murmured something but did not stop, and she opened herself to him like a blossoming flower welcoming a bee, writhing beneath him. Waves heightened and crashed, taking her far, far away, filling her with a churning, giddy ache.

'Just hold on, honey,' he whispered. She clenched his shoulders but couldn't grip him tightly enough. The fire in her middle consumed her, radiating like sunbeams. His fingers grazed her inner thighs, and his prolonged kiss was drawing her farther and farther into a mindless, whirling pool of sheer pleasure. Before she had a chance to think about it, she was careening down a water slide, screaming in surprised delight as spasm after spasm sapped the longing from her.

Just as she was realizing what had happened, he filled her, overpowering her with iron maleness. Tears puddled in her eyes so she could barely see. She didn't need to. Raising her hips, she clasped herself to him. He captured her hands, entwining his fingers through hers.

His lips covered hers, his tongue claiming her mouth as his lean hips moved to a slow, steady rhythm she remembered from so long ago. She moved in time with him. It was as if she could hear the creek rippling below them again, feel long-ago sunshine on her shoulders in this cold, dark room.

She closed her eyes, her only thought that of plunging him into the basin of sweet release he had taken her to. His skin felt tough as leather, as hot as a branding iron.

He clasped her closer to him, and she felt him dipping deeper and deeper within her. Closing her eyes, she began floating higher and higher into the darkness. She grew giddy and weightless, until a spectacular starburst exploded in her head.

As she cried out, she heard his voice blend with hers, and she pulled him to her in a trembling frenzy, catching the flow of spent desire streaming from him like lava.

Then, everything was still. Time stopped as she lay there on the floor, holding him. The tears she'd been holding back spilled freely now, rolling down her cheeks. Through all the years away from him, the times she'd convinced herself she'd forgotten, she'd never felt truly connected to anyone. Until now. She didn't deserve his lovemaking.

Matt was gazing down on her, stroking wisps of her dark hair.

'No crying,' he admonished, kissing her eyelid. 'Are you sorry?'

'Are you kidding?' She was laughing and crying at the same time.

'Good,' he concluded. 'Because I'm not finished with you yet.'

Even now, fresh desire stirred inside her as she anticipated his making good on his promise. Sierra whooped as he scooped her up in his arms and carried her into the bedroom, where he deposited her, naked as a jaybird, in the middle of his bed. Sierra knew the night, along with the rest of her life, had just begun.

When Sierra opened her eyes the next morning she found herself alone in Matt's bed, buried beneath a pile of blankets. A quick glance out of the window told her the morning was gray and still and cold.

Leisurely, she stretched, her body still sated and filled with him as though he'd driven a fever from it. She smelled his scent in the sheets. Although she'd had little sleep last night, she felt rested and deeply relaxed.

For the first time in years, she'd awakened with hope in her heart.

But why had he left her here by herself?

Throwing off the heavy blankets, sitting up to find herself unclothed, she pulled one off the top of the heap and gathered it around her. Barefoot, she padded across the cool floor.

Matt was standing in the kitchen, his back to her as he stood staring out the small square window that looked out over the pasture. Bare-chested, he was wearing only his jeans. The thumb of one hand was hooked on his back pocket, while he held a mug of steaming coffee in the other.

For several minutes she stood back, reveling in the sight of him, so fine and straight and strong. She couldn't help wondering, if circumstances had worked out differently, whether she could have ever been enough to drive away the demons that plagued him.

'I wondered where you'd gone to,' she said.

Matt turned. He smiled.

She smiled back. In the morning light she felt suddenly shy with the man whose arms she'd freely rolled into time and time again during the night.

'I didn't want to wake you. You were sleeping real pretty. Sorry about keeping you up half the night.'

A schoolgirl blush painted her cheeks. 'Don't be sorry. I'm not.'

'Come here.'

Dragging the blanket behind her, she walked to his side. Hair tousled, eyes still sleepy, a rosy glow to her skin, she looked like a woman who had been properly made love to. Already, Matt wanted her again. He slipped his hand out of his pocket and looped a long arm around her shoulders, folding her against his side.

Resting her head against him, she closed her eyes. He couldn't guess how much last night had meant to her.

'Any reason in particular why I woke up under a ton of blankets?' she asked, forcing a light tone.

He chuckled. 'I was afraid you'd get cold, not having any clothes on and all. You weren't too hot, were you?'

'No, just weighted down. I was fine, really.'

'Look,' he instructed with a nod towards the window.

Sierra followed his eyes. The world before her was frozen, silent, and eerily beautiful. Ice coated the grass, the bare tree branches, everything.

'If I were a painter,' she suggested, 'I would put this on canvas.'

'So paint it.'

'I wouldn't even know where to begin. It would all melt before I even sketched it.'

'Imprint it in your mind, so you'll have it with you when you're ready.'

She shook her head. 'My kind of painting is for the idle rich. I'm not good enough to make a living at it. I need to devote my time to the farm and Will, not daydreams.'

He handed her the coffee mug. Grasping it in both hands, she sipped the hot, bitter liquid.

'I guess that's what growing up is,' he said. 'Learning to abandon your dreams gracefully. I always wondered what made my dad so angry at everyone and everything. Now I'm beginning to understand, and it scares me. He worked hard, but instead of getting ahead, he stayed poor. The rewards he expected never came, and he saw his life slipping away.'

'It didn't give him the right to vent his frustration on you.'

He raised an eyebrow. 'Nor did being wealthy justify your father using it to control you.'

'He didn't do that out of meanness. I was all he had.'

'Then if he loves you so much, Sierra, how can he stand to turn away from you now?'

'I'm sure it's hard for him. He thinks he's doing the right thing. He wants to take care of Will and me, but in his way. He's yet to accept I'm a grown woman capable of standing on my own and making my own decisions.'

'You're making excuses for him, darlin'. In truth, your background isn't any more privileged than my own undistinguished upbringing.'

'Sometimes I think we become what we are despite our families rather than because of them.'

'Depends on who you are, I reckon.'

She rested her head against his side. With all the ice outside, she felt as though they were encased inside a glass dome, where nothing else could get in or out.

'Let's not talk about our families,' she said. 'Please. Not this morning.'

He grinned down on her. 'Are you hungry? The power's back on, and I think there's an egg or two in that itty-bitty refrigerator.'

She shook her head. 'No, I'm not hungry right now.'

He shrugged. 'Well, I can't turn the horses out in this and I don't have a television set here, so I can't see that there's much to do.'

Stepping back, she let go of the blanket corners she clutched at her throat. The blankets slid across her shoulders and dropped to the floor.

Matt studied her appreciatively.

'I guess you already have something in mind,' he said.

'A nice hot shower.'

'Sounds like a damn good idea.'

Her smile dropped briefly. 'Matt . . .'

'What?'

'You changed things for me last night. I wanted you to know I appreciate it.'

'Because I exorcised Ben for you? That just happened. Wasn't anything I could have done without your co-operation.'

'It's more than that. After all that's happened, we're still good together . . . better. After what I did to you, I don't deserve . . .'

'How do you expect to take care of yourself and the boy if you can't say anything good about yourself? Besides, as much as I loathe the idea of you living as another man's wife, Ben at least provided you with a fine son, something I never could have given you.'

When he looked down at her, something flashed in her eyes he couldn't read. Quickly, she diverted her glance.

'I know I can't expect you to believe this, Matt. I had obligations to my husband. I wanted us to be happy together. I'd thought making love with any man would be the way it was with you. I was wrong. He never touched me the way you did.'

'I've got no call to be jealous of a dead man.'

'I just was so afraid you hated me.'

'Hate you, darlin'? You probably spared us both from needless suffering. Face it, you and I never could have had any kind of life together, not in this town. Why can't we just enjoy what we have without circling around to last time? It's different now, and we both know it. Rest your mind, I'm not entertaining any delusions about hanging around. Not any longer than I need to, anyway.'

Her mouth dropped open and remained that way as he set the coffee mug on the table and captured her scarlet lips in a deep kiss. His words faded from her mind as her body quickened to his keen touch.

Hours later, Sierra stood over her bathroom sink, splashing warm water on her face and scrubbing it with a green bar of gardenia-scented soap. She was wearing a pair of cream-colored jeans and a cable-knit sweater the deep green of pine. Her hair was brushed back from her face. She was entertaining the idea of letting it grow long again.

She studied her face in the mirror: bright eyes and glowing skin. She looked like a woman who had spent the night in the arms of her lover. Will would be home any minute, and she prayed her son wouldn't detect the change in her. Of course, he was just a child, not sophisticated enough to guess exactly why she was different, but little in her household escaped his keen observation.

The house smelled pleasantly of chillies and onions as her pot of taco sauce simmered on the stove. Chicken tacos were Will's favorite.

Last night, Matt had given her everything, then taken it away just as quickly. What had she expected? She'd abdicated any claim she ever had to being special to him. Just because she'd never stopped caring hadn't prevented him from changing. Had she thought he'd rearrange his life just because she'd bounced into his bed?

Really, she told herself, would she want that even if she could have it? He'd given her a good time, tapped into a place she'd thought was locked up tight forever. There was more to life than making love, and she had to get on with hers. If he stayed, she was bound to start hanging on to him, needing him. And ultimately he'd learn the truth about Will and despise her in a way he'd never get over.

No, Matt was right. For the time being, they could enjoy each other. At least she could cherish the small satisfaction of knowing she pleased him physically. She owed him that. She owed him something. And when he left this time, there would be no hurt, no lingering sense of betrayal, no regrets. She shouldn't have been surprised to learn he wasn't giving her any more than she had coming after all.

Realizing that once the ice melted Will would be coming home, that he might try to call the house and worry when she failed to answer, she'd finally torn herself away from the tiny apartment and its tenant. Matt had dressed and gone out to the stables. A while later, she'd heard his truck drive off. Even knowing he was probably on his way to Leeann's, to help her with the house and the kids, she experienced an odd sense of desolation. There had been a time when he would have done anything she asked, but that time was long past.

Patting her face dry with a towel, she heard a car pulling up outside. Assuming Luke's parents had arrived with Will, she raced to the front door, throwing it open.

She paled as a silver Lincoln stopped in the drive. The driver's door opened, and a tall man with dark eyes and thick, expensively styled hair as metallic as his car stepped out. Dressed in a dark blue suit, white shirt and waistcoat, he stood tall, his shoulders squared stiffly.

His eyes swept over his surroundings as though he'd emerged from a space capsule to find himself on some unknown planet. Then they set on the woman standing in the doorway.

'Hello, Sierra. Are you going to gawk at me all day or invite me in?' he demanded finally.

Still dumbfounded, Sierra swung the door open wider. 'You needn't wait for an invitation,' she replied. 'You know you're always welcome in my house, Father.'

She moved aside to let him pass.

Matt noticed the house with wreaths on the doors and windows as he passed, but the approaching

Christmas holiday had nothing to do with his good spirits. Christmas to him was like a second Sunday added one week out of the year. More an inconvenience than anything else. When he was lucky, he worked through it so the day would pass quickly. Otherwise, finding a decent restaurant open was a pain in the butt.

No, it was his night with Sierra that inspired a tenuous serenity within him. She'd brought him his Christmas last night. No woman had ever inspired such poignant longing in him. Even now, after coupling over and over through the night, his midsection tightened at the thought of her. She was a rare flower, blooming in winter, spicing the cold air with her exotic, delicate fragrance. He'd never tired of watching her bloom, watching her face soften in ecstasy as his name spilled from lips as deep red as holly berries.

God, she made him just want to sink inside her and stay there. But this time he wasn't entertaining any foolish notions about the two of them lasting forever, about wanting to love her. He didn't dare. Now that she realized that arrogant husband of hers had brainwashed her into believing she was frozen inside, she'd find herself another man just like him, some rich dandy like the doctor who owned the Arabian.

No, he was facing facts: they were merely passing time together. She was on her own and scared and coming back for a while to a place she knew was safe. Good old Matt. Always a nice guy, always finishing last. But this time he'd know when to walk out, jump ship before she decided again she didn't really need him.

He'd been smelling trouble in the air ever since he got here, and trouble was the last thing he needed. Maybe he'd already walked too far out on to a ledge by making love to her, but he was only human. For the past week he'd been watching her, his flesh constricting at the sight of her, and he'd suffered physical pain keeping his distance. When she'd come to him, resisting had been impossible.

He pushed from his mind the tears he'd discovered on her face last night. At first, he feared that he'd hurt her somehow, but she claimed he hadn't. Still, knowing he'd made her cry bothered him, and he didn't know what in tarnation he'd done wrong.

Was she regretting her impulsiveness in giving herself to him, descending once again from the exclusive residential area in the hills ingrained in her to find something real. Something her daddy's money couldn't buy her?

Now, he wondered if she'd come to his bed again at all. When he returned, Will would be back, and he knew she'd sooner die than let her son suspect she could be close to any man other than the kid's father.

And he respected that. He liked the kid well

enough, and the boy had loved his dad. Far be it from him to intrude on those memories. All he knew about Ben, aside from having seen him around town driving flashy cars and wearing preppy, pressed clothes, was that he had to have been an idiot to have had a son who adored him and a woman like Sierra and not taken care of them in every way.

But that was their problem, not his. He was too well aware of his own failings ever to tackle the responsibility of a family. Never having had one of his own, he wasn't about to take charge of someone else's. Once, he'd begun to think Sierra might change all that. She'd loved him in a way he hadn't felt himself worthy of, and he'd started pondering whether she'd care for him like that if he was all that much like his old man. In a child that was half hers, her kind, loving nature might counter his inherent harshness.

What he'd been looking at was an illusion, like a mirage in the desert, he knew now. No sense at all thinking about what might have been. He hadn't been the one to give Sierra a child, and he never would. Their parting had been inevitable. He'd been young and grasping at straws. Better in the end that he'd never spawned a child who'd grow up to loathe a father who'd resent his very existence, the way his old man hated him.

God, he detested himself for the way he felt about his father. The festering resentment he felt was the last thing he wanted to carry around with him. But nowhere in his heart could he muster the slightest inkling of love for the old man . . .

Matt huddled in one corner of the frayed old sofa, watching his father pace the front room in long, frantic strides, holding the infant in his arms as though someone had handed him a sack of rotting potatoes.

Lester Rollins turned, pinning his sharp, hawk-like glance on Matt. It was early, but getting dark outside. The lamps cast a yellowish glow on the shabby, polished furnishings, the tattered upholstery.

Matt's heart turned over and rose to his throat. He was only six years old, and woefully thin, shorter than most of the other boys in his class. His daddy loomed over him taller than a skyscraper.

Daddy stopped, leaning over him, staring accusingly. Matt knew he hadn't done anything wrong, but he'd already learned Daddy had his own particular code of justice. Sometimes innocence wasn't enough to make a difference.

'Where's Dylan?' he demanded.

'He hasn't come home yet,' Matt answered. He shrank against the cushions as his father continued glaring at him. 'He took Darcy over to play with the Marshall kids.'

Daddy's look hardened, and Matt wondered what

he'd said wrong. Finally, Daddy ordered, 'Hold your arms out.'

Puzzled by the command, Matt complied. He hadn't yet learned to rebel and still hoped he could one day please his father the way Dylan did just by walking in a room.

His father placed the tiny wriggling baby in his arms.

Every muscle in Matt's body tensed as he stared down at his baby sister, so small, so fragile. He was bad about dropping things. Especially when his Daddy was around, making him nervous.

'Take her back, Daddy,' he pleaded.

The old man laughed. 'Stop whining. You just sit there with her and don't move.'

Matt didn't dare move. He was scared to breathe.

His daddy headed for the front door. 'I'm going to get your Ma from the diner. I'll take Gage with me. You be sittin' right there when I get back or I'll have your hide.' He snickered. 'And don't drop her. Them teeny young 'uns break real easy.'

Matt watched incredulously as the old man walked out of the door, leaving him alone with the baby. He heard the roar of the old pickup and knew he was really going.

Frozen, he sat there helplessly, clutching his baby sister to his chest with trembling arms. He heard his own heart drumming in his chest, the ticking of the clock. His hands were so slick and sweaty, he feared Leeann would slide out of his grasp.

Outside, the shadows deepened. He felt as though he were the last person left in the world. God would never forgive him if he let anything happen to his sister . . .

'Uncle Matt!' Tanner barreled out of the house with outstretched arms as Matt approached and leaned down, snaring Matt's neck in a bear-hug.

'Howdy, cowboy,' Matt greeted him, tousling the boy's hair. 'Where's your ma?'

'In the kitchen.' Tanner trailed happily along behind him.

Leeann was grating onions. 'Kind of expected to see you back here last night,' she said without looking up.

'Decided to stay, since I needed to tend the horses this morning anyway.'

She cast him a glance that told him she didn't believe for a minute it was horses he'd been tending to. 'Tanner, why don't you go play in your room until dinner? I need to talk to Uncle Matt.'

Tanner looked none too happy about the request.

Matt reached down and patted his shoulder. 'Go on,' he urged. 'I'll come in after while and tell you a story.'

'About the rodeo?'

Matt gave a slow nod, and Tanner took off down the hall.

When he was gone, Leeann turned to Matt. 'Hellfire, Matt. I knew there was gonna be trouble when you went out there.'

'There's no trouble.' He peered over her shoulder. 'What are you cooking?'

'Coleslaw. There's a meat loaf and macaroni in the oven. If you're home to stay for a while, I'm goin' down to the hospital to eat with Jerry. Woulda gone earlier if it hadn't been for all that nasty ice on the roads. I was kinda worried when you didn't come home right away.'

'I guess I should have called, but there's no phone in the apartment out there.'

She nodded. 'I called her a while ago, to see where you were. She said you'd left and she figured you must be on your way here. Sounded awful chipper.'

'Sierra's a gracious woman. She's got no call to be unfriendly to you.'

Leeann chewed her bottom lip. 'I hope she's not bein' overly gracious, Matt. You never mentioned you'd be workin' out there on the weekends too. Be careful, please. I know you've been away a long time, but things don't change as fast in Winter as they do everywhere else. I don't want to see you get hurt again, not by her.'

'I can take care of myself. You have enough to worry about, Leeann.'

'I'd worry about you less if you'd find some woman who was worth your time and marry her. One of Jerry's friends has a sister who's single, and I could invite . . .'

'Forget it, Turtle. I'm not getting married and I'm not staying in Winter. That's what you want, isn't it? You'd love for me to tie myself down here.'

'I ain't denyin' it, Matt. It's good havin' you back. But I'd sooner run you out of town myself than to think that she-devil was toyin' with you again, like a cat playing with a ball of string.'

'You overestimate Sierra's power over me. Do you think I'm spineless enough to fall into the same pit twice?'

He wondered why he shied away from telling her the flat-out truth as he always had. He told himself it was because she'd assume his sleeping with Sierra meant he was falling in love with her again, and he truly hadn't come here to add to his sister's troubles, real or imagined.

'She is awful pretty. I can see where she'd be hard to resist. Especially bein' out there all alone on that ranch and everything.'

'I'm not stupid, Leeann. I don't go around asking for punishment. We're both grown-ups now, with our own lives. I leave you to manage yours, and I'd appreciate being left to deal with mine on my own terms. I'm sorry I wasn't here to help you with the kids last night. I thought ya'll might enjoy having me out of the way for a while.'

Not wanting to argue with her, he walked into the living room. The glossy jacket of a hard-cover library book sitting on the table with a paper marker sticking out of it caught his eye.

Idly, he picked it up. Leeann must have got it to read during all those long hours at the hospital. He'd never noticed his sister reading much except romance and mystery paperbacks. As he scanned the title, his blood began simmering.

'What the . . .?' he muttered. 'Leeann!'

She appeared in the doorframe, her face reddening as she spotted the book in his hand.

'*Finding Your Family*?' he asked, waving the book. 'Who – I'm afraid to even guess – are you searching for?'

Her eyes dropped. 'It's different for me than it is for you. My whole life is about my family. When Jerry got hurt and I didn't have anyone else, wasn't even sure I'd be able to find you, I got to thinkin' about how alone we all are. I think I can get in touch with Darcy and Gage, Matt. Maybe they can help us find Dylan. It's almost Christmas, and you're already here. I'm hoping Jerry will be home, even if I have to push him around in a wheelchair. Wouldn't it be great, Matt, just one year to have all five of us Rollins kids together for Christmas dinner?'

'No!' he protested louder than he meant to. Leeann, astonished by her brother's fierce, unusually quick anger, stepped back.

Realizing he'd frightened her, Matt lowered his voice. 'Count me out. I mean it, Leeann. Let it be. Let it be or I'm gone.'

'Just us kids, Matt. That's all I want. We always liked each other.'

'You start rootin' out Dylan, and somehow Daddy'll show up. Bank on it. And personally, I never want to see him again.'

'Matt, for all we know he could be dead by now.'

'He's not. He wouldn't have died that quietly. He's out there somewhere, Leeann. I can't explain it, but I can feel it as strong as if he were standing right here looking over my shoulder. I can't think of anything I'd want less for Christmas than a family reunion.'

He turned towards the door.

Her voice stopped him. 'OK, Matt. It was just an idea. I don't have to. Where are you going?'

'Outside. I need a smoke.'

Remembering the kids inside the house, he shut the door quietly behind him.

CHAPTER 7

Sierra watched incredulously as her father marched into her house with the air of an expected guest arriving for Sunday dinner.

'Is something wrong?' she asked, following him inside and shutting the door.

He turned, and she suddenly felt as though she were the guest. Refusing to cower in his presence, she held her spine stiff, her chin high.

Even when his dark gaze zeroed on her. 'Why should anything be wrong? You're looking remarkably well . . . considering.' He swept his disdainful glance through her living room. 'Where's my grandson?'

She twisted her hands. 'Will slept over at a friend's house. They'll be dropping him off shortly. Actually, I'm glad you've come to see him. You're welcome to wait.'

'Just as well he's not here right now.' He sat down without waiting to be asked. 'Sit down, Sierra. We've some business to attend to.'

She balked. 'What business is that? If you've come here looking for another argument, I'm not in the mood.'

'Please, just hear me out.'

Stunned at hearing William Ross use the word please, she studied her father and saw that beneath his distinguished, well-groomed appearance he was so much older than she normally thought of him as being, and maybe just a tad tired.

Without arguing, she sat, ashamed at having assumed the worst about his motives for coming here. 'How are you feeling?' she asked.

He waved one hand in the air. 'Too impatient for small talk, Sierra. I've come here hoping we can reach an agreement. This silence between us has stretched out long enough, don't you think?'

'I think it's senseless, but it wasn't my choice. I never wanted it to begin with.'

'You're too mule-headed for your own good – standing by a man every thug in town was after, endangering yourself and your son in the process.'

'I didn't realize Will and I were in any danger until after Ben was killed. If I had, I probably would have had to leave him. But there's no going back. Are you going to hold that against me forever? Haven't you ever done anything in your life you regretted, Father?'

'Everyone in town thinks you've lost your mind, living here, trying to make money with horses. You don't know a horse from a raccoon.'

'I'm learning. And last I saw, *you* were telling everyone in this town what they think. I'm a single parent who wants her own life and her own home. Is that what you believe, that I've lost my mind?'

He shook his head. 'You and Will both could have a better, easier life. All you have to do is say the word.'

Her dark features tightened. 'So Will can have everything handed to him and turn out like Ben? I want him to learn how to take care of himself one day, not expect to have someone always looking out for him. I want him to learn to be responsible for his actions. We're not moving back to the house with you.'

'You're one of the most stubborn people I've ever come up against,' he conceded.

Her frown curved into a laugh. 'Wherever might I get that from?'

'Your mother, undoubtedly – you become more like her with each passing year.'

'Good; if I'm like her, I'm glad.'

'You look much the way I remember her . . .'

'You're getting sentimental! That's not like you, Father. Are you sure there's nothing wrong?'

'Just more time to think lately. It'll pass. Your mother had her failings, Sierra. Of course, you couldn't remember her, but don't be so quick to want to be like her.'

Sierra studied her father carefully. She had always considered her mother's death in terms of *her* loss, never stopping to think of all the years her father had endured alone. How awful it must be to love someone you could never see again.

Her face heated as Ben's photo on the wall reminded her that her own husband had died and she should be mourning for him that way. But Ben's memory, ever-dim, had been pushed aside. She'd been grieving for Matt longer than she knew. It was Matt she thought of today, her blissful abandonment in his arms, the improbability of his coming back, of their being together, even if last night was the only time it would ever happen. The prospect of losing him forever filled her with emptiness. Should she feel guilt over finding joy with the man she'd loved before Ben had taken over rights to her bed?

'Can I get you a drink?' she asked.

'No. No, thank you. Just tell me I'm allowed to see you and my grandson again.'

'I've never barred you from it. I never would.'

'I've missed young Will. Oh, you too, of course. He is a good boy. Surprising, considering he's Matt Rollins' son.'

Her face glowed crimson. 'Never say that!'

'It's the truth.'

'What if Will should overhear or someone else should and tell him?'

'It's only the two of us alone here, isn't it? Why

are you so upset? I'm the last person who'd ever want to acknowledge the shady side of my grandson's heritage.'

'Being Matt's son is nothing to be ashamed of. I'm proud of how much of Matt I see in him. But Will would be devastated to learn Ben wasn't his real father, that's all.'

'I don't know how you can defend that low-life, after he got you pregnant and sneaked out of town.'

'If he'd known I was pregnant, he never would have left.'

'He's lucky I didn't come after him.'

'Father, it's not as though 'd been raped. I don't want to talk about this. If it weren't for Matt, we wouldn't have Will at all, would we?'

'I suppose. Still, if I ever see that worthless philanderer . . .'

'I did what you wanted me to, Father. Fortunately, Matt left town and spared you the necessity of avenging my honor. In retrospect, I wish I'd married him. The Davenports would still be speaking to me, their son might still be alive, and Will would know who his daddy is.'

William Ross grunted. 'I'd rather see you dead.'

Trembling, she paled to the color of a freshly bleached sheet. 'You can't mean that!'

'Why him of all the men in this town, SiSi? His daddy ran all over town bragging about all the women he bedded down with when he took off in that truck of his. Wasn't a woman in this town would have him except his wife, and I guess stuck with his five brats she didn't see much choice.'

'That was his father, not him. He's not like that.'

'You don't know how he turned out. It's been years since you last saw him. And good riddance, I say.'

Sierra realized that between his frequent business trips out of town and the small elite crowd he socialized with, her father didn't have a clue Matt was back in town, let alone working for her here. Matt's name didn't come up very often at the country club. She suspected her pal Alison had been reporting to her father after her visits, for what Alison believed were altruistic reasons. But even Alison wouldn't have gone so far as to tell William Ross that Matt Rollins was staying out in the country with his daughter, and looked damn good shoeing the horses.

'Please don't ever say it aloud again. Ben is Will's father. That's the only reason I married Ben, as you well know, and it's about all I got from the marriage. Let's at least preserve that.'

'Fair enough. You're right. God knows I wouldn't want anyone to know otherwise either. Whatever, he's still a Ross. I'd like to take him to New York with me next weekend.'

'New York?'

'It's an exciting place this time of year. All the decorations, bright lights . . .'

'That's not the part you have to sell me on. He's never been that far away from me before.'

'Why don't the three of us go?'

'I can't leave the horses. I have work here.'

'No sense in punishing the boy for that. Besides, you could probably use some time to yourself.'

'I could, but . . . look, I want your word you won't try to interfere in our lives again. Will loves you without your spoiling him.'

'It's Christmas. Nothing elaborate.'

'Fine.'

She knew her father's generosity. He showered those he loved with comforts they grew to depend on, then controlled them by threatening to take them away. She supposed he was like some upscale drug dealer, and she didn't want her son dependent on him. Will would grow up to stand tall on his own like his father. But, unlike Matt, Will would not grow up doubting his own capacity to love.

If only she'd been stronger so long ago, had had some way of making a living on her own. No, she'd been weak, allowed her father to wield too much power over her. He'd rot in hell, he'd claimed, before he'd support Matt Rollins' bastard child. But he knew of a clinic where the problem could be eliminated quietly. Sierra would suffer only mild discomfort.

Knowing Matt never wanted children, she'd had only Ben to turn to. She would not kill the child growing inside her. And it was the only other option agreeable to her father.

The front door burst open, and Will sped into the house, dropping his duffel bag on the floor and marveling at the sight of his grandfather. Arms spread wide, he tore straight at him.

'Mom said you were mad at us,' Will told his grandfather as he hugged him.

Arms folded, Sierra blinked misty eyes as she watched the reunion. She'd always wanted a real family – she'd tried hard to make her and Will and Ben into one. She sighed. Sometimes you just have to make the best of what life hands you, she reflected. And whatever miracle had brought William Ross here today presented a good start, a new start. Perhaps with age, he was mellowing. She wanted what little family she had close to her.

'Just a misunderstanding, William,' he told the boy as he patted his back. 'Your mom and I have worked it out.'

'It's good to have you here, Father,' Sierra agreed. 'Can you stay for supper?'

'No. No. I've got to get back to the house and make some calls. But why don't you let me take Will back to the house for a while? I'm sure the cook's making something good.'

Will's face lit up like Christmas. Sierra set her hands on her hips.

'He just got home.'

'Aw, Mom.'

'And you and Luke were probably up most of the night too, weren't you?'

'I'm not tired.'

Overriding her son's protests, she refused to let him go.

'That's all right, William,' his grandfather assured him. 'How would you like to come to New York with me next weekend?'

Sierra couldn't help smiling as her son's eyes nearly popped out of his head. Will's head whipped towards her.

'Can I?' he asked.

'We'll see.' She turned to her father. 'We need to discuss this more before I make a decision.'

'Fine,' he agreed, rising. 'I'll call you.'

She hugged her father. He received the gesture stiffly. Sierra smiled. Emotional displays had always made him uncomfortable. 'Don't be a stranger,' she told him.

She and Will stood watching by the window as William Ross walked to his car.

'What made Grandfather William come back today?' Will asked. Even at his age, he understood that people didn't get over being angry unless something happened to change that.

She set one hand on her son's shoulder. 'Maybe he just got tired of being alone.'

'Maybe he saw the ghost of Christmas present . . . like in my play.'

Smiling softly, she shook her head. 'No, I don't think he's seen any ghosts.'

She looked down at her son – the dark handsome face with the proud straight lines. With each day, he looked more like his father.

Even a man as detached as her father couldn't resist loving this boy, his grandson and sole male heir. She knew her father must look back on his suggestion that she undergo an abortion with as much alarm and regret as she did. Will would be a wealthy man one day, but she hoped by then he would be prepared to deal with controlling a fortune.

So what had prompted her father's gesture? Never in her life had she known him to give in to anyone. Wondering why he had now left her unsettled. If he would go so far as swallowing his pride to reclaim his grandson, what else might he do?

Sierra nearly gasped out loud as she thought of it. Had her father merely devised an alternate plan for getting Will under his roof, even if it meant bypassing her? Her heart clenched, and she tightened her grip on the boy's shoulder.

Surely even her father wasn't callous enough to resort to that? she mused. Still, with Ben gone, his family turned away from her, she'd be helpless against a powerful man like her father. As much as she wanted to believe he wouldn't do that to her, he hadn't minded watching her marry a man she didn't love. Once Will had the Davenport name and the legitimacy of married parents, William Ross hadn't seen any need for his daughter to stand behind her husband.

She chewed her lip, reminding herself that he'd believed for practical reasons that her marriage was the best thing for her and the baby. And, like locating the clinic, it was something he'd done long ago. Maybe, for men, love was only a minor consideration in life's plan. It certainly didn't matter to Matt any more.

And maybe a daughter paled into insignificance beside a grandson. Whatever her father was up to, an echo in her heart told her that, if not for Will, he never would have made peace with her.

Will looked up at her, his eyes bright and eager. 'So can I go to New York, Mom? Please?'

Monday dawned cold but sunny. Once Will was off to school and the house was quiet, Sierra struggled to concentrate on her household chores. She cleaned the kitchen until it shone, threw a load of clothes in the washer and dusted the furniture.

When she heard Matt's voice outside, giving orders to the hands, her heart clenched and her skin bristled. Memories streamed through her of that night out of time when he'd made love to her so thoroughly, she'd lost herself to him. She hadn't meant for that to happen. She couldn't afford to lose her heart to him now. Still, he was taking it without even trying. Taking something he didn't want.

She looked out of the window and saw him, lean and rugged as he turned the horses out into the pasture. His only concession to the cold was a thin denim jacket. As she remembered how he'd tucked a mass of blankets over her, her lips curled into a smile.

Matt never failed to provide for the small consideration of other people's needs. Maybe it was as if he knew first-hand what it was like to have no one really care what you needed. Sierra winced. Everyone in town knew what kind of man Lester Rollins had been. But they'd looked the other way because his wife was the most popular waitress in town; just about all the ranchers knew her by her first name. And she loved him and needed him when he was around. The kids weren't being beaten.

Sierra had heard stories about Matt's family before she'd ever met him. When she had, he hadn't been at all what she'd expected. He carried himself with a quiet dignity, a sense of purpose, that certainly didn't come from his old man, as he called him.

And she hadn't anticipated the tug in her heart as she stood on tiptoe looking over Matt's shoulder into the complex workings of her car engine that summer day he'd rescued her. He seemed to know so much about everything.

The leathery muscle of his arm had brushed against hers, sending a ripple of warm, tingly electricity through her body, a feeling that drew her closer to him. Since high school she'd been dating boys from fine upstanding families, and she couldn't remember one who'd held her interest beyond a day or two, nor one who hadn't tried to coax her into the back seat of his car. She'd perceived that day a connection between herself and Matt, a force ruled by the universe and unrelated to anything on earth.

Intrigued and fascinated, she'd sought to understand it, refusing to go away until she did. Unlike the other young men she'd known, Matt was a gentleman. He treated her with respect, so much so that she'd wondered if he wasn't afraid of her, and she'd realized she'd found the man who would unravel the mysteries of lovemaking free of fear or shame. For her, trust came hard. She blamed her father for instilling a suspicion of the human race in her. He constantly drilled into her how everyone was after the Ross fortune – his oil, his company, his stocks.

Propping her elbows on the windowsill and her face in her hands, she leaned closer to the window, watching her cowboy. Today, she didn't mind if he caught her looking. There was a side to Matt he kept locked away from everyone, a part of him haunted and scarred. Maybe he could exorcise Ben for her, but he'd never allow her to touch that wounded part inside him, to soothe his pain. No, ultimately she'd only added to it.

Was this a second chance, or was she fooling herself? Were they, as he claimed, simply good together in bed?

An ache in her breasts reminded her how much she wanted him.

Dropping her gaze, she studied the linoleum. Was lovemaking ever enjoyable without love behind it? Maybe Matt cared for her more than he'd admit. But she needed more than that. She needed his forgiveness. And how could she hope to gain that without revealing a truth she could never tell?

In a few weeks, Matt would leave again. Will's well-being was her permanent responsibility. She would never sacrifice her son for anyone.

Maybe she could just grab the fleeting joy she had found with Matt and stop questioning it. Do things the way Matt wanted.

With the horses turned out, Matt was leaning against the fence, chewing on a piece of hay and watching them.

Sierra fetched her jacket and threw it on over her sweater. Suddenly, she couldn't stand to have even the window between them.

Texas sunshine bathed her face as she flew out of

the door, her hair streaming behind her. Thunder, who'd been sitting by the door, trotted along at her feet. Matt was still standing by the fence, one boot propped on it.

'Morning,' he greeted her, his expression solemn, unreadable.

She came to stand bedside him and leaned against the fence. 'It's a beautiful day,' she noted idly, wondering why she felt so awkward in the presence of a man she'd shared herself so freely with the night before last.

'Glorious,' he agreed, pulling at the brim of his hat.

Sierra felt her heart sinking. What had she expected? That he'd pull her into his arms out here in broad daylight in front of the hands and everything? Well, no, but he seemed so distant. Maybe he'd got to thinking things over, recalling how she'd betrayed him the last time he let her in close.

'You taking up grazing?' she asked, referring to the straw he held between his teeth.

He removed the hay and tossed it on the ground. 'Trying to give up smoking as usual. This is a darn poor substitute.'

Sierra laughed lightly. 'From what I've seen, you're pretty close to having given it up altogether.'

'Yeah. I'm close. I stay close. I'll get there.'

'How about some coffee? I could bring a Thermos out.'

He shook his head. 'No, thanks. I've got a lot to do this morning. The horses are due for their worming, and I need to drive in to the veterinary supply.'

Sierra nodded. Alarm nipped at her as his expression darkened and he continued looking at her as though he had something he wanted to get off his chest.

'What's wrong?' she asked.

'They've been asking about your bill.'

She colored. 'I'll give you a check to take them.'

'Money getting tight?'

Embarrassed as she was, she wasn't going to tell him another lie. 'I had no idea keeping horses was so expensive. Compared to what we're bringing in . . .'

'You're not trying hard enough. A couple of boarders, a handful of riding students . . . you need to bring in some more business.'

'I've had some enquiries about boarding over the holidays, but I don't see that there's room . . .'

'I can build you a couple of board stalls in the corner of the corral. Lumber won't cost much. If that's OK . . . We can move a couple of our . . . your horses over there temporarily.'

'Well, yes, sure . . .'

'What about getting some more people out here to ride?'

'I don't think I could do much about that until

after the first of the year. But to be honest, Matt, I can't offer something I'm not sure I can provide. I don't know how long you'll be here.'

'Sign 'em up. Jerry's not going to be on his feet for a while. And I'm not going to leave without giving you proper notice. You'll have time to find a replacement.'

'All right,' she agreed.

He looked down at her hard, his blue eyes glistening in the morning sunlight. The air smelled fresh and clean.

'Are you serious, Sierra, about making a go of this place?'

'Of course I am.'

'Because I don't want to throw myself into helping you get it up and running to turn around and find you abandoning it to work for your daddy or marry some millionaire. I know how you're prone to sudden changes of heart.'

Her chin rose indignantly. 'I told you before, I'm not getting married again.' Especially not if I can't have the one man I'd want to be a wife to, she added silently. Why did he have to be so sarcastic?

He gave her a long, low appraisal. 'Sorry. No offense. That last part kind of slipped out.'

'Forget it. So what's the deal? What's on your mind, Matt?'

'Buggy rides.'

Her dark eyebrows knit into a V. 'Buggy rides?'

'A guy I knew in Wyoming did it. He had a carriage and rented it out. Drove people around in the rig. You know how people get all sentimental and romantic around the holidays. They'll pay a high price for a few hours of caroling or partying.'

'You're serious.'

'As taxes. It's the quickest way I can think of for you to make enough money right now to keep you afloat through the winter.'

'Problem is, I don't have a carriage.'

'I know someone who has one. At least he used to, and I've never known Sam Burke to get rid of anything.'

'Sam? Do you think he'd let us use it?'

'No harm in asking. I've been needing to go see that old coot anyway. He probably thinks I'm ticked at him because of his grandson turning me down for a job. There's not much that old guy could do to make me stay mad at him. I love the hell out of him, always have, always will.'

Sierra's lips parted. She wanted to warn Matt before he went over there, but, remembering Sam didn't want anyone telling Matt about his problems, she closed her mouth quickly.

'Who's going to drive it?'

'I will. You take care of advertising it and booking it. Any of these horses trained to harness?'

'I don't know. Why are you doing all this?' she asked.

'It's my job.'

'It's more than your job.'

He turned his eyes towards the sun and squinted. 'I'd feel better being able to leave without worrying about how the two of you are getting on,' he admitted.

'Oh.'

'There is a string attached.'

'What?'

'Since this is extra, if I get the carriage, I want my own cut of the profits. I don't want to be worrying about how I leave my sister behind either.'

'How much?'

'Thirty per cent.'

'Twenty-five.'

'Thirty or I'm not going to mess with it. And you'll have seventy five per cent of nothin'.'

'Thirty,' she conceded. Getting into her pants hadn't softened his bargaining savvy, she observed.

In one quick motion his hand caught hers, hanging between them at her side, wrapping it warmly, squeezing it. Surprised and thrilled at the contact, she looked up into his eyes, smiling. His eyes were intense and compelling, and she glimpsed the tenderness, the lingering intimacy, the silent promise of more. She felt as though he'd reached out and put his hand on her heart.

He leaned closer. 'This is business, Sierra. One

thing doesn't have anything to do with the other. I can't afford to let it.'

His tactics reminded her disturbingly of her father's, and a thread of trepidation coiled inside her as she wondered what might happened if these two strong men ever confronted one another. Father's statement that he'd rather see her dead than with Matt Rollins echoed in her head. William Ross wasn't prone to making statements he didn't mean. Of course, she knew he wouldn't actually kill her or anyone else. He had little to hold over her any more. But Matt, Matt was the one who'd bear the brunt of her father's rage. And he had ways of making people wish they were dead.

Silently, she nodded her understanding. He was reaffirming his independence. But he needn't have bothered. She'd already received his message. She accepted it. She'd never measured up to being worthy of a place in his heart.

Driving up the road to Sam's house, Matt felt as though he'd fallen back in time.

Walking up to the door, he recalled the time Sam had come out to meet him, to tell him Star was dead, and an odd sense of foreboding he couldn't shake overcame him.

Foolish, he told himself. He was just feeling antsy over seeing Sam again after all this time.

He rapped on the door.

A young blonde woman he'd never seen before opened it. He tipped his hat in greeting. 'I've come to see Sam,' he said.

She didn't move. 'Who are you?'

'Tell him Matt Rollins is here.'

Her cautious expression burst into a smile, and Matt realized she was prettier than he'd first thought.

'So, you're Matt Rollins. I've heard about you. Come on in, Mr Rollins. I'll go get Sam.'

'Thanks. And I'd rather you'd just call me Matt.'

'Matt, then.' She led him into a warm red and white kitchen with good smells of baking lingering in the air. 'I've heard so much about you. Would you like some coffee?'

'Don't mind if I do.'

She found a mug and filled it. 'Take anything in it?'

'Black's fine.'

Removing his hat, he sat at the oval-shaped wooden table facing the window. She set the mug before him.

'You staying here with Sam?' he asked.

Clutching a splayed hand to the bodice of her corduroy jumper, she laughed nervously. 'I'm sorry. I was so surprised to see you, I forgot my manners. I'm Jamie Burke, Dunc's wife. We're living here now, looking after the place and Sam.'

'As I recall, Sam never needed much looking after.'

She shrugged. 'Things have changed while you were away. Sam's gotten older. I'm glad you've come to see him. He needs a boost right now. He talks about you all the time. I hope you're not upset because Dunc couldn't hire you on. Times are tough for all the cattle ranchers. We're all losin' money, struggling to get by.'

Guilt washed through Matt. He should have come to see Sam first off without waiting for business to bring him here. But when he'd come last time, his grandson had said Sam'd gone away for a few days.

'I understand,' he told her.

She wiped her hands on a dishtowel. Matt glanced up from his coffee and wondered why she was looking at him like a messenger with a bad telegram.

She scrambled out of the room. Nervous type, he thought, but she made a good cup of coffee. Funny to think Duncan had found him a wife. Matt remembered him mainly as a younger kid who was always getting underfoot while he worked. Sam's only son, Clyde, had never cared much for ranching. He'd already finished college and gone off to become a big-city journalist instead before Matt ever knew Sam. Sam had never admitted his disappointment, but Matt had glimpsed it in his eyes when he spoke of Clyde.

Sam had showed him a man could be tough and

strong without being mean. He'd made him believe he could be that way too. As a teenager, he'd often wished Sam had been his father, and sometimes he just pretended he was, especially when the old man was around and things got tough at home.

In a few minutes Sam came waddling out in his jeans and flannel shirt, looking as grizzled and cheerful as ever. Rising, Matt broke into a grin, extending one arm for a handshake.

'You are one sight for sore eyes,' Sam assessed, looking him up and down, then clasping Matt's hand and, instead of shaking it, using it to pull Matt into a hug. 'I thought you'd given up on me.'

As he drew back, he grinned like a cat who'd just sashayed past a sleeping dog.

Matt stared at him blankly. Sam Burke was many things, but never affectionate.

'It's good to see you, Sam.'

'Took you long enough to come around here.'

'You were gone last time I was here. I've been working for Sierra Ross and trying to help Leeann.'

Sam waved him off. 'She's a Davenport, not a Ross now, and I know what you've been doing. Glad to know the two of you are takin' care of each other. I keep an eye on things.'

'How are you, Sam?'

'What brings you out here in the middle of the day?'

'I came to see if you still have that old carriage in

the barn. Thought maybe we could strike up a deal about letting Sierra use it for a couple of weeks.'

'Hmm. Maybe we can. Jamie makes some fine coffee, doesn't she?'

'Great,' Matt agreed.

Sam's eyes narrowed. 'Why don't you sit down and finish yours and let's talk a bit before we go see the carriage.'

Sam's tone made Matt feel downright uneasy. He knew in his gut the old man was leading up to something he wasn't going to like. He sat rigid, not touching the coffee.

Sam sat opposite him, leaning forward and looking him in the eye. 'I was nearly hoping you wouldn't come so I wouldn't have to tell you this, Matt. I've spent a lot of years thinking of you like as if you were my own son. So many times I wanted to reach out and jerk you away from that nincompoop who mistreated you, but I had no claim, no right. If you'd been my boy, I would have done ya' differently.'

'I've always known that, Sam. None of us gets to choose our families.'

Sam nodded. 'Sometimes strangers grow closer than people who share the same blood. Quirk of nature, I reckon. And we can't change what's gone on in the past. Fact is, I don't have much time to be lamentin' over it. Doctors tell me I'm dyin', son.'

The whole world went black, and Matt felt as though a mule had kicked him in the stomach.

'No.' The feeble protest fell from his lips.

'Don't you fall out on me. They're all tiptoeing around, pretending it's not going to happen. We've always played it straight with each other, haven't we, Matt? Don't you dare start sending me daisies. I've still got enough fight in me to go hand-to-hand with you if it comes down to that.'

Matt wasn't sure whether he was going to laugh or cry. Somehow he couldn't picture Sam holding a bouquet of daisies.

It was Sam who decided what came next. 'Come on, let's go take a look at that carriage.'

He shot out of the house. Matt, still dazed, got up and trailed after him. The old cowpuncher didn't look or act sick.

Getting up slowly, he reached for his hat, put it on, and followed Sam to the barn.

The old carriage had been sitting for a spell, but mostly all it needed was cleaning up.

'I don't see no problem with lettin' Sierra have it,' Sam said.

'Both of us,' Matt qualified, stooping down to inspect the spokes. 'This is a joint venture.'

'Suits me. You'll have to worry over draggin' it outa here. I imagine Duncan'll be glad to have it outa his way.'

'Let me pay you something for it, Sam.'

Sam shook his head. 'The money don't mean much these days. Don't see any point in takin' it from you nor Sierra. Glad ya'll gettin' along well enough to be startin' a business enterprise.' He brushed his hands against his trousers. 'Now that that's over with, let's stop standin' here starin' at our boots like we was at a wake and saddle up some horses. Great day for a ride.'

'Are you sure you're up to it?'

'I said I'm dyin', son. I ain't dead yet.'

Shaking his head, Matt followed. He still didn't believe it. The doctors had made a mistake. Mix-ups like that happened all the time.

He and Sam rode out to the far north end of Sam's property, the prettiest part where the flat earth rolled into gently sloping hills and thick stands of live oaks dotted the landscape.

Sam dismounted. Matt followed suit.

Sam stared out beyond the trees and pointed in that direction with a finger crooked from his roping days. 'Creek's over yonder,' he said.

Matt gave a brief nod. He knew the creek.

'This over here, Matthew . . . this is yours, son. There's about fifty acres.'

'What?' Sam wasn't dying; he was just loco.

'You heard me right. I'm leavin' it to you in my will.'

'Sam, I don't want your land. I just want you to be all right.'

'Well, I ain't gettin' better. I got cancer all through me.'

'God, Sam.'

'It's not so much as you'd think. Now I brought you out here, because some folks might say you've got no claim to this, and I'm tellin' you now flat out, it's yours and don't let no one tell ya' differently. This here's part of the universe, and we all got our place in it. Not everybody fits in where they'd expect to, and the trick is to find that little niche where you fit into the puzzle.'

'But it belongs to your family, your grandson.'

'There's plenty left over for him. And Clyde, he's never cared about the land. If I ever knew a man who needed some soil to dig his heels into, it's you. Do what you want with it . . . make a home here or sell it and move on. I'm not makin' any requests except that you follow your own gut instincts.'

'This property is worth a fortune.'

'If you know how to make it work for you. And you can. Lord, I wish your ma had lived to see how you are now, all grown-up. You're nothin' like your daddy, Matt. Don't ever think you are. It was Dylan got that curse.'

'This is mighty generous of you, Sam. But I can't take your land. I wasn't around to know you were sick. Your grandson's here, working the place, looking after you.'

'He's a good boy, and he'll get what he needs. Call this conscience payment, if you will, for all those years your father treated you like dirt and I couldn't do nothing about it.'

'It was never your problem, Sam.'

'I think it was. Now, if you ever repeat what I'm about to tell you to a living soul, I'll swear you dreamed it. You weren't born yet, so of course you wouldn't have known I was sweet on your ma once.'

'On my ma? But . . .'

'I was old enough to be her daddy? Didn't matter. After Dylan was born, your Daddy started going out with the boys nights he wasn't on the road, leaving her at home after work with the chores and baby. Nothing sadder in the world than a pretty, young lonely woman. I'd go in to the diner for breakfast a couple mornings a week . . . it was a couple o' years after Annie died, and I was feelin' kind of down myself. She got to talkin' about her problems, and I'd hang around to listen. She came out here a couple o' times. Stop lookin' at me like that, I know this is your ma I'm talkin' about. Nothin' happened, but not for lack of my wantin' it to. We kissed a few times, and I guess we both knew if we didn't break it off, things would go farther real quick. She already suspected she was pregnant again, and she still believed your Daddy would turn himself around if she didn't do something foolish like cheat on him. Being the honest, God-fearing woman she was, she admitted the whole thing to him and repented, begging his forgiveness. Being the hot-head he was, your Daddy never believed she'd told him the whole truth. When you were born, so different inside than he was, he planted it in his head you were my son and not his. Dylan had always been a difficult child, and when you came along, quiet and easy, it was natural for your ma to favor you. Kind of made up for the other. That just fired up your Daddy's jealousy all the more. I watched him. Oh, I watched him. I wished you *had* been my son so I coulda at least tried to get you away from him. But he was sly, Lester was. He wasn't the kind of tormentor who leaves bruises, was he?'

'My father treated me like cowdung all my life because he thought I was your son?'

'He knew you weren't. But he wouldn't let go of it, even when he could see his own features on you. A blind man doesn't recognize much. I guess you reminded him of how much of a fool he was, nearly losing his wife. He did love her, or he wouldn't have taken her back, not believin' she'd cheated on him. I'm telling you this because I know how it was between the two of you, and I know you've always wondered what you'd done to him. Now I'm telling you, it was what I done, not you. He believed he had a reason to resent you. Damned if I'd ever make excuses for him. Believe me, he's the one who's the worst off for it. I've seen his kind before, raised to believe bein' a man means you do whatever you feel like and worryin' over how you make other people feel is for sissies. I'm gonna tell you something else. I'm saying this just once because all this tirin' me out some. What it all boils down to in the end is hate is an awful heavy load to be totin' through life, and when you get to the end of the road, you see you been haulin' one useless saddlebag. I just hope one day you'll find it in your heart to forgive Lester and free yourself of him forever. There's too many good things in life to enjoy.'

'I doubt I could ever forgive him, Sam. It runs too deep.'

Sam shrugged. 'God gave ya' life; he didn't. Let me do this one thing for you, Matthew. You deserve better than what you got.'

'Your family should have it.'

'You are family to me. Like I said, you can sell it or whatever, but it will be yours because I'm not changin' my will, and by the time you get it, I'll be too dead for you to argue.'

'Blackmail doesn't become you, Sam.'

'I ain't got my sweet time to convince ya.'

Matt turned to him, deep lines creasing his tanned face. 'You scared, Sam?'

'Scared as hell, but I ain't got no other road to take. I've made my peace.'

CHAPTER 8

The sound of hammering interspersed with the intermittent whine of the electric saw echoed across the open fields. Early winter darkness was stealing across the horizon. Peering through her back window, Sierra strained to see Matt. He appeared as a dark speck in the distance, tossing boards around in the corner of the corral.

Her arms folded across her chest, she jutted her bottom lip and paced. Ever since he'd mentioned his intention of going to Sam's, she'd worried over how he might take the news of Sam's illness. Now, she knew Sam must have told him. Well aware of how Matt admired the grizzled old rancher, she sensed how deeply he must he hurting inside. She longed to comfort Matt, cushion the pain he must be feeling. But he hadn't come to her with it, as she'd been hoping he would.

Damn him. A tractor could run over him and he'd refuse an anesthetic. He held his pain inside, but then he'd been trained to, never having had an outlet for it.

She left him to himself as long as she could stand it. The silent house mocked her. Will had stayed late at school for a play rehearsal, leaving her here alone with her thoughts.

She had no right to intrude on Matt's privacy. But he had come back here, to the ranch, hadn't he? He could have gone elsewhere, somewhere he knew he'd be alone or among strangers. Maybe this was the closest he could come to asking . . .

The last of the light was fading as she resolutely threw her jacket over her shoulders and marched outside.

Matt was kneeling on one knee in the dirt, a lit cigarette dangling from his lips. He glanced up at her briefly, not saying anything. He continued working.

'There's not much light left out here. Why don't you stop working now?' she suggested mildly.

'I'm fixing to set up some portable lights from the barn,' he informed her.

'It's late – you must be tired.'

'Can't always stop because you're tired. You want to have shelter to board the extra horses over the holidays, don't you?'

'Yes.' A gust of cold wind blew across the field, sending her hair streaming sideways.

'Then let me be. I know what I'm doing.'

'May I help?'

He cocked one eye as he looked up at her. 'You know anything about carpentry?'

'No.'

'Then you'd just be in the way. Go back inside, Sierra, and leave me be.'

'I'm a fast learner.' She lowered her voice. 'And I should know how to nail boards together. For when you're gone . . .'

He cast her a disparaging look. 'I'm not in the mood for giving lessons right now, Sierra. You should have learned how to take care of yourself a long time ago.'

Considering his ill mood and the reason behind it, she saw no point in arguing with him. He was skittish as a wounded bear. She turned to go.

His voice halted her. 'Sierra?'

She turned, watching him toss away the half-finished cigarette.

'I'm sorry. I'm just not in a real good temper. I've got no call taking it out on you. Don't feel like chattering with anybody, you know?'

She stepped towards him. A full moon was rising in the blue velvet star-studded sky. Her voice blended with the wind. 'You saw Sam today, didn't you?' she asked.

His eyes diminished to pinpoints. Slowly, he nodded. 'Uh-huh. You knew about Sam?'

She nodded.

'You might have mentioned something, prepared me for it.'

'I was respecting Sam's wishes. He didn't want to

be fodder for the local grapevine. And he didn't want you to find out unless he told you himself.'

'Good at keeping secrets, aren't you?'

'Last time we were together, Sam wasn't what was on my mind.' Her face heated at the memory of what had occupied her thoughts.

Abandoning his construction efforts, Matt tossed the hammer aside and sat back on the hard, damp ground. 'Ah, hell, it's not your fault. Sounds just like Sam, not wanting the whole town flocking around him, staring at him with pity in their eyes. I'm just kicking myself for not staying in touch with him, for staying away since I've been back because I was disappointed that he'd broken a promise to me. Here I was, thinking of myself, oblivious to what he was going through.'

His face was twisted with pain. Sierra wished she could hold him close, stroke his hair, and cradle his face in her breasts.

'You couldn't have guessed. Don't be so hard on yourself.'

He shook his head. 'Sam's been up there on that ranch ever since I can remember, kind of watching over his own little piece of the world. I took it for granted he always would be.' He shrugged. 'But nothing good ever lasts, does it, darlin'? I should have learned that a long time ago. What little good there is just slips away like dirt in a rainstorm.'

With a sharp pang of regret, Sierra wished she

could tell him he'd made something that would last for a long time, something fine and strong and good – a son named Will.

She held her chin high. 'I don't believe that, and I don't think you do either. We live and we die, but that's all the more reason to hold on to what's precious while we can.'

His eyes swept over her. 'As I recall, you never focused much on holding on to things.'

Feeling the heat of his gaze, she dropped her eyes. 'I've changed, Matt. I'm not that flighty, spoiled rich girl you knew. Everything came too easily. I never realized I had to hold fast to anything. Maybe that's what drew me to you back then. Despite everything that had happened to you, you always believed there was something better. And maybe a part of me was wanting to find it with you. When did you stop looking?'

Tingling, she felt his eyes skimming over her in the darkness that was dropping over them like a heavy curtain.

'After all that's happened to you – being married to a man who gambled away a fortune and got himself killed – you haven't given up?'

'No, I never will.'

'But you already have. You say you'll never marry again.'

'Will and I will be happy on our own.'

'Face it, Sierra, years change people. Reality takes

over, and you give up dreams, like your painting, like my wanting to be a vet.'

'Maybe those weren't the right dreams.'

'Sam has done more for me than anyone on this earth. I don't know what direction I might have gone if I hadn't had him to look up to. While my old man was laughing at me, making me believe I was nothing, Sam taught me to do something I was good at, made me feel like I was something more than a thorn in my old man's side. I wanted to be just like Sam. He never tried to be anything more or less than just Sam, but I doubt he would have hurt even a rattlesnake unless it had its fangs in his arm. Over the years, I thought about him all the time, every time I was near a horse. I owe him everything, and yet I couldn't take the time to make a phone call or send a Christmas card.'

Sierra bowed her head. If not for her, Matt might not have run so fast and so far. Then he wouldn't be feeling so guilty now.

'Well, you can't go back, you don't get to do it over. That's one of life's little jokes, don't you see? By the time you realize what you should have done, it's too late.'

Matt shook his head, raising his hands at his sides. 'I don't know what to do.'

She spoke gently. 'Be here for him now.'

'And watch him die? I don't know if I can. And Sam would hate it.'

'Would he? Do you think he would have been so kind to you if he didn't love you as much as you love him? Oh, yes, I know men like you and Sam don't use that word to describe how you feel about each other. Too thick-headed, I suppose. Why do you think he told you the truth? He didn't have to. For once, stop looking at everything in terms of yourself. Maybe he told you because he's missed you, because he needs you here to see him through this.'

'Sam's always hated having anyone hovering over him.'

'Ask him.' Her words tumbled softly in the rising wind. 'Ask him if you can share some of the little time he has left. Or else don't. You can always just forget it and run away again. That would make it a whole lot easier on you, wouldn't it?'

Clutching the lapels of her jacket together, her head bowed and her black hair whipping in the fierce wind, she turned on one heel and headed towards the house.

Matt felt like a giant lying in Tanner's narrow bed. Clad in only his briefs, he had his hands clasped behind his head and his eyes wide open. The rest of Leeann's household had long been asleep, but he didn't feel much like sleeping tonight.

He longed for the feel of Sierra's sleek, slender body tucked against his. God, how he wanted her.

He wanted to be inside her, moving slowly, feeling real and alive.

Had he really thought he could have her again and forget her? Even when he'd never forgotten her the first time? He shouldn't have made love to her. Too hard to separate the physical act from having once loved her. Too much lingering tenderness. He didn't want to start depending on having her around.

Just thinking of her, the mass of dark hair, those spellbinding eyes nearly the color of coal, the full cranberry lips pliant and warm, trim, curving coppery flesh that yielded to his touch . . . He hardened at the memory of her naked body glistening in a sheen of sweat, quivering to his touch, writhing beneath him as he played to heighten her pleasure. He remembered watching the lines of her sweet face soften as she surrendered the last of her resistance to the fiery waves of pleasure he stoked, feeling her sway to his tempo, pressing her skin against his until she trembled and moaned as he took her over the brink of ecstasy.

His throbbing member warned him she was getting under his skin again, far beneath it, and he propelled his thoughts in another direction.

He had to decide what to do about Sam. Back in Wyoming – Montana before that – he'd done his job and no one had expected much else of him. He'd come back here to help his sister, make some money to help her and the kids, then be on his way. He'd forgotten home wasn't like any place else you moved into and settled in. Home was where people you knew and once loved maybe were. When you came back around, people began wanting more out of you than an honest day's work.

Sierra wanted him to teach her how to make a living from the stables on her own and now to stave off a widow's night-time loneliness. Will wanted him to teach him the stuff a boy his age needed to know and wouldn't find out from his mother. Leeann wanted him to be part of a family reunion from hell, and Sam wanted him to forgive a cruel father he still had nightmares about.

Home-folks sure could worry the hell out of a fella.

Feeling as though he were suffocating, Matt got up and cracked open the window. Cold air swept through the small room.

He smelled trouble coming, bad trouble. Every nerve in his body yearned to be in a sleeping bag out under the stars somewhere in a place he had no ties to, some nameless place where he couldn't disappoint anyone.

But he couldn't abandon any of them – Sierra and Will, Leeann and the kids, nor his mentor, Sam. He couldn't help wondering whether the old man had known Sam was watching him, whether life might not have been worse if Daddy thought no one was paying attention. That single fact could have been why the old man had stopped short of physical abuse. Lester Rollins had never laid a hand on him, but Matt had sometimes felt his father wanted to kill him.

Maybe Sierra was right about Sam not minding if he stayed close. But she had been wrong to think the old geezer would admit it if he did. Yeah, he'd hang around long enough to see Sam through this, no matter how much Sam protested. Damn him for dying anyway. Sure, Sam was old, but he'd been old ever since Matt could remember. What was it like, he wondered, to live with no hope greater than seeing the sunset one more time, wondering if each would be the last? But did anyone really have more than that?

He had to persuade Sam to change his will. He didn't want to take the old man's land. Nothing Sam owned had come easy to him, and Matt didn't want the responsibility of inheriting it. Taking it would oblige him to stay. He knew he could never bring himself to sell it.

Groggily, he yawned. Stretching out as best he could, hugging the thin pillow, he closed his eyes. His thoughts drifted into blackness, then re-emerged from a place inside him beyond his control . . .

His Christmas gift that year was the realization that he hadn't simply failed to please his father. The old man hated him and always would. And now the old man blamed him for depriving him of Dylan.

He was thirteen that bleak, rainy Christmas Eve, the grayest day he ever remembered. Ma was working late at the diner. Daddy'd been on the road for weeks, and they hadn't heard from him. He hadn't sent any money back either. Now Ma was looking tired and worried over how she was going to pay the bills on her waitress's salary and tips. She'd sat them down last week and told them not to expect presents or a tree this year. Dylan, who was fifteen, had gone straight to the woods and chopped down a pine tree, then pulled out the lights and ornaments from the shed. Ma had cried. Instead of being happy about it, she'd told Dylan all he was doing was reminding the younger kids there wasn't much else.

Now, Matt and Dylan had the kids on the porch. Through the window the sparse strand of colored lights was shining. Matt began to think his ma was right. They had the kids outside, trying to make-believe it wasn't Christmas. Darcy was eleven, tall and kind of spindly with short, straight brown hair. She was the quietest and the smartest one of the lot. Daddy said she was lazy because she usually had a book in her face. Gage was nine, fair like Leeann and full of mischief and laughter. He was always doing something nutty, clowning around. Leeann, at eight, was the baby of the family. The kids at school had filled her head with talk of Santa and expensive presents, and she took everything the hardest. She refused to believe Santa wouldn't be dropping by their house tonight.

Matt tensed when he heard the rig rumbling up the road.

'Daddy's home!' Leeann squealed with delight. She snapped her head around. 'You see, Matt.'

While she raced into the yard behind the others, Matt hung back. The rig ground to a stop out front. Lester Rollins emerged majestically from the cab, Gage and Leeann leaping joyfully into his arms.

'What's all this?' their father asked, prancing like a returning warrior.

Matt glanced sideways, wondering why Daddy'd let Ma worry so. He was surprised to see his own guarded expression mirrored in his older brother's eyes. He knew his brother was puzzling over the same thing.

Daddy rounded the truck, opening the door on the driver's side to reveal a stack of wrapped packages. Leeann and Gage's little eyes rounded with awe as if Santa himself had just landed his sleigh in the front yard.

'Picked up a couple o' things for y'all, seein' as how it's Christmas and all,' Daddy said.

Reaching inside, he began handing out the packages one-by-one right there in the rain. Leeann got a doll, Gage a metal fire engine. Darcy unwrapped a book.

Matt watched as Dylan tore the foil off his package and extracted a blue and white football jersey.

'Wow!' Dylan exclaimed, letting the box and wrappings fall on the wet ground and waving the garment like a flag. 'Thanks, Daddy.' Apparently, his reservations over Daddy's unannounced return had dissolved.

Matt would never forget the way Daddy stood there beaming down on Dylan, grinning at him as though he'd burst with pride.

Suddenly, Leeann paused from hugging her new doll. 'Where's Matt's present, Daddy?' she asked.

As Matt peered inside the truck and saw no more presents on the seat, a thick lump began forming in his throat. Time seemed frozen as Lester Rollins shifted his stance, shuffling in the mud and leveling his gaze on his second oldest. He cleared his throat. 'Sorry, Matt. I couldn't find nothin' to suit ya, and I was pressed for time. I'll make it up to you later.'

Matt felt his brothers and sisters staring at him. He didn't know what to say. He wished the earth would open up and swallow him. Not for a minute could he believe he'd been left out accidentally.

'It doesn't matter,' he sputtered, refusing to let the old man see he hurt so bad he wanted to cry, determined not to spoil this for the other kids. He knew as dead sure as tomorrow was Christmas Daddy had no intention of trying to make this up to him. And Daddy knew he knew it. He was just saying it, thinking he was slick because he thought the rest of them would believe it, and he didn't want them to know how cruel he was.

'No. It does matter.'

Both Matt and their father whipped around to see that the protest had come from Dylan standing beside Matt, holding out his new jersey. 'Here, Matt,' he offered 'Take this. I'm the oldest, and if one of us does without, I guess it should be me.'

Daddy gawked at Dylan as though his favorite son had stuck a knife in his chest. He'd always been jealous of the two brothers' closeness, sometimes going so far as trying to goad them into fights. Then his eyes shifted to Matt, settling on him. Matt recoiled at the dark fires of pure hatred burning there.

Not taking the shirt, Matt pushed his brother's arms back. 'No,' he objected evenly. 'He meant it for you.' He knew if he even thought about taking Dylan's jersey, their Daddy would make him regret it every minute for the rest of his life. Without looking back at either of them, he marched away, blinking back tears and holding his head high.

On Christmas morning, the jersey was still lying out there in the mud.

Matt awoke, drenched in sweat. He had the devil inside him, and no matter how far he went or what he did, the old man was never going away. Maybe Sam was right, getting rid of him was a matter of working from the inside out. But he truly didn't know where to start.

Turning over on his side, he untangled himself from the sheets. Risking the torment of his own horniness, he brought Sierra into his thoughts so he could sleep.

Sierra sat hunched over the kitchen table, her tongue sticking out of one corner of her mouth, trying to master the intricacies of the portable sewing machine she'd borrowed from Luke's mother. When Helen had demonstrated its operation, the procedure had looked simple. Sierra couldn't figure out why her stitches were coming out loose and uneven instead of neat and straight. Will's performance was only a few days away. He needed his costume, and it had to look good.

Once, she would have simply found a dressmaker in the classified, obtained references, and dropped off the pattern and material. Now, she couldn't afford such luxuries. Growing up without a mother, how was she expected to know how to sew?

Will shot through the door.

'William, I've told you about running in the house . . .' she began automatically.

'Come quick, Mom,' he panted. 'Fancy kicked Matt. I think he's dead!'

'What!' she cried, shooting out of her chair before she realized it.

'Hurry, Mom,' he urged, running back out the door.

She followed. Halfway to the stable, she realized she should have called an ambulance before she left the house. Fear threaded through her. She couldn't face the thought of being left without Matt again, and her apprehension had nothing to do with running the stables. Everything to do with her heart.

For a wrenching moment, she debated between going back or forward. No, she had to go to Matt. She could send one of the hands back to the house. God, she couldn't just stand here.

Forcing herself to move, she raced the rest of the way to the barn.

Matt, sprawled on his back, was struggling to right himself, brushing straw off his jacket. Relief flooded through her as she saw her son had exaggerated his condition.

'Stay back,' he warned, gesturing towards Fancy.

'Do you need a doctor?' she asked.

'No, but call the vet.'

'Really, Matt, if you're hurt there's no need to cut corners . . .'

'Not for me, for Fancy! She's got a tick in her ear and won't let me near her. She'll have to be tranquilized so we can get it off.'

Startled momentarily, Sierra burst into laughter.

'What's so darn funny?' Matt asked.

'You, on your butt.'

He was on his feet now, grinning. 'Well, you'll be lucky to see that again.'

Her eyebrows flared. 'We'll see. At least now I know you're human.'

'Did I leave any doubts about that?' He glanced down at Will. 'Thanks for saving my life anyway, Will. That was quick thinking. You did the right thing.'

Will was staring up at him in awe. 'You're not even hurt?' he asked incredulously.

'Shook up is all. I'll be fine once my brain stops rattling.'

'Wait till I call Luke and tell him about this!'

He raced out of the stable, leaving Matt and Sierra face to face among the horses.

'Are you really all right?' she pressed.

'Fine.'

'Matt, Will's going to be gone this weekend. I don't know what your plans are, but . . .'

He was shaking his head. 'Maybe our seeing each other isn't any better an idea now than it was all those years ago, Sierra. The other night, maybe we just needed to circle around and see what it would be like again.'

She shrunk back, looking wounded. 'I'm not asking for anything more than to be with you. I believe you made your intentions quite clear.'

His expression toughened. 'But I'm not so sure I can go through with it without feeling anything.' His eyes shot up to her. 'I can't keep the old times from coming back when I touch you. Let's leave behind the mess we made of the past and go on with our lives. I thank you for the other night. You make me feel alive – that's never changed. Whatever you think I did for you can't possibly match what it meant to me. But it's too much too fast. Maybe it's not a good idea with us working here together.'

He moved past her.

But Sierra's soul was soaring at his admission that he'd felt more for her than physical need. Because she'd felt so much more.

She knew he loved Will. Even Matt had found hardening his heart to the endearing little boy impossible. If by some miracle Matt's love for her had survived, could they ever find happiness now? Matt would love Will as his son, and, when he discovered what he was capable of, realized he wasn't a monster, he might want more children.

But Sierra realized withholding the truth would become increasingly impossible.

No, there was no hope of their being together permanently. Matt had come here with his mind made up to leave as soon as he could. She knew better than to push him.

But she wanted him for this one weekend at least. And he wouldn't permit it.

'I guess you're right,' she said, not meaning it. She walked back towards the house, determined to conquer the sewing machine.

Will was in the kitchen.

'Honey, why did you say Matt was dead?' she asked.

'He wasn't even moving at first, Mom. I guess I was thinking about Dad.'

'I know you miss him.'

'Yeah. Matt knows lots of things about animals and plants and Indians. I'm glad he's here taking care of us.'

Sierra smiled softly. 'He's helping us for a while, son. You can't think he's going to stay permanently.'

'Why not? He likes it here. He shows me how to take care of the horses. He likes you too, Mom. I can tell when he looks at you. I bet he'd stay if you asked him. Lots of kids at school have more than one dad.'

'Will, Matt's not the kind of person who's happy staying in one place. And you can't just pick someone to be your dad.'

Will's forehead creased, and as he contemplated this information, he reminded her so much of his father that her heart constricted.

'Maybe nobody's ever asked him to stay anywhere before. I'll ask him if you won't.'

'No!' she commanded in a voice so threatening it seemed not to be her own. She'd never spoken this harshly to her son.

He shrank back, staring at her wide-eyed as though she'd been transformed into a space-alien before his eyes.

'I thought you liked him.'

'I do, Will, but we can't always ask people to do what we want them to. Now promise me you won't ask Matt to stay.'

'But Mom . . .'

'William, you know this is important or I wouldn't ask you to promise. If Matt should decide to stay here, it's got to be because he wants to, not because we need him.'

'All right . . .'

William Ross sat back in his leather-upholstered easy chair and jingled the ice cubes in his Kentucky bourbon and water. 'Mighty kind of you to stop by, Jake. Sure you won't have a drink?'

Jake Everheart shuffled papers in his leather portfolio. 'No, thanks. Sorry it had to be so late, Bill.'

'No problem. Let's just get to the chase, though. What are my chances?'

Jake, sitting in the gold-flecked green-upholstered chair opposite the oil tycoon, tapped his fingers on the arm-rest. 'It's not usually easy to take custody of a child away from his mother, even in this day and age. I've been your attorney for some time now, and personally I'd like to ask, considering your age and health, do you really want to be responsible for a nine-year-old boy?'

'Personally, Jake, I don't pay you to ask questions.'

The lawyer blushed to the roots of his thinning blond hair. He took a deep breath. 'Considering your position, I don't anticipate any problems.'

'Good. That's good.'

'Bill, I need to know what you saw when you visited the house a few days ago? Any signs of neglect?'

'My daughter would never neglect her son. The place is clean as a whistle. And she does it all herself.'

'What about her moral conduct? You say the boy's father is dead? Any male guests staying overnight at the house?'

William Ross shone like a beet. 'This is my daughter you're talking about. She's a widow, still grieving for her husband. She's a good mother, and I'm not taking her to court to prove otherwise. I just want to see the boy is well provided for, and she won't let me do it any other way. She doesn't have the means to bring him up properly. She's not making a decent living. You can use that.'

'I think that will help.'

'Just remember, don't file anything until after the

first of the year. She's liable to get a little huffy about all this, so I want to wait until after Christmas.'

'Your sentimentality astounds me, William.'

The elderly man chortled. 'Getting soft in my old age, I guess. Once young Will is living here, she'll come around. Just might take her a month or two is all. No sense ruining the boy's holiday over it.'

Jake raised his wrist to check his watch. 'I've got to get back to Houston. I'll be in touch after New Year. In the meantime, if you detect any behavior we might be able to use in court, document it. I don't think you want to make a try at getting the boy and fail.'

'I haven't hired you because I expect to fail.'

'I'll do all I can. Maybe over the holidays you and your daughter can talk, come up with a more amicable solution. I know you don't want to hear this, Bill, but he is her son. Morally she does have priority in deciding how he's raised.'

Ross waved him off. 'Her stubborn insistence on keeping those smelly horses and living amongst them shows she's not thinking clearly. If she were putting Will's welfare first, she'd have him back here in my house. Ben never meant that little ranch to be their livelihood. She must still be in shock over his death.'

'Doesn't seem her husband left her much of anything that would provide a livelihood.'

'Quite sad the way he turned out. He had so much potential for a good future.'

'Bill, you realize your daughter is a grown woman. She may resent your interference in her life, regardless of your motives. I know she's the only family you've got. Have you stopped to consider she may be angry enough to sever her relationship with you completely?'

'Sierra wouldn't dare do that. Oh, she'll see things my way eventually. She always does. Besides, I'll have her son here, and she'd never turn away from him. She'll come around. She's always left it to me to look after her well-being. Just get me the boy. Let me see you to the door, Jake.'

CHAPTER 9

Matt was passing by the side of the house when he noticed Sierra atop the ladder, all long and stretched out in jeans and a white top, reaching for the gutter.

He paused to appreciate the view, tracing the contours of her sleek body, watching the wind play with her hair. A drowsy, warm desire stole through him. Nothing, he reflected, would ever make him stop wanting her.

It was late afternoon, and the horses were in for the evening, the hands gone home. He'd been about to call it quits for the evening himself, but Sierra looked mighty shaky up there.

A warning in his head told him to leave her be. She'd always done what she damn well pleased anyway. Let her break her neck if she had her mind set on it. He wasn't responsible for the fool things people did to themselves. But what if she fell with no one around? He scanned the yard and recalled that he hadn't seen Will this afternoon. Will's dog sat at the foot of the ladder.

Suddenly, she turned. 'What are you grinning at?' she called, then, nearly losing her footing on the rung, she grabbed for the gutter and spun back around.

Cursing himself because his life was getting more complicated every minute and because he'd been remembering how good her lithe body had felt next to his without realizing the memory had him smiling like a damn fool, he headed for the ladder.

'I was just admiring how good you look, getting one last eyeful before you fall off that ladder and kill yourself,' he called up to her. 'Don't you have a lick of common sense?'

Each time he was around Sierra, his emotions heightened. Despite his expertise in blocking out disturbing feelings, when it came to her he always felt too much.

Reaching the ladder's base and bracing it, he called up to her again. 'Sierra, what the blazes are you doing up there?'

As she looked down, he saw the strand of multicolored lights in her hand, and he glanced briefly at the pile of boxes stacked on the front porch. At first he'd thought they contained trash, but now he noticed a plastic snowman peeping over the rim of one. Glory! Christmas decorations. More holiday hoopla. So that was what had pushed her to the brink of insanity. But he knew she must be doing it for Will.

'I'm getting in the spirit of the season,' she insisted.

'Can't you do it from down here?'

When she failed to answer, he reluctantly offered, 'Want some help?'

'I can manage, thanks.'

'You want them up before Christmas, don't you?' he asked.

'Of course.'

'Then you'd better come down and let me do that.'

With a heavy sigh she began descending the ladder. Matt stood at the bottom, holding its base, enjoying the sight of her. A hot, constricting rush shot through his midsection, slinking lower. He nearly groaned aloud. When he reached for her waist to steady her, his hand fell lower than he'd planned.

Sierra stiffened at the unexpected pressure of his hand scooping her buttocks, hot desire seeping through her, nearly knocking her off the ladder. Fortunately, only a couple of feet remained between her and the ground.

The last few days had been torture, having him so near, watching him, wanting him every minute. Going to him last weekend had not sated her desire, merely whetted it.

She didn't know how much longer she could control her longing. But she'd already shed her pride that once. No matter how much she hankered for him, she refused to fling herself upon him. She craved more than he claimed he was offering, and she needed at least the small concession of his admitting he wanted her.

By the time she set her feet on the ground, her heart was racing, and she was breathing rapidly. With Matt waiting below, tumbling into his arms was unavoidable. Her chest mashed against his, and she felt the squeeze of her nipples tightening. Reaching out, she rested a palm against the hard muscles of his chest.

His face hovered inches from hers. 'Sierra,' he said. 'Sorry, I didn't mean to . . .'

But the evidence of his desire grew obvious as his jeans pressed against hers.

In a half gasp, her lips parted slightly.

Impulsively, Matt swooped, capturing them in his, nibbling teasingly at first, then clasping her elbows and sinking his mouth down farther to drink in the taste of her.

A kaleidoscope of colors swirled in her head as he slid his tongue through the narrow slit between her lips, prying the opening wider, skimming his tongue around the rim of her mouth and probing more deeply. Her senses filled with his musky scent, the taste of him, the pressure of hard muscle against her. Boldly she met his tongue with the tip of her own.

Light-headed from the floral scent of her perfume, he lost every sense except wanting her, urgently. How he needed something good to hold on to. And the places Sierra had taken him to were the most peaceful vistas he'd ever been to. His open palms traveled the length of her, hot as a branding iron, shooting icy shivers up and down her spine.

A whimpering sound escaped the back of Sierra's throat as she pressed herself against his hard body. Already moist inside her jeans, she abandoned thoughts of Christmas decorations. She'd done a bad job of pretending to love Ben, a job that had got more difficult as time wore on. Loving Matt came easily to her. Quickly, she reminded herself that she didn't, couldn't love him now. Her rational thoughts ebbed away as her need mounted. Her knees threatened to buckle. So intense was her longing, it hurt.

Heat seared through her as his hand cupped her breast. She arched her back to him, closing her eyes as he gently kneaded the soft flesh.

'Oh, Matt,' she purred, sinking deeper into his arms.

Suddenly, she remembered they were standing in the front yard. If anyone walked up to the gate . . .

Matt seemed to think of the same thing. 'Where's Will?' he asked.

'Rehearsal,' she breathed. 'He won't be back for a few hours.'

'I guess it's obvious what I'm thinking.'

'You said we shouldn't . . .'

'I've been needing you so bad, Sierra. I was trying to convince myself I didn't. I reckon it must be the same way you felt when you showed up on my doorstep the other night.'

'We can go inside.'

Matt looked at the door, his pickup truck parked beside the stables, then back at her.

He caught hold of her hand and led her towards the door.

'Come on,' he said.

Once inside, he hesitated. Sierra pulled him down the hall towards her bedroom. He stopped in the door-frame, briefly taking in the copper and turquoise comforter on the bed, the matching ruffled curtains, lace-trimmed pillow shams. Copper planters along the windowsill spilled lush green foliage, and a mammoth oak dresser along the wall was lined with a rectangular doily and a row of tiny, colorful cosmetic bottles. The room exuded Sierra's spirit.

Sierra stepped inside, pulling down the comforter to expose lilac sheets.

'Are you sure it's all right?' he asked.

At first, she wondered why this powerful man who so easily brought her to a melting point would balk at entering her room. Then she realized that while she'd thought she'd once loved him in every way possible, she'd never once admitted him into her world.

Until now. Hiding something as pure as the love they'd shared had been her biggest mistake, she realized. She'd been proud to be with him, and she should have walked at his side openly – damn anyone who didn't like it.

Turning to him and smiling, she systematically began shedding her clothes. 'Please, Matt,' she told him. 'Come into my room. I'm not going to make love to you in the doorway.'

His groin hardened to granite as she stood before him, pulling the clingy top over her head. She reached behind her to unhook her bra, her firm breasts springing free. Her skin was the deep reddish pink of roses.

Closing the bedroom door behind him, he moved towards her. The rest of the world ceased to exist.

Clad now in only her panties, Sierra shook her hair back, her heart pounding as he approached. She met his gaze directly, smiling tentatively. He gave her a leisurely Texas grin as his eyes raked appreciatively over her.

Reaching out, he lifted her in his strong arms.

Holding her in midair, he bowed his head to her chest, catching in his mouth a nipple as red and hard as a ruby. Latching her arms around his neck, Sierra closed her eyes, blocking out everything but the sensation of his lips against her tender skin. As he suckled her, delight bubbled inside her. A sweet lava flowed between her legs.

Pausing, he leaned back to gaze at her, eagerly glimpsing the dark eyes heavy with passion. 'Oh, darlin', I have missed you,' he said.

Gently, he set her on the bed, lying her across it and sliding his toughened hand across her bare belly. Moving over her, he sniffed her delicate, perfumed skin, then kissed her quivering tummy, caressing the flat of her midriff, savoring the feel of her squirming with pleasure beneath him.

Raising his head, he looked into the richness of her eyes, moist and shining with desire. To him, they were the pistils of an exquisite orchid. He smiled into them, watching her lips curl in reply. Watching her eyes, he eased a trembling hand beneath the narrow elastic band of her cream-colored satin panties, unfolding her delicate petals to dip into the intimate womanly core of her. He saw with satisfaction how the pleasure of his touch slackened her pretty features. He relished feeling her tremors. Tenderly and deliberately, he probed deeper into the hub of her need.

Her breath caught as he dabbed into the hot, dewy niche, stroking inside her. Her eyes fluttered shut, and she parted her legs obligingly, feeling full of him and wanting more. The power of his masculinity overwhelmed her.

Matt had been everything she'd ever wanted. She'd dared to give herself freely to him because he needed so much. Now, she knew he could need her as much as she required him, in body, heart and soul.

Bowing over her, Matt thought he'd never encountered anything as fragrant or as smooth and soft as her skin. He inhaled her feminine scent, enhanced by the heat of desire like perfume oil simmering over a lit candle.

With a sweep of his hand, he lowered the scant garment that covered her. Dipping lower, he nibbled at the swell above her moist core.

'No,' she protested.

Pausing, he looked up at her questioningly, puzzled by a hesitation he'd missed when he looked in her eyes. If she didn't want to go through with this, she had miserable timing.

In answer, she rose up and began unbuttoning his shirt. Matt realized he was still fully dressed. 'It's not fair,' she explained with a toss of her head. 'I want to see you too. I want to feel you.'

Slowly, she undressed him, pushing his hands away when he moved to help.

'Let me, please,' she pleaded.

The shirt quickly gone, his muscles clamped as, after discarding his jeans, she released his swollen maleness from the confines of his briefs.

As she reached out and took him into her hands, longing surged through him, making him shudder.

'Sierra, honey, what are you doing to me?' he groaned, skimming his hands over the contours of her torso. He reached for her, but she pushed him back.

'It's always been you giving to me. Lie back and let me make love to you. Let me show you how good you make me feel.'

Matt eyed her skeptically.

'Go on, please,' she crooned, prodding him towards her bed. 'Trust me.'

He fell back, his nostrils flooding with the light fragrance of her wafting from the linens. The mattress was as soft as she was.

His loins tightened achingly as she fluttered over him like a scarlet butterfly, her small hands caressing the tender underside of his thighs, stroking and probing. Sinking back against the pillows, he reached down and meshed his fingers in her thick hair. She knelt over him, tentatively kissing his belly as he had hers, tickling his skin with the tip of her tongue.

The tingling sensation ebbed through him. He stiffened and groaned.

A swirling blackness gripped him as she moved her mouth over him, capturing his pulsating desire, heightening it until he thought he would explode.

Smiling, she moved over him, swinging one leg over his prone torso and mounting him.

'Like it?' she whispered.

'You're amazing.'

'I want you to be happy, Matt.'

Emotion washed through him like a hurricane's surge. So few people had ever really cared whether he was happy, he only vaguely remembered having heard that before.

He looked into those dark infinite eyes and wondered how this woman who gave so freely could have taken away everything he cherished and believed in. Was it a mistake they could ever undo?

He moaned as she slipped over him, taking him inside her and relieving his mind of all conscious thought.

'Oh, Sierra,' he said, swinging his hips to climb higher inside her, holding her slim waist and pulling her to him.

Pushing himself up, he captured a rigid nipple in his mouth, molding the pliant flesh around it. Her eyes closed as her body softened, moistening around him.

He thrust upwards between her splayed legs.

Sierra inhaled deeply at the hot rush of pleasure. She trembled as his hands played over her belly, fingertips skimming the velvet patch of curls at its base, delving lower to fondle her aching core.

She whimpered as a fire more intense than any she'd ever known shot through her, rendering her mindless. She felt him propel deeper into her like a soaring rocket.

He grasped her hips firmly, wrenching her to him

as she writhed madly, his name spilling from her lips. She could never have enough of him.

She cried out as fierce spasms rocked her, and she felt him holding her, moving beneath her to the rhythm of her desire. As she spent herself, he whirled her around, plummeting and plummeting, burying his face between her round breasts, until his passion crested with hers.

For a long time, she didn't move. He was still inside her and she longed to keep him there. His breathing was smooth and even, his chest falling rhythmically against hers. She inhaled his rugged, musky scent.

Once before, she'd known this kind of happiness. She wanted desperately for it to last.

He planted a kiss just below her ear. Her neck was damp with a glistening sheen of sweat. He glanced out of the window. 'It's too dark to put the lights up now,' he noted.

'I didn't care about them anyway. They're for Will.'

'I figured. I'll get them up tomorrow,' he promised.

She wondered if there was anything he wouldn't do for her son. But she knew he let his guard down because he considered the boy to be safe to love, another man's son. Why couldn't he see that being a father wouldn't change that?

He moved off her, lassoing her around the waist and bunching her close against him.

'I'm sorry, Sierra. I can't keep my hands off you. I didn't mean for any of this to happen.' He kissed the back of her neck.

'Please don't be sorry, Matt. There's something between us . . . we weren't meant to be apart.'

'I used to think that.'

'Maybe we should give it a chance. Maybe we owe each other more than a few stolen moments in bed.'

He sat up, reaching for his shirt. 'Something keeps drawing me back to you. But I don't see what more we can give each other. You're forgetting I'm not going to be around long enough for much more than that. I thought we understood each other, Sierra. Can't we just enjoy this without analyzing it?'

'I don't think that's what you really want,' she accused. She feared he was right, that it was too late for them. But to have something as precious as this . . . she refused to believe there couldn't be a way.

With his shirt hanging open, he stepped into his briefs. 'To tell you the truth, darlin', I don't know what I want, and I can't see any point in dragging you into all that.'

He looked down on her, lying on her side across the bed, her skin flushed and shimmering from their lovemaking. He loved the shape of her body, the ruddy hue of her skin. Fresh passion stirred in his loins.

Bending down, he pulled the sheet over her nakedness. 'I feel something with you I've never felt with anyone else,' he confessed. 'But you deserve better than me, you always have, and we've both always known it. Isn't that why you were crying the last time? That's why I didn't want this to happen again.'

She caught hold of his arm. 'Matthew, I wasn't crying because I regretted what we'd done.'

'I saw your tears.'

'I was crying because I'd forgotten how good you always were to me. Because nobody else has ever treated me the way you do. There is no one better,' she insisted. 'You're honest, hard-working, and you live by your ideals. I don't know a better man than you are, Matt Rollins. You're the finest person I've ever known, and I'd entrust my life to you. I'm the one who's flawed.'

'I don't want anybody's life in my hands. Giving you a good time in bed isn't enough, Sierra, and it never was. You need a man who's going to be around for you and Will both, some guy with a lot of money who'll give you all those thousand kids you used to talk about.'

'I don't care about money. There's only one man I want.'

'Don't talk like that. You're asking more from me than I could ever give you. Don't you see how that hurts me?'

'Damn if you aren't the most unyielding man I've

ever known. I know how proud you are, and I know how badly I hurt your pride once. But that was an eternity ago. If I don't mean anything to you now, if you don't feel anything more when you make love to me than you've felt with any other woman, say it, and I'll accept it.'

When he said nothing, her heart quickened. 'Matt, we were younger than we knew last time. I see now that I should have done things differently. I should have gone to you before I let my father pressure me into anything. You were still living in your father's house, still bitter. But you're over thirty now. I'd like to believe I've changed. Can't you give me the chance to know if I have?'

His eyebrows tangled over the bridge of his nose. 'Why come to me? You knew how I felt about you. You had a mind of your own.'

Sierra realized her near-slip.

'I should have explained to you that my father threatened to throw me out of his house if I didn't marry Ben right away.'

Matt's eyes widened. 'Downright cantankerous critter, isn't he?' He shrugged. 'I can see you'd get used to living in a big house, eating in restaurants, traveling and wearing fancy clothes.'

She flashed him a dark look. 'I didn't have a choice. I didn't know how to take care of myself because I was raised to not have to. Ben had proposed to me. You hadn't.'

'What did you do to make your father so angry?'

She diverted her glance to the pillowcase. 'I told him I slept with you.'

'Why? Just to piss him off? What was the point? You knew he wouldn't approve. Or were you just trying to get his attention off his busy business schedule and back on his poor-little-rich-girl daughter?'

Sierra seethed under his undeserved scorn. If he knew she'd been pregnant, he would understand that she hadn't acted on a whim. But of course, he couldn't know that and she couldn't tell him.

She raised her chin. 'You don't understand how it was between my father and me. I'd never kept anything from him until I met you. I should have brought you to meet him before I told him so he wouldn't jump to false conclusions about you.'

Matt emitted a cryptic laugh. 'Like I didn't have a nickel to my name and came from a very unstable family? Like how my father would abandon us for months on end and the only good times I recall are when he was gone? Honey, he would have been right on target. Fact is, I couldn't have supported a pet mouse. Hell, if I had a daughter, I wouldn't have let her marry a kid like me. Why'd you have to rush things? I was saving every penny to get some land. For what it's worth, I was planning to ask you to be my wife one day. Had it on my mind most of the time. If you'd just waited . . .'

'You talked about going away, but you never mentioned marriage.'

'I don't say things until I'm ready to back them up.'

Her raven eyes glistened as her head sank back against the pillow. 'Father was so afraid I'd run away with you. He has to control everything, everyone. He wasn't about to let me slip away from him. Did you really want that, Matt? For us to get married and have a home and a family?'

'Whoa. I didn't say anything about a family. You know how I feel about that.'

'I know how you said you felt. Hasn't time changed anything for you? Haven't you ever thought about having children? I see how you are with Will. He adores you. And I see how you feel about your niece and nephew when you talk about them. Your eyes light up, and I see how proud you are. I accepted your terms, Matt. No entanglements, no commitments. And I'm not asking you to promise me anything. But we're not prisoners of the past. Maybe we should both open ourselves to the possibilities . . .'

'It's different with them. They don't belong to me. I don't have to concern myself with shaping their future. I'm not going to make some child miserable all his life just because I give in to a whim. My old man had five children, and the only one he ever loved, in his own warped way, was

Dylan. Why didn't he just stop after that? Dylan was first. He kept on having them, so he must have thought he wanted more. Birth control wasn't exactly non-existent thirty-some years ago.'

'But you're not your father.' Something he'd said struck a chord inside her, and after pondering it, she realized something unusual had happened here. She nearly gasped out loud. Balling her hand into a fist, she bunched the sheet over her chest. 'My God, Matt, we didn't use any protection.'

Her cheeks flamed. She felt like an idiot. Maybe he'd assumed since she'd been married so long without having any more children that she'd stayed on the Pill. And she couldn't very well tell him Ben had been sterile without letting on to the truth about Will.

Still, Matt felt so strongly about this that he wasn't likely to have assumed she had taken precautions. He would have taken responsibility for them, as he always had.

He stepped into his jeans. 'Don't worry about it. I had a vasectomy a couple of years back.'

Her mouth formed an astonished O. 'You didn't!'

'I started thinking I didn't want to get trapped into tying myself down the hard way, so I made sure it wouldn't happen.'

Sierra suspected a close call must have inspired his surgery, but she couldn't bear to hear about him and another woman. Yet she'd caused him to endure knowing about her and Ben. Whoever she was, Sierra was glad he hadn't wanted to marry her.

'So drastic,' she murmured. 'So permanent. Matt, what if you change your mind some day?'

'I'm not going to.'

'I wish, Matt, that you could know the kind of love a child brings into your life. It's awesome, having another person you would give your very life for. Having Will taught me something about love I'd never known before, the responsibility for nurturing it.'

His eyes narrowed as he looked at her, and she saw an inkling of suspicion creeping into his eyes. Had she said too much already? Aware of the strong bond between parent and child, she wondered now if by instinct Matt was feeling that love for Will without understanding why. She was wondering if Matt was thinking back, starting to figure things out. Sooner or later, he was bound to guess the truth. She dreaded the prospect of the contempt he'd feel for her, knowing the scope of her lie. He wouldn't want to touch her again the way he just had.

She averted her gaze.

He leaned over and kissed her. 'You're a good mother to him, Sierra. I've watched the two of you together. But not everyone feels things as deeply as you do. Not everyone is suited for parenthood.'

'I know you too well to believe you're unfeeling.'

'I've never been less than straight with you, Sierra. You know I've always detested lies and liars. My father contrived so many excuses for what he did, I don't think he ever knew himself what the truth was. You're sweeter than strawberries in summer, but I doubt anything in this world could make me stay in this town.' He sat on the edge of the bed, stroking her hair. 'I guess if anything ever could it probably would be you. But when I'm here, I have to remember how it was growing up, how it was with us before. Nothing ever goes right for me here. And nothing ever will.'

Guilt gnawed at her. He deserved to know the truth. He probably wouldn't tell Will, wouldn't want him to know. Still, she feared his sure, slow fury at learning how she'd deceived him. How could she not have, though? If she'd come to him all those years ago and told him she was pregnant, he would have done the right thing, then resented her and Will both for it. He'd never asked her to marry him and he'd made it clear he never wanted children. And maybe that resentment would have turned him into someone like his father, the one thing he most feared becoming. She'd loved him too much to do that to either of them.

'What do we do about this weekend?' she asked.

'You still want me here?'

'I want to be with you now. No matter what your plans are.'

'Sierra, don't make me fall in love with you again.'

'Are you?'

'I've got to go. I have something I have to do for Leeann and the kids. And I know you don't want Will to come home and find me here.'

She blinked her reply.

He looked down at her, tenderness softening the bold lines and angles of his face.

'You do make me happy,' he whispered. 'Happier than I can remember being for a long time. But that's the way it is for me – happiness comes in little pieces and disappears like a burned-up firecracker. I wish things were different. I wish *I* were different, so I could give you what you need.'

With blurred vision, she watched him go. And she knew he was taking her heart with him.

Tanner emitted a stream of giggles as he sat in the infant seat of the grocery basket his Uncle Matt was whisking across the supermarket parking lot.

'Giddy-up, horsey,' Tanner commanded as Matt trotted behind the basket.

'Matt, stop!' Leeann implored, coming along behind with Sally at her side. Her face was knitted tightly into a stern expression, and she was struggling hard not to laugh. Her older brother was a sight, prancing along like a wild stallion. 'You'll both be hit by a car!'

Matt glanced from side to side. 'Nothing's coming!' he called back.

Tanner squealed as Matt brought the cart to a halt behind his pickup. A pool of light fell from the lamp Matt had parked beneath.

'Honestly,' Leeann muttered as she and Sally caught up. 'You behave like a wild man sometimes. What kind of impression are you making on the children?'

'I thought it was funny,' Sally noted. At seven, she was slender and pretty and blonde like her ma. But with her serious demeanor she reminded Matt more of Darcy than Leeann. He wondered what his elder sister had done with all her intelligence and no one at home to care about finding a way to send her to college.

Matt gave his niece an approving nod. 'I rest my case,' Matt declared, spreading his arms in the air.

A frown creased Leeann's face. 'Watch out. Don't let the cart get away from you.'

He pointed to his boot, which was hooked over the cart's bottom rung.

'No runaway carts tonight,' he predicted. 'Here, let's get you outa there, Tanner.'

'He's almost too big to sit in the baby seat,' Leeann reflected.

Matt squeezed his nephew out of the cart. 'He's a big guy.'

Sally was reaching in the cart for a grocery bag. Matt took it from her.

'That's kind of heavy for you, isn't it?' he asked.

'I've lifted heavier ones,' she said simply.

'Not when I'm around,' he countered. 'None of this 90s woman stuff. I don't believe in it. Your grandma taught me to be a gentlemen.'

Leeann cast him a crooked smile. 'Don't listen to him, Sally. If he found himself some swooning old-fashioned belle, he wouldn't know what to do with her.'

'How come you don't have a wife, Uncle Matt?' Sally asked.

'Don't want one,' he said. 'Some people don't.'

'Just wait,' Leeann predicted. 'I've got a premonition you're going to have one sooner than you think.'

'Not likely. And you sound like Ma. Since when did you start having premonitions?'

'Sometimes I just feel things. Don't you ever wake up in the morning and know it's gonna be a good day or a bad day?'

'No. I'm always surprised.'

She shook her head. Matt studied his sister's face. Beneath the forced brightness, her face was laced by dark lines of fatigue. This was the first evening he could remember that she hadn't gone back to the hospital.

'Don't take it so lightly. That's the trouble with you. You see signs and ignore them. The morning of Jerry's accident, I woke up dreamin' I answered the phone and it was the hospital callin' to say he'd been hurt. All day I tried to shake it off, you know, disregard it as nonsense like you're doin'. Then that evenin' it really happened. I kept hopin' I'd wake up again and find I was still dreamin'.'

He set a hand on her shoulder. She flashed him a strained smile.

'Ma was right about there bein' some things in life that control us and we can't do nothin' about them. But I keep thinkin' if I'd believed, made Jerry stay home . . .'

'Would he have stayed home if you asked him to because of a dream?'

'Probably not. I coulda begged him . . .'

'Come on, Leeann. How many times do you dream about things that are totally meaningless? How could you have known this one was different? Is anything wrong?' he asked.

'No, things are great. Jerry's being moved to a nursing home tomorrow. The people at the hospital are bein' real nice to us.'

'Will he make it home for Christmas?' He knew this meant a lot to her.

'Nobody will give me a definite answer.'

The groceries loaded, he slammed the tailgate shut.

'Hey, everything's going your way. It's just taking a little longer than you'd hoped. That always happens.'

'I'm hungry, Ma,' Tanner announced impatiently.

She gave him a slight nod. 'I'll bet you are, after an hour of staring at food on the shelves. Let's go home and I'll make cheeseburgers.'

'No,' Matt objected. 'You're not going home and cooking. We'll stop at the diner – I'm treating. Then we can grab a video, and you can go home, put your feet up for a while. After it's over, I'll see the kids are ready for bed on time. You can take a hot bath or read your book.'

'Matthew Rollins, you're an angel, you know that? If you weren't here . . .'

Her eyes misted over.

Embarrassed by her outburst, Matt reddened. 'But I am. Aw, come on, Turtle, don't get all sloppy on me now. Here I am planning to take you inside a public place.'

She was laughing and crying at the same time.

They all packed inside the truck's cab and headed for the diner, enjoying the greasy cheeseburgers and home-made french fries. The jukebox played as though the years had never passed, and Matt thought he recognized the same red tinsel garland and lighted plastic Santa Claus that used to decorate the place when Ma had worked here. At Christmastime, people just plumb lost their minds, he reflected. Having flung himself into Sierra's bed this afternoon, he was living testament to that. But he knew that compulsion had zilch to do with the season.

Sierra. She was the sweetest, softest thing on earth, but God help him, now he had thoughts bouncing around in the back of his head about that plot of land by the creek and wantin' to hang around for a while. She'd put a spell on him and was driving him loco. All her talk about giving them a chance together. Sure. Even if he fell in love with her again, when it boiled down to declaring that to all the world and their families, the same thing would happen all over again. As long as they shut the world out, everything was great. But out in the open their feelings for each other were some shameful little secret Sierra would never reveal to her father and his fancy friends. And even if she dared, Matt wouldn't let her. Why should she lose the place in this community she'd been born to? She'd no more chosen her background than he had his.

He needed some breathing space. He glanced around the booth at Tanner dunking a fry in a pool of ketchup, Sally trying to look grown-up as she demurely munched her cheeseburger, and Leeann, so bone-tired she couldn't do much more than toy with her food. He couldn't cut out on them, and, in helping them, he couldn't avoid being around Sierra.

On the way out, he moved to pay the bill, but Gillian Evans, the owner, waved him off. 'After all the years y'all's mama worked here for my parents, I can't charge you, Matt,' she insisted.

Matt looked across the counter, now recognizing the pretty young woman with sparkling blue eyes and the long, subtly waved tawny hair pulled back in a ponytail. He'd gone to high school with her. Her parents had been good to his ma, letting her bring cartons of leftover food home to her children at night.

'Gillian,' he said. 'I'm sorry, I thought that was your ma back there. I mean, not that you look . . .'

She laughed. 'Lots of people make that mistake. My parents retired last year. I came home from Dallas to take over the place.'

'Big change, I reckon.'

Nodding emphatically, she chuckled. 'Are you still riding?'

'Every chance I get. No more rodeo stuff, though.'

'It's a shame. You were good at it.'

He turned and saw that Leeann and the kids had vanished. 'I've gotta go. Good to see you, Gillian. Are you sure I can't pay?'

'Put your wallet away, Matt. And have a merry Christmas. Maybe we can go riding some afternoon.'

'It's kind of hard to get away right now.'

'Call me if you get a chance to sneak off.'

'Maybe I will,' he said, backing out.

Already he knew he wouldn't. He couldn't get Sierra out off his mind. Even a woman as attractive and friendly as Gillian failed to interest him. He'd surrendered more of his freedom to Sierra than he knew.

Leeann and the kids were waiting in the truck.

'I hadn't even thought of Gillian,' Leeann said with the tone of a general plotting war strategies. 'She's divorced, you know. That's really why she came back here.'

'I always liked Gillian.'

'Didn't you used to go out with her?'

'I took her riding at Sam's a few times in high school. We were just pals, Leeann, so don't waste your energy cooking up any match-making schemes, OK? This wedding you're fantasizing about will not be mine.'

He pulled the truck up in front of the video store.

Sally took Tanner by the hand and rushed on inside with him.

'You realize it will take them an hour to decide on a movie,' Leeann informed him.

'I'll give them ten minutes, tops,' he said, rushing in behind them. Searching for his niece and nephew, he rounded the end of the aisle leading to the family viewing movies, running nearly smack-dab into Sierra and Will.

Startled, Sierra looked up, her lips curling into a smile as she recognized him. Just a few hours ago, he'd been kissing that smile. The recent memory of their encounter rolled heat through him, and something in his chest tugged sharply. Those dark eyes shone so prettily, he yearned to reach out and touch the skin as soft as peach fuzz. His loins constricted with newly awakened desire.

Leeann's shuffling footsteps behind him came to an abrupt halt. He felt his sister's glare burning through his back like lasers.

Sierra's smile dropped to a worried frown as she spotted Leeann over his shoulder.

But it was Will who broke the silence, glancing up at Matt and breaking into an excited grin. 'Matt!' he shouted. 'Mom and I are getting a movie. Can you come over and watch it with us?'

He stopped short as he noticed the unfamiliar woman standing behind Matt.

'No, Will, not tonight.' He turned and nudged Leeann forward. He took a deep breath. 'Sierra, Will, I don't believe you've met my sister, Leeann.'

Sierra extended one hand. 'It's good to finally meet you,' she said.

Matt watched his sister, her weary expression unreadable. He knew she harbored bad feelings towards Sierra on his account, but he wished she'd let them go.

And the thought echoed in his mind that Sam had advised him to do the same thing with his lingering resentment.

To his relief, Leeann forced a grudging smile and finally grasped Sierra's hand. It was a start. 'Hello,' Leeann greeted her stiffly.

Sally rounded the corner, her arms folded across her chest. Tanner trailed behind her. 'We wanted *The Santa Clause*, Uncle Matt, but all the copies are gone.'

'Then we'll just have to find something else tonight,' Matt reasoned. 'We'll get that one another time.'

Will looked at the box in his hand, then at the two younger kids. He held the box out to Sally. 'Here, he said. 'I've got the last copy. Mom and I can watch it another night.'

Leeann stared at the tall, handsome young boy. Suddenly her countenance darkened, and she turned away. 'I'll be waiting in the truck, Matt,' she said, tearing off down the aisle.

Matt wondered what had possessed her. He turned apologetically to Sierra. 'Leeann's real tired,' he explained. 'I think she forget her manners.'

'It's OK,' Sierra insisted. 'I know I'm not one of her favorite people, and I have a pretty good idea why.'

Matt grasped Will's shoulder. 'Mighty big of you to give up your movie,' he told the boy.

'Thank you,' Sally echoed.

'Yeah, thanks,' Tanner joined in. 'You could come over and watch it with us.'

Matt and Sierra's faces both registered an uncomfortable shock at this suggestion.

'That's a nice idea, Tanner,' Matt told him. 'But your ma's too tired for company tonight.'

Matt grinned at Sierra, the corners of his eyes crinkling. A current passed between them, and he wished he could kiss her right then and there.

'I'll see you tomorrow,' he told her. 'Goodnight, Will.'

Leeann was waiting in the truck.

Matt waited until everyone was in and he'd started the ignition before he said anything. 'Leeann, knowing how you feel about Sierra, I can't express my appreciation over how dignified you acted towards her back there. But why'd you have to go tearing out of the store like you were on fire or something?'

She turned to him. 'Because I looked up to you and counted on you to tell the truth, even when it wasn't always so nice. And I just realized you weren't always telling the whole truth. I'm . . . well . . . I'm disappointed. You know no matter what you do, I'd never think any less of you. I'd know you musta had a darn good reason.'

'What the hell are you talking about?'

She scowled at him, and he remembered the kids.

'Sorry,' he muttered.

She glanced at her children, both of whom were abnormally silent, listening intently, especially now that hell had been mentioned.

She smoothed her coat with both hands. 'It'll keep till we get to the house,' she announced.

CHAPTER 10

As it turned out, Sally and Tanner ended up watching the video while Leeann and Matt sipped coffee at her kitchen table. The movie score played a backdrop to the silence between them.

Leeann searched her brother's face. From the opposite side of the table, he met her worried gaze.

'What's going on with you, Leeann?'

She drummed her short fingernails on the tabletop. 'I can't think of a delicate way to say this. Then again, maybe I should never have said anything at all.'

He gave her a weak smile. 'It's not like you to be delicate when it comes to speaking your mind. Not to me anyway. Spit it out, Sis, and get it over with so you can watch the rest of the movie with the kids. If something I've done bothers you this much, we'd better talk it out.'

Still she hesitated. 'Matt, I know you'd never get somebody in trouble and run out on them.'

'I'd like to think I wouldn't. What kind of trouble are we talking about?'

'Like getting a woman pregnant.'

His face registered his bewilderment. 'But I haven't . . . you're going to have to be a mite clearer on what you're driving at. Is someone claiming . . .?'

Shaking her head, she sighed heavily.

'Is that why you're so upset that I'm working for Sierra? You think something like that will happen? Kind of a notion from out of the blue, isn't it?'

Leeann shook her head. 'This is coming out all wrong. Have you ever taken a good look at that boy of hers?'

'Will? Yeah, he's a good kid.'

'I looked at him tonight, and I saw the spittin' image of my big brother, and I ain't talking about Dylan. If you look past the darker coloring, you'll see he looks a lot like you. Be straight with me, Matt. Is that why you packed off and ran off like a spooked deer? Because Sierra was pregnant? I won't think any less of you for the truth. I know you were young and broke and scared . . .'

'I didn't abandon Sierra, and I certainly wouldn't have stranded her with a baby. I was young, but I was never careless. For Pete's sake, Leeann. Ben Davenport didn't really look that much unlike me. And Sierra wasn't pregnant when I left. Not by me anyway.'

'No, Matt. Ben Davenport's face was weak as dishwater. The boy has a bolder profile. Look at his nose, his chin, his cheekbones and tell me he doesn't have Daddy's bone-structure, your bone-structure.'

'Don't be bringing up that I look like him.'

'You don't really, Matt. It's hard to explain, like two different kinds of houses with the same foundation. Daddy had a harsh face. He always looked angry, and even when he smiled he looked like he was in pain, sneering. Your eyes and mouth must come from Ma's side of the family. But young Will, he carries himself like you. He moves like you.'

'He's imitating me. It's only natural. After all, his father's not around any more, and we've been spending some time together. He's an impressionable kid, that's all.'

Leeann dipped her head and raked splayed fingers through her feathery hair. 'It's not like you to be so thick-headed. I mean, considering the boy's age and what was going on between you and Sierra before you left, what I'm suggesting is physically possible, isn't it?'

Something flared in Matt's eyes. 'Not really. Even as young as I was, I knew to be careful.'

Rolling her eyes, Leeann lowered her voice. 'Yeah, Jerry and I were being careful when I got pregnant with Tanner. How old is the boy? Do you know when his birthday is?'

Matt shrugged. 'Well, no. He's nine or ten.'

'After you left, I never really saw Sierra around town until her baby was several months old. Odd, that Ben's family was so hot to announce their son's engagement in the newspaper yet never sent in their grandson's birth announcement.'

'Maybe you just missed reading the paper one day. Leeann, that boy is not my son. I would never have run off if he were. I never wanted kids, but I'm not that much of a coward that I would have abandoned Sierra and let another man pretend to be my kid's father.'

'I don't believe you would have, either. Maybe she just neglected to tell you so you wouldn't interfere with her marrying Ben. How can you be so sure?'

'Sierra would never have lied to me about that.'

'After all she's done to you, you trust her so much? Why did she marry Ben so quick? Maybe she used your baby to get Ben to marry her. Some women do things like that.'

'Not Sierra. She was young and beautiful and smart and rich. She didn't have to trick anyone into marrying her.'

'If you're so sure, then why don't you ask her?'

'Can't you see how insulting that would be? Just asking would imply I believe it. If she says the boy is Ben's son, he is.'

Leeann shook her head. 'It's started again, hasn't it, between the two of you? I saw how you looked at each other in the video store.'

'That's my business, Leeann. I'm a grown man, and I can look out for myself.'

'I hope so. Matt, what would do if you found out, just suppose, that she did lie to you?'

'I don't know. I don't think I'd be able to stand to keep working for her, no matter how much we need the money. Hell, I probably wouldn't even want to look at her. But she would never have lied about something that important. Why do women always have to be suspicious of each other? She's had a whole other life while I've been away. And she had a child with another man. I accept that. If you really knew Sierra, you'd understand why I believe her.'

'You believed she was in love with you when she turned around and married Ben.'

'Her father forced her into that because he found out about us and he was afraid she'd run off with me.'

Leeann shook her head. 'Hell'd be drippin' icicles before I'd have let Daddy tell me who to marry.'

'Yeah, well, after practically raising ourselves, the prospect of being poor and alone wasn't exactly a threat to any of us. Her daddy raised her to be dependent on him. It's taken her this long to finally break free.'

'If his hold's that strong, she'll never really escape it. I feel responsible for your coming back here, Matt. I just don't want to see you get hurt again. Last time, it was like she drained the life out of you.'

'I like being with her, Leeann. Nothing about it feels wrong. She knows I'm not staying. But for now . . . I don't want to argue with you about this.'

Leeann gave her brother a long, worried look. 'Butt out, you mean? I'll try. That was real nice of you, takin' me and the kids out to eat tonight. Things like that mean a lot to them, and I'm afraid I've been short-changin' them on attention lately.'

'They've been pretty brave through all this with Jerry.'

'They have.'

'Leeann, I've been thinkin'. How much does finding Dylan and the others mean to you?'

'Not so much that I'm going to do it if you're set against it. I just thought, you know, when we were growin' up, we never had an aunts or uncles comin' around. I guess we have some somewhere. I want my kids to have like a base. Shucks, I want *us* to have a base. Just findin' each other again would be a start.'

'Maybe I'm a little afraid to find how we all turned out. None of us was really prepared to go out and face the world. But I've been thinkin', I wouldn't mind seein' them again, if you've got your heart set on finding them.'

'Are you sure, Matt?'

It was nice to see Leeann's face light up. She'd been looking so grim lately.

He nodded. 'Let's have our reunion. Just as long as you don't contact Daddy. He's the one person I never want to see again as long as I live.'

For the first time in weeks, she broke into a genuine smile, one as bright as the sun coming out after a long rain.

Matt knew the prospect of seeing his family again should have kindled warm feelings inside him, but instead it gnawed at him the way Leeann's premonition had troubled her.

'I'll have the last of these up in a minute,' Matt called down from his precarious perch atop the ladder. 'I still don't see why we can't just put them on the shrubs.'

Sierra, having finished hanging wreaths on the doors and positioning Mr Snowman on the front porch, stepped back to get a better look at her decorated house. The lights had previously gone on their old house, a much bigger place. Ben had hired someone to put them up every year. There were too many for this little house, and she hadn't intended for Matt to hang them all. He had anyway. Strands snaked up the porch pillars like candy cane stripes, lined the porch railings, bordered the front window. Will was going to love it. She refused to think about the whopping electric bill she'd get in January. She'd been feeling better about life lately than she had in ages.

The most appealing part of her view at the moment was Matt reaching over the gutter.

Guiltily, she reflected she shouldn't have let him

do this. There were so many things she'd never learned for herself, whereas Matt had grown up doing everything for himself. At least, after ripping the seams apart several times, she'd finally finished Will's costume in time for tonight's dress rehearsal. Still, she worried now that she'd begun to rely too much on Matt. He made it easy to do that.

More than anything, she relished the way he came to her bed and made her feel like a woman. She'd never known a thrill quite like the way he took pleasure in her from head to toe. And lying in his arms brought a peace to her heart. It was something she wanted to hang on to.

She knew he was determined to leave. And when he did, her heart would snap in two. Nothing she could do or say would make him stay, and that was her own fault. But the past couldn't be rewritten. She began to wonder if her inclination to tell Matt the truth about Will wasn't a subconscious ploy to get him to stay.

Oh, he would. Out of obligation. But he'd resent her not only for saddling him with a child he'd never wanted, but for withholding the truth so long. He'd stay all right, but he wouldn't ever be making love to her again. She'd remained silent this long; she'd have to continue to do so forever.

The sound of her phone ringing inside the house interrupted her thoughts. She dashed in to answer it.

'Sierra, this is Neal.'

Confused, she tried to place the name and the voice.

'Neal Adamson.'

'Oh, Neal, how are you?'

'I was calling to see if you found a babysitter . . . for the Winter Hoedown, Saturday.'

She remembered she'd half-promised she'd go to the dance with him. That conversation seemed light years ago. With her father taking Will to New York, she'd have the whole weekend to herself, so a babysitter wasn't a problem if she wanted to go.

From above, she heard the scraping sound of Matt attaching lights to the gutter. He hadn't given her an answer about this weekend, and she knew he was reluctant to commit himself to giving her even that small block of his time. Her heart and soul were filled with him. On the practical side, if she were looking for another husband, another substitute father for Will, dating Neal was probably the first step in that direction. He was nice enough, good-looking, amiable. But she looked on the prospect of an evening with him with as much enthusiasm as a dentist's appointment.

'Neal, I'm so sorry. I've been so busy here, I just don't feel up to going to a dance.'

'Oh, well, I understand, of course. Maybe some other time.'

'Thank you for understanding. Bye.'

Slowly, she replaced the receiver. Damn Matt Rollins anyway. He'd ruined her for any other man, yet he wasn't going to hang around town long enough to get involved with her again.

Fuming, she stormed out the door, nearly colliding with Matt, who was packing away the extra light bulbs.

Glimpsing her fierce expression, he did a double-take. 'Who are you so mad at?'

'Myself. Matt, when I married Ben, I never thought you'd leave town. I ruined your life.'

At that, he laughed. 'Sierra, if anyone ruined my life, it damn sure wasn't you. I had to get away from my father. He's the one who really ran me off, not you. You just gave me the last reason I needed to go.'

'But you could have finished school.'

'I did finish school.'

'Really?'

'I transferred my credits and went to school nights here and there.'

'Why didn't you go on and become a vet like you'd wanted to?'

'I decided that wasn't for me. I never was much of a scientist. By the time I got a bachelor's degree in business management, I was tired of spending half my life with my nose in a book.'

'But if you have a college degree in management, you could get a terrific job . . .'

'And be inside some store or factory all day? No, thanks. It would be like jail to me. I like what I do just fine. Do you have any idea of what the world looks like at night, Sierra, without a roof over your head, all open? I guess to a lot of people that would look pretty scary, exposing themselves to the elements. But to me, it makes me happy, as if there's a path leading straight to heaven.'

'Can you show me, Matt?'

'It's not a place anyone can take you to. You've got to find it for yourself. You're the only one who knows where you're comfortable.'

'Why get a degree you're never going to use?'

He shrugged. 'You did.'

'That was different. My father expected me to go to school. I had to study something.'

'Mine thought I never would. Maybe I just did it to spite him. Show him I accomplished more than he ever did. Most parents would be proud of that – he'd hate it.'

'Is there anything you do that isn't connected with him? I mean, you haven't been near the man in ten years, but you're still letting him rule your life.'

'He doesn't have anything to do with my life.'

Sierra laughed. 'He dominates you more than my father affected me. At least I'm working to free myself of the last of his control. But you center your life around getting back at your father – you go to school, you move from one town to another, you have yourself sterilized so you can never have children, by God! Leave his actions to be his problem, his conscience, Matt. He's got to live with himself now. Go for what you really want in life. That's what you deserve to have.'

Matt's expression twisted into one of incredible sadness, one that made Sierra's heart ache.

'I try to shake him off. But sometimes it's like I hear his voice over my shoulder.'

She stepped closer to him. 'Stop listening, then. Stop running and hear instead the voices of the people who love you . . . Sam, your mother, Leeann, Will, me.'

She saw the light flash in his eyes, and for a long moment she feared he was going to bolt and flee.

Instead, he placed his hands on her shoulders, pulling her close. 'Why did you ever want to get mixed up with someone like me, anyway?' he asked. 'Weren't you just trying to get back at your father?'

'Maybe in the beginning. Then something happened I didn't expect. I wasn't prepared.'

'Sierra, I have feelings for you I don't know what to do with.'

'There's no shame in having them. I'm glad you do, Matt. I want you to feel them. Don't you realize, if you were like him, you wouldn't.'

'I don't know, Sierra, I don't see any future for us.'

'If there's one thing I've learned, it's not to be

afraid of the future. Being scared is what prompts us to do that wrong thing.'

His lips pressed down on hers, tasting like warm syrup in the cool air. His whiskers grazed her soft cheek, and he pulled her closer against him. She fitted her body neatly to his hard muscle, the inner stirrings of desire rolling through her.

As his hand moved to cup her breast, heat radiated through her chest. Her nipples throbbed beneath the restraint of her bra, her belly quivered pleasantly, and she moistened in anticipation at the thought of drawing him inside her.

Growing delirious with desire, she would have made love to him right there on the front porch if she hadn't suddenly remembered where she had to be.

She pulled away from him. 'Matt, I've got to change clothes. I promised Will I'd watch his dress rehearsal tonight.'

Disappointment evident in his eyes, he released her. 'You'd better get away from me pretty quick, then, darlin'. As it is you're about a hair's breadth away from being made love to.'

Stepping back, she beamed at him. 'Rain-check?'

'You bet. But I'm not waiting for rain.'

'Good, then let's go camping this weekend. You can show me that open sky.'

'Sierra, it's December now. You'll freeze.'

'I have sleeping bags. Show me your world, Matt. Or is it a place where I'm not allowed?'

'What about the horses?'

'I'll get Jules to tend to them over the weekend.'

He shrugged. 'You'll be begging to come back to your warm house before one night is over,' he challenged.

'I'll wear longjohns.'

He laughed. 'Might be interesting.'

'I hope so. I wasn't exactly planning on going for birdwatching.'

He wrapped his arms around her, holding her close and burying his face in her scented hair. God, he loved the way she felt in his arms. He planted a kiss below her ear, then reluctantly released her.

He moved to step down off the porch.

'Matt?' she called after him. 'Will's counting on your being at his play tomorrow night.'

'I haven't forgotten. I'll be there.'

'Does it bother you, that I said I love you?'

He shrugged. 'I suppose it does. Makes everything more difficult.'

He turned away too quickly to see her worried frown.

Amid the buzz of scattered conversations and mingled scents of heavy perfumes, Sierra sat in the front row of the middle school auditorium, twisted like a pretzel in her seat as she scanned the back of the auditorium. It was nearly curtain time, and Matt hadn't shown.

Of course he'd be here if he said he would. She'd been excited all day long about both her son's stage debut and seeing Matt tonight. She'd taken great care with her appearance, happy for a chance to dress up for him. She was wearing a winter suit that set off both her complexion and her curves. Of course, it was last year's, because any new clothes she splurged on had to be for Will. But it was one of her favorite outfits, and she knew she looked good in it.

With her hair at such an awkward length, she hadn't been able to do much with it. After extensive experiments, she'd shaped a mass of curls at the top, allowing them to frame her face. She couldn't help remembering how she'd once worn her hair, flowing long and free down her back. Matt had always loved it that way. He used to delight in running his hands through her tresses. But Ben had preferred the more sophisticated look of a shorter haircut. She had decided to let her hair grow out again.

She couldn't help wondering if she hadn't made a terrible mistake, telling Matt she loved him. But pretending she didn't was too hard. Let him go if he must, but this time he'd know exactly what he was walking away from.

She heard rustling behind the curtain, teachers' hushed voices, and she knew the young actors were taking their places for the opening scene. By now, she thought she knew every movement, every line by heart. Turning again, she scanned the back of the auditorium, hoping to catch Matt's attention as he came in and wave him over here to the seat beside her she'd saved for him.

How strangely domestic it would feel to sit beside her son's father and watch their boy perform.

Knowing Matt was unaware of his ties to Will left her feeling hollow. Matt had every right to know he was Will's father. Each time she was with him, her guilt over shielding him from the truth deepened, like an invisible wedge. But she couldn't stand to shatter the fragile bond developing between them. She was almost beginning to hope Matt would find it in his heart to love her again. Selfishly, she dreaded destroying that.

Luke's parents, seated over to one side, waved to her. She waved back. Then, her bright smile dropped as a familiar figure she hadn't expected to see tonight strutted through the auditorium entrance.

'Father,' she murmured.

Her head swam. Certainly he was welcome here. She wanted him to see his grandson's play. But their meeting the other day had taken her so by surprise that she hadn't thought to mention it.

And she'd been too preoccupied with thoughts of Matt to call Father and invite him, as she should have.

Now, his head snapped up, and he spotted her

immediately, strolling up the aisle and settling in the seat she'd saved for Matt.

'Sierra, you're looking well, as you have been lately.'

'Hello, Father. Will will be glad to see you here.'

'Hmm. You might have told me he was starring in a play. I would have missed it if he hadn't mentioned it on the phone the other night.'

'I didn't know he'd spoken to you. Honestly, Father, I wasn't trying to exclude you. I've just had a lot on my mind.'

'Will said he gave Ben's ticket to one of the ranch hands. Misplaced generosity, no doubt, but of course I don't mind having to buy one.'

Sierra watched the back of the auditorium through the corner of one eye as she spoke to her father. Her heart lurched as she saw Matt come through the door, his hat in his hands. If not for the beard, she might not have recognized him in his suit and vest. Obviously he'd gone to a lot of trouble for her and Will both tonight. Her first instinct was to rush to him.

But, glancing at her stern-faced father beside her, she caught herself. Her truce with him didn't extend far enough to make her believe he wouldn't act to keep her and Matt apart if he knew Matt was back in town, if he guessed what was going on between them. He'd do something terrible to make sure Matt left town before he discovered the truth about Will. That was for sure.

Spotting her, Matt grinned and began walking in their direction. Sierra's chest tightened, her heart skittered. Discreetly she gestured with her eyes at her father. For his own sake, Matt couldn't come to her.

Go back, she willed him. She believed telepathy was sometimes possible between two people who were very close, like when she'd know Will was going to ask for a peanut butter sandwich right before he did.

As Matt neared, a new worry turned her blood to ice. What if Matt caught her warning, saw her father, and proceeded up here anyway? She recalled how he'd confronted the hospital's business manager, and she knew he believed in standing his ground against anyone who bullied him or those he cared about.

His glance shifting to William Ross, Matt stopped short on the sloping linoleum, his expression reflecting astonishment then a dark anger as he gaped at the man beside Sierra. Taking an abrupt turn, he found a seat somewhere in the middle to one side.

Exhaling deeply in relief, Sierra tried to send him a silent apology. She knew he was angry when he refused to acknowledge her glance.

Relaxing a little, Sierra swung her eyes to the curtain. Would he ever believe she hadn't known William Ross would be here tonight?

'What's wrong, Sierra? You look as if you've seen a ghost,' her father demanded. Turning, he scrutinized the crowd behind them, trying to determine what had drawn her attention.

Sierra held her breath until he spun around. Silently she thanked God for Matt's awful beard. It had kept her father from recognizing him.

'Don't you know it's bad manners to be twisting around like that? You're more fidgety than a child.'

She turned to him. 'You just did it,' she countered.

'Honestly, I don't know what's gotten into you lately. You haven't been yourself since Ben died.'

'Actually, I think I finally am being myself. Sorry. I'm just nervous, for Will.'

'Yes, well, let him get this foolishness out of his system while he's young. When he grows up he'll have more important things to attend to.'

She raised her eyebrows. 'That, of course, will be up to him. Or are you assuming he'll be working in the oil business?'

'Naturally.'

'I'm bringing Will up to make his own choices. He's quite talented. He may grow up and decide he wants to be an actor.'

'Nonsense. I won't . . . I'm sure you won't allow that.'

'He'll be free to choose the direction of his life, Father. No one should be forced to have decisions made for them that make lasting impacts on their lives. You won't interfere with that.' Realizing she was raising her voice, she quickly dropped it.

'Don't be so defiant, Sierra. I've always considered your best interests first, and I intend to do the same for my grandson.'

'He's my son. And I know how I want him to grow up.'

The lights dimmed and a hush fell over the crowd. Well, Sierra thought, at least she'd made her position clear. But as she felt Matt's eyes on her back, her short-lived sense of victory diminished. If she was as independent as she claimed, why had she balked at bringing Matt up to sit with her?

She told herself it was because she feared what her father might do to Matt. But in her heart she was terrified of once again finding her life fashioned according to her father's will. When it came down to it, she didn't know if she had the courage for a head-on battle against him.

CHAPTER 11

Throughout the play, Matt felt as fidgety as if ants were crawling inside his stiff clothes. Unaccustomed to sitting still for long periods, he was itching to know what was going on with Sierra and her father.

It wasn't surprising that William Ross should want to see his grandson's stage debut. But Sierra had claimed they weren't even on speaking terms, and here they were sitting together.

The look he'd seen in her eyes as he'd approached her earlier, the look of a terrified, trapped kitten, warning him away, had struck him with the force of a jackhammer. Why was Sierra so afraid of her father? And why had she been so desperate to keep him from knowing Matt was here? With all her talk of independence, would she ultimately allow her father to keep running her life?

Matt tugged at his shirt collar. The heat in the auditorium was turned up too high, and the large, crowded room was stuffy. He propped his elbows on the narrow arm-rests. Maybe some things never changed so much after all. Was he still some secret vice Sierra was ashamed of, like sneaking a quick smoke behind the barn? Or had she simply wanted to delay the inevitable scene her father would make until they were outside Will's school?

A deep-rooted possessiveness surged through him. Hadn't he been the one insisting on no strings? He didn't much like feeling shut out of Sierra's life. He realized he wanted to be a part of it every minute. Making love in secret had never been enough for him, and it wasn't now. But he wasn't sure what he could do about that.

For now, he'd assume she was simply trying to avoid a nasty scene for Will's sake. No reason to push. Not now anyway. But he wasn't cowering to anyone in this town anymore. Lester Rollins had carved his reputation as a loser. But Matt refused to stand in that shadow any longer.

Trying to concentrate, he smiled at Will's exaggerated facial expressions. Earlier, Matt had made his way backstage, feeling like a Colossus from a science-fiction movie let loose in the elementary school hallways. He'd found Will pacing in the hallway. He was dressed as a white-haired old man in a suit with a pocket watch.

'Aren't you a sight?' Matt had asked.

At the sound of his voice, Will's head had jerked up. He cracked a grin through his heavy stage make-up. 'Matt!' Will's smile melted into an anxious frown. His glance shifted from side to side. 'You're not supposed to be back here.'

Matt shrugged. 'Figured I'd come and tell you to break a leg. Not that I'm superstitious. I know you're going to do a good job. All that rehearsing you've done is going to pay off.'

'You look neat, Matt. I've never seen you all dressed up before. Has Mom seen you?'

Matt shook his head. So, the boy was starting to notice how close he and Sierra were growing. He was a bright kid, and Matt thought he picked up on more than his mother sometimes gave him credit for. Sometimes she didn't see that he wasn't a baby any more.

'Thanks, Will. Get a good look, because I wear this get-up about as often as you put on your costumes. I'm going to go sit down out front now. You're not getting butterflies, are you?'

Clutching his stomach, Will admitted. 'Just a little.'

Matt reached out to tousle his hair, then, thinking better of messing it up, drew his hand back. 'Just remember, you've come this far, so just have fun with it now. It's like the rodeo. You sit in the shoot getting that clawing feeling in your stomach, and all you can do is make up your mind you're going to have the best darn time you can riding that bronc. Works every time. You stay on, because you forget you have to.'

'Matt, do you think acting is for sissies?'

'Someone been picking on you?'

'Yeah.'

'I'll bet they're kids who didn't have parts in the play.'

Will nodded. 'I've been trying to ignore them like Mom says, but it's getting tiresome. And when I ignore them, they do it more.'

'Sometimes you've got to hold your ground and not walk away.'

Will nodded soberly. Matt clasped the boy's slim shoulder. 'See you later,' he said.

'Bye, Matt. Will you be here after the show?'

'Sure.'

Walking back through the hallways, Matt pondered Leeann's charge that Will could be his son. Damn her for planting the suggestion in his mind. As usual, his sister was over reacting to a series of innocent coincidences. But Matt had to admit, he'd found himself looking at the boy a little harder. Because he'd never considered siring a child, he'd never contemplated what his offspring might be like.

In some aspects, Leeann's notion wasn't as far-fetched as it first sounded. The boy had affected Matt's demeanor, his walk. But Matt attributed that to the kid's impressionable age and the fact that he didn't have any other grown man around him much. He was kind of flattered.

Sierra had made some mistakes, and so had he. But had his seed sprouted inside her, she never would have withheld that information from him. He would have been the first person she told. He hadn't left town until after she'd decided to marry Ben.

Except she hadn't mentioned she'd been dating Ben while they were together, he recalled, and that bothered him. Perhaps if he'd known, he would have sensed the betrayal coming, realized how far she'd go to please her father. Still, he couldn't believe she would have lied to him and Ben both about her son's paternity. If she'd deceived him about a fact of that magnitude, she was deceiving him now. He had to believe in her, had to believe her when she said she saw now she was wrong to have caved to her father's will, that she was stronger now, than she loved him. He needed to believe in that, believe in her.

Will seemed to be the only good thing that had come out of her union with Ben. Ben had given Sierra the one thing Matt never would have. If he ever had a son, he'd hope it would be a kid like Will. He couldn't really explain the kinship he felt towards the boy. Maybe it was a natural extension of his feelings towards Sierra. And maybe he felt sorry for a boy left without a father to guide him, because he'd been left to figure life out for himself. And he'd at least had Dylan.

This afternoon she'd told him she loved him, and

he was still sorting out how he felt about that. She'd said it once before, then married someone else. He wanted to believe in her the way he once had. But here she sat beside her daddy, shooing him away like a fly in the potato salad. And damned if Will looked a hair like the portrait of Ben Davenport in Sierra's living room.

His backstage visit had been prompted by his memory of that first rodeo his daddy couldn't be bothered attending. He'd wanted Will to know he was here, just as Sam had been there for him, making sure he caught Matt's attention to let him know he'd come.

He had to shake the small seed of suspicion Leeann had planted in his mind. Will had to be Ben's son, just as Sierra said he was. If he ever found out differently, he wouldn't be able to stand in the same room with her.

But what was going on with her and her father? Was this the beginning of her allowing him to separate them once again? It had been all Matt could do to restrain himself from charging up front. But this was neither the time nor the place.

Matt wished he'd never come back. Life here was getting too complicated, too fast.

Through Sierra's eyes, the play was the best she'd ever seen. Her son portrayed a startlingly convincing Ebeneezer Scrooge, none of the scenery fell over, and none of the actors forgot their lines.

As the cast came on stage to receive a standing ovation from enthusiastic parents and friends, the house lights came on, and Sierra suddenly remembered her father standing at her side and their earlier confrontation. And Matt was somewhere behind them. She didn't dare speculate what he must be thinking about her father's sudden appearance.

Turning, she scanned the audience. Matt had disappeared.

At least he and her father wouldn't be accosting each other tonight. A temporary reprieve. But it was only a matter of time before William Ross discovered Matt was back in town and working for her. Standing her ground against her father was worth the effort it cost her, but she was reluctant to see him attack Matt, as she knew he would. Her father preferred having Matt as far away from her and Will as possible. He'd made that clear.

She had to warn Matt.

When Matt returned to his sister's house, anxious to change out of his suit, Leeann and the kids were nowhere around. The house was strangely silent, and Matt welcomed the quiet. It tempered a mood that was anything but serene.

In his haste to change into comfortable worn jeans and a white T-shirt, he nearly didn't notice the red light blinking on his sister's answering machine. He spotted it as he was grabbing a beer out of the refrigerator, and, thinking it might be a message from Leeann to let him know where she and the kids were, he automatically pressed for a playback.

'Howdy, Leeann.'

As Matt recognized his older brother's drawl, the beer bottle slipped from his hand and shattered on the floor. To have located him this quickly, she must have started looking even before Jerry's accident. She must have already known where everyone was before Matt agreed to the reunion.

The voice on the machine continued. 'Darcy called and said you're trying to get the family together for Christmas. Talk about a bolt out of the blue. I'd nearly forgotten I had a family, it's been so long. I've been thinking about seeing all of y'all again . . . I'll call back later when I don't have to discuss what I think about it with this fool machine. Matt, Darcy says you're there. I've wondered how things turned out for you, but it's easier to not look back, isn't it? I know this reunion idea is Leeann's and not yours. It's been a long, long time, hasn't it, little brother? I sure have missed you . . . I'll call back.'

The machine snapped as the message clicked off, whining as the tape rewound.

Dylan. His eldest brother had been the one

person who understood how things had been for him. Daddy'd thought the sun rose in his presence. The old man had been too self-absorbed to see how Dylan resented all the responsibility dropped on him every time Daddy took off, getting the chores done, looking after the younger kids, looking after Ma. Dylan took it seriously. Just as he'd tried to shield Matt from Daddy's meanness. And Daddy had never looked deep enough to see Dylan's spirit, longing to be free. He wanted to climb mountains and swim in oceans and touch the stars.

No, Daddy couldn't love even Dylan unselfishly enough to see that. He saw Dylan as being just like him and never got to know him well enough to realize he wasn't. And breath by breath Daddy'd been smothering him, making him old before his youth played out.

Matt had never blamed Dylan for leaving him and the others behind. He knew why his brother had had to go. But that hadn't stopped him from missing him. Matt would have looked him up, but he'd always figured Dylan would have looked for him if he wanted to be found . . .

Matt ambled towards the house, in no big hurry to get there because the rig was parked out front. He nearly lost his lunch when he was suddenly nabbed from behind and dragged into the woods.

'Hey!' he protested. Adrenalin pumping, he

struggled to free himself, scrambling to his feet and coming up with fists raised.

'Whoa,' his older brother cautioned, stepping back with his hands raised defensively over his chest.

Matt sucked in a deep breath as he recognized the familiar long face with the sharp nose and jutting chin, brown hair dipping over Dylan's forehead.

'Ya goin' loony, Dylan?' he asked. 'I always knew ya' were bound to one of these days.'

'Take it easy, Matt. How would ya' like to go to the movies tonight with Mary Lynn's cousin? Remember we saw 'em in the diner together the other day?'

'The girl with the blonde curls?' Matt asked incredulously, his interest piqued. She'd looked like an angel off a Christmas tree.

'Yeah, that one. Mary Lynn says she won't go out and leave her cousin sittin' home, and I'm not gonna have a good time draggin' an extra person along. Mary Lynn says her cousin thinks you're real cute.' He paused long enough to grimace, indicating her assessment was beyond his comprehension. 'You see, you can keep her occupied so Mary Lynn and I can enjoy some time by ourselves.' His expression indicated he planned on something beyond quiet conversation.

Matt's eyes dropped, and he shook his head. 'I don't have money for any movie.'

Dylan smiled slyly. 'I already got it. Just asked Daddy for enough for both of us.'

'Asked him for more than you needed, you mean? He wouldn't give me a bean if he had a potful.'

'It doesn't matter. Don't worry about him. He's stupid.'

'Dylan!' Matt had thought it, but he'd never said it aloud. Dylan knew their father doted on him. Matt used to think Dylan looked up to him. But ever since the football jersey incident, Dylan had been playing the old man like a fiddle, coaxing him out of not only everything he wanted, but everything he wanted for Matt and their Ma too.

'You know it's true. He wants me to grow up to be just like him. I'd rather be dead.'

'You wouldn't.'

'You comin' tonight or what?'

'Yeah, I'll go.'

Grinning, Dylan reached in the back pocket of his jeans, pulling out his wallet. He plucked out a sheaf of bills and handed them to Matt.

'Put those in your billfold. A girl likes to think you have your own money.' Two years older than Matt, Dylan was always teaching Matt about the way girls were and had been the first one to tell him why Daddy and Ma always closed the bedroom door whenever Daddy'd come home off the road. Nobody else bothered to explain these things to Matt, who was impressed by Dylan's vast store of knowledge. When he'd asked his brother how he knew so much, Dylan shamelessly confessed to having spied on their parents through the thin curtains. Shocked, from then on Matt stopped asking where Dylan picked up his information.

'What difference does it make?' he asked now.

Dylan shrugged. 'It just does.' He reached into his wallet again and extracted a crumpled foil packet. He held it out to Matt. 'You're gonna need this too.'

Realizing what it was, Matt recoiled as though he were dangling a scorpion.

'I won't,' he insisted. 'I'm not gonna do that to her.'

Dylan pressed it into his hand anyway. 'Take it just in case. You do know what to do with it, don't you?'

'Course I do. Just can't imagine some girl I barely know wantin' to do it with me.'

Dylan laughed. 'Boy, don't you know you've been blessed with the kind of good looks drives girls mad? Now me, I've got to get by on charm and wit, but all you've gotta do is wink at 'em. Ma even seen it, that's why she'd always carryin' on about you being born with the rising sun and that crap. Daddy hates it that he accidentally gave ya somethin' better than what he ever had. A couple years from now, you're going to have your pick of women. I bet you could even have one of those snotty rich bitches from up in the hills rubbin' all over you.'

'Come on, Dylan. I ain't plannin' on spendin' my whole life chasin' women who think they're better than everybody else. Or chasin' women, period.'

Dylan shrugged. 'Have you ever even kissed a girl?'

'Sure.'

'Just wonderin''. Look, what you do is your business, but with the age you're getting to and the way you look, you be careful about carrying one of these here packages with you and not forgettin' to use it. Don't let some girl get herself knocked up by you. You'll be trapped in this town forever, and you'll start hatin' your own guts, just like Daddy hates himself.'

'How do you know so much about all this, Dylan? Are you sayin' Mary Lynn lets you . . .'

Dylan nodded. 'Every chance we get. It ain't so hard to persuade 'em, Matt. You just tell her she's the prettiest thing you ever saw, over and over, and you hold her hand a lot. If you want to see her with her clothes off, you wait for a real hot day and take her for a walk down by the tanks. Then real innocent like, you suggest a swim.'

'That would have to be some real stupid girl, Dylan. I'd feel like an idiot doin' that.' Girls, after all, were people too. While he couldn't figure them out, he didn't imagine ones with any brains shed their clothes that easily. Especially with his brother watching.

Dylan shrugged. 'Wait a couple years and you'll change your mind. But I'm too smart to stay around here for anything or anybody. After I get a little more money saved, I'm takin' off.'

'For where?'

'Somewhere Daddy'll never find me. And if you're smart, you'll do the same. He thinks I don't see what a jerk he really is, that I should be proud to be his son. When I look at him, I feel sick inside. Folks in town laugh at him.'

'You can't have much money saved . . .'

'When he comes home after a long haul, he's always carryin' a load of money in his pocket. He drinks beer til he passes out. And if his wallet's a mite lighter in the morning, he don't ever notice.'

'You steal money from him, Dylan?'

'He's always got money for himself, but Ma has to keep workin' to pay the bills. He owes us, Matt.' Dylan extracted a cigarette from a rumpled pack and lit it. Matt knew Dylan had sneaked those from Daddy's room too. Dylan held the open end of the pack out to him, and Matt pulled out a cigarette. He didn't enjoy smoking much, but he savored the sweet revenge of burning the old man.

Matt shook his head. 'Still stealin''. Cigarettes are one thing, but money's serious. I'll get away from here on my own some day.'

'Suit yourself. You can come with me if you want.

I'd hate leavin' you on your own to deal with Daddy.'

Matt was beginning to wonder if there was anything Dylan wouldn't do.

'I can handle him. I ain't scared any more.'

'Let's go. You have to take a bath if you're going out with a girl. They don't like it if you stink.'

'Aw, hell. I don't stink.'

Matt fell in step beside his brother. Dylan was about the best friend he'd ever had. He was dying to ask what it felt like to slip into that silk between a girl's legs. The logistics of that had been occupying his mind pretty much lately. He found it hard to imagine it could feel as mind-numbing good as it was supposed to. His urges to find out were becoming more insistent.

But he couldn't flat-out ask without admitting he was still a virgin. And he wanted to appear every bit as worldly as his big brother.

Despite Dylan's predictions, Matt had no call to open the packet in his wallet that night or any night for a couple more years. But he did enjoy kissing the teenage girl who resembled a porcelain figurine with spun-gold curls. She seemed to like him well enough.

Later, he studied his face in the bathroom mirror. As Dylan had pointed out, it wasn't as horselike as their father's. He looked OK. Combing his hair, he started feeling a little better about himself. Ma always said nice things about everybody, but Dylan didn't pass out compliments unless he meant them. Matt had always felt nothing about himself was good enough to make Daddy happy. Now, he considered Dylan might be right. Did Daddy only wish Matt were the no-account he made him feel he was . . .?

Leeann and the kids burst through the front door.

'Phew!' Leeann noted, wrinkling her nose as she headed for the kitchen. 'Smells like a brewery in here.' She stopped short. 'Matt, what happened! Mind you don't cut your feet.'

Matt realized he was standing barefoot in a pool of beer and glass shards. Carefully, he stepped clear of the mess.

'Sorry,' he told Leeann, who was already reaching for a rag. 'It slipped out of my hand.'

'Accidents happen, but why are you standing in it like you're in a trance?' She plucked one of the larger fragments out of the debris and flung it in the trash can.

'Here, let me,' he said, crouching beside her. 'Where have you been?'

'I took the kids to see Jerry. The nursing home allows them in. We stayed till the nurses kicked us out.'

'You had a phone call.'

Her glance swerved towards the machine on the counter.

'I thought it was a message from you and played it back. It was Dylan.'

Her puzzled expression brightened. 'Is he coming?'

'He said he'll call back.'

'Did he leave a number?'

'No.'

'What's wrong, Matt? You and Dylan were always so close. I know you're wanting to see him again. You're not having second thoughts, are you?'

He shook his head. 'Reckon I thought none of 'em would actually come. Hearing Dylan's voice again made it seem kind of real.'

He sopped up the last of the beer.

Leeann stood and washed her hands off in the sink. She moved to play back the message, but before she punched the button, the phone rang again.

She answered it.

'Yes, just a minute,' she said softly. She held out the receiver to Matt, planting her palm over one end. 'It's your boss,' she announced.

Matt took the phone from her. 'Sierra?' he asked, unable to keep the warmth out of his voice, even though Leeann was standing there listening. She turned and left the room.

'Matt, I called to apologize. I didn't know Father was coming to the play. Will had talked to him on the phone and invited him. He didn't mention it to me.'

'Thought you and your father were on the outs these days.'

'He came here to make peace the other day. No matter what he's done, Matt, he's still my father, Will's grandfather. And it's Christmas-time.'

'I've got no problem with that. But are you sure you're not just getting tired of trying to make a go of the stables?'

'Just because I'm not taking anything from him, it doesn't mean I have to shut him out of my life. Matt, if you knew him, you'd know how hard it was for him to make the first gesture.'

'Maybe it is time he and I got to know one another.'

'I want that. And I appreciate your not forcing the issue tonight.'

'You know I wouldn't have done anything to spoil Will's play.'

'Matt, I'm not ashamed of what I feel for you. Father was angry a long time ago because I'd made a choice that wasn't thc one he would have made for me. He doesn't recover from his anger easily. But he's seen how Ben fell short of his expectations. I don't expect you to avoid Father forever, but I need time to prepare him.'

'Sierra, I'm not sure where everything that's happened is taking us. But I do know I'm not going to hide in the shadows where you're concerned. You and I both know we waited too long last time to tell anyone the truth.'

A long silence spun across the phone line. 'Are you saying you're considering staying, Matt?'

'I can't make any promises, Sierra. But I know for sure I don't want to be some phantom in your life. Everything inside me is telling me to go, but I keep wanting to hold on. I'm finding it harder and hard to imagine going away from you.'

'I don't want you to leave, ever.'

Now it was his turn to struggle for words. 'I'm wrong for you.'

'You're all I've ever wanted, Matt. If you have to leave, I won't try to stop you. But please, think long and hard before you go.'

'Listen, tell Will I'm sorry I couldn't stay and see him after the show. I hate breaking my word to him.'

'I told him something unexpected came up. I don't know how to begin to explain . . .'

'Maybe once your father knows how things are, you won't have to.'

There was a long pause. 'Maybe.'

'Goodnight, Sierra.'

'Goodnight, Matt.'

CHAPTER 12

Sam poured steaming coffee from a Thermos, staring disdainfully at Matt as he wiped years of caked-on dirt off the old carriage.

Aware of the rancher's scrutiny, Matt tried to ignore it but couldn't help wondering what he had on his mind.

Finally, Sam blurted out, 'Why don't you shave those whiskers? They make your face look like it's ate up with steel wool.'

Rubbing the offending beard self-consciously, Matt chuckled. 'Funny you should mention that. I've been contemplating shedding them.'

'What are ya' waitin' for? Quit contemplatin' and take a razor to that dog fur. There's some of us around here who enjoy seeing your face. Not that you're any movie star, mind you.'

Matt's amusement faded. 'How have you been feeling, Sam?'

Leaning against a stack of baled hay, Sam sipped his coffee, then shrugged. 'There's good days and there's bad days. Course there's pain-killers. I try not to think so much about how I feel. Time's runnin' out for me, runnin' fast.'

'Don't say that, Sam. You look terrific.'

'I look like a tired old dyin' man. You've never been one to toss a lot of bull around, Matt. Don't start now. Doesn't suit you.'

'I hate this for you.'

'And damned if I don't love you for that. But pretendin' it ain't happenin' ain't gonna change nothin'. I don't think it's goin' to be so bad. I'm gonna get through it whether I want to or not. Of course, I'll miss gettin' up in the mornings and watching the sun rise over the hills. All the little routines that make up your life and get to seem boring are some of life's sweetest pleasures. Pretty soon, ya' start takin' 'em for granted. I'll miss all the damn critters, but I've been thinkin' maybe there's something better. Last night, well, I guess I was half dreamin', but I saw Annie.'

'Your wife?' Matt asked, trying to mask his surprise. He knew she'd been dead for decades.

An uncharacteristic dreamy look came into Sam's eyes. That itself was enough to alarm Matt. 'She was staring at me, looking all soft and pretty like I remember her. She had the quietest way of talkin'. Never said a word unless it was important. At first it scared the blazes out of me. Then I felt real calm. I guess it's her way of gettin' me to accept the way things are. Those years we had together sped by quicker than a whirlwind crosses the prairie. I never gave much thought to the hereafter, but the idea of bein' with my Annie again is kinda soothin'.'

Matt shifted uncomfortably. 'Do we have to talk about this?'

'Yes.' Sam focused back on Matt. 'Because when I'm not here to keep telling you, I want you to know I may not be going willingly, but I'm all right with it, not kicking and screaming. I've never been much of a philosopher, but you can bet, Matthew, life is over in the blink of an eye. The good parts anyway. And all that's left are those few good things you've found. Hold on to them while you can.'

'Sam, suppose you got a sour taste inside you that mixes up your knowing what the good things are? What do you do if things someone's done to you eat at you all the time and make you hate that person so bad you can't ever forgive them?'

'Things blow up inside you til they don't fit any more. I'd face him head-on. Once, when I was younger, I was on a cattle drive with a hand who didn't much like me being promoted to foreman. Started findin' little things tampered with, like sand in my coffee and a snake in my bedroll. I knew he was doin' it. Finally just duked it out with him and run him off. Soon as he was out of my sight, I forgot all about it.'

Matt laughed. 'What if it's not someone who's around to punch it out with?'

Sam's white brow furrowed. 'Like your old man, you mean?'

'Yeah.'

'I don't know. That's a tough one. Maybe just stop trying so hard to get over it, you know? Accept the past and how he was for what it was and go on. One thing I know for sure, if you keep running from your troubles, sure as shootin', they're going to catch up with you.'

'Mine sure have done that. I never gave much thought to the way I grew up until I came back here. Now, it seems there's nowhere to escape it. Leeann's trying to get the family together for Christmas?'

'Your old man coming?'

'He's not invited. And wouldn't be even if we knew where he was.'

'So, how long are you gonna be in town, Matt?'

Matt shot him a startled glance. Then he shrugged. 'I reckon I'll hang around for a while. Just to make sure you have somebody here you can talk straight to.'

Sam broke into a grin. 'You're not holdin' up here on my account, are you?'

'Don't get a swelled head over it,' Matt joshed. 'I've got some other business to take care of. And it's not like I'm staying forever.'

'You could, you know. This is your home.'

'Sam, about your will . . .'

'I'm not changin' it. And I'm not goin' to tolerate any more arguin'. Don't you think it's about time you got a break? You deserve your own hunk of land. If you wanna hang around, that's one thing, but don't spend your time hasslin' me about my will.'

'I don't mean to sound ungrateful. I know what you're trying to do.'

'Well, ya do belong here. And don't be so sure you can read my mind. Maybe I'm just doin' this to ease my conscience about all the trouble I caused you and your ma. I don't have any inclination to squabble about it.'

Matt chuckled. 'Sorry. Sam, you're the only person besides my ma who's ever done anything for me. I guess I really don't know what I should do.'

'Humph. Just say thanks and be done with it. I should have done more. I would have offered you a room out here but I knew your ma needed you around the house.'

'You gave a damn, Sam. That mattered to me more than you'll know.'

'How are you and Sierra getting along?'

Matt's head jerked up. He told himself Sam must be referring to their business venture. He couldn't know their true relationship. Sam wasn't clairvoyant, and Matt had never told him about her. Still, Sam sounded as though he knew.

'Fine,' Matt shot back, returning his attention to the wagon.

'Ahh, touchy subject. Maybe you'd prefer to talk some more about my dyin'.'

'Of course not. Say your piece, Sam.'

'Sierra's a beautiful young woman. Don't tell me you haven't noticed, because I see it in your eyes when I say her name. I saw it just now, as a matter of fact. And that's a fine-lookin' son she has, a good boy. Never could figure out why she married a rogue like Ben Davenport. She deserves a man who knows how to do more'n toss money around.'

'Guess Ben appealed to her.' Matt tried to sound dispassionate.

Sam swallowed the last of his coffee and rubbed his grizzled jaw. 'Guess William Ross bullied his daughter into marrying someone he saw as upstanding in the community. I know William Ross, although I wouldn't consider him a friend. He's a crafty bastard. When I wouldn't sell him an oil lease on my land, he came in on the adjacent property and drilled in at an angle. You watch out for William Ross. He's capable of doing anything he thinks is in his best interests. And I doubt you top his list of favorite people.'

'Why should he care about me one way or another?'

'We both know why, son. He's had you stickin' in his craw for a long time now. Because of Sierra.'

'You knew?'

'I guessed. That last summer you worked here you used to rush out of here so fast in the evenings, I knew you were meeting a girl somewhere. Funny thing was, a young man has him a steady girl, he likes to show her off, you keep runnin' into them together around town. I never saw you with anybody. So I figured it must be a girl from up in the hills. Then, you took off right after Sierra's engagement was announced. Still, I was just guessing. Then every time I saw her in town, she'd ask if I'd heard from you. That's when I really knew. Sometimes she'd come across the street or into a store just to ask me.'

'You never said anything?'

'Wasn't any of my business.'

Matt's gaze hardened. 'Is that why you sent her to hire me?'

'She needed your help; you needed a job. And I promised you a long time ago you'd always have one here. Problem was, I've turned my place over to my grandson. I figured whatever happened beyond that was between the two of you. I ain't runnin' no dating service, if that's what you're gettin' at.'

'I was in love with her, then she up and married Ben. She's got a way about her nobody else has. Everything happened by accident. I never had any sights on those hills, Sam. No one from up there had ever impressed me much. Until Sierra. Now, it's happening all over again.'

'And you're afraid she'll disappoint you again?'

'I suppose. Sam, you know what my life was like. Then I thought I'd found something pure and good and lasting. Something that was all mine like nothing ever had been. I've been sharing all my life, and I guess it's made me a little selfish. She made me feel alive from so deep inside it hurt. Then suddenly, everything gone.'

'So, you've got a second chance. Sometimes you run out of those. You know how strongly the way your father treated you affected your actions. Sierra's father never allowed her much freedom. Personally, I think he sank the lowest when he refused to let the girl's mother see her.'

Matt gave him a blank look. 'You're mistaken about that. Sierra's mother died when she was a baby.'

'Maybe she's dead now, but she was very much alive a couple years after Ross and his daughter moved here from Brownsville. A pretty black-haired woman – she looked almost as striking as Sierra does now, except she had real long hair all the way down her back. She showed up at the door, asking if this was William Ross's house. She acted real nervous, and I got the feeling she might have come across the Rio Grande illegally. She was so soft-spoken, ya' had to kind of lean forward to hear her. I think she was self-conscious about her English, but when I switched our conversation to

Spanish, it seemed to set her at ease. She said she'd come to visit her baby daughter, and she showed me this Mexican doll she'd brought to give her.

'I gave her directions to the Ross house, but I found out later he never let her past the electric gate. All the security around that house? He wasn't scared of robbers as much as he wanted to keep her out. Damn shame if you ask me, a self-respecting woman like that associating with the likes of Bill Ross. I always thought he must have brainwashed the girl into believing her mama was some kind of witch, to keep her from looking for her and explain why she never came back. Never occurred to me he might have told the child she was dead.'

Listening incredulously, Matt seethed with indignation. Apparently Sierra didn't realize how much of a tyrant her father was. Why would he keep Sierra's own mother away from her? How could he? How could he tell his daughter her mother was dead when she was outside trying to get past his gate? No one had the right to keep people apart who wanted to be together. No one.

Matt kicked the buggy wheel. The carriage shuddered in protest.

'Sierra always thought her father loved her too much. Yet he perpetuated a lie through her whole life. She wanted to go to Mexico and find her mother's grave, not knowing that if she really went, she might find her mama. No wonder her father told her the trip was too dangerous. He knew if she learned the truth her anger would give her the strength to break away from his control.'

'Are you gonna tell her?'

Matt hesitated. 'No.' he said finally. 'It's not my place. And I can't tell her something that will destroy everything she believes in. Despite it all, she loves her father and she believes he loves her. She has a right to hear the truth, but it's not going to come from me.'

He wouldn't, but he silently swore he'd see to it William Ross finally confessed the truth.

He was so preoccupied, he nearly missed Sam's next question. 'So, when are you gonna shave?'

When Matt, polishing the buggy so hard that the finish was in jeopardy, failed to answer, his old friend shook his head.

'Don't matter,' he muttered. 'Everything always comes in its own time.'

'You sure you want to go through with this?' Matt asked, casting Sierra a sidelong glance across the darkened cab of his pickup.

'It was my idea,' she insisted. Her head resting against the back of the seat, she looked relaxed and especially beautiful tonight, the way Matt remembered her from so long ago. Her light fragrance filled the cab, and Matt felt a tug in his loins. For tonight, at least, she was his. The prospect of making love to her again was driving him to distraction. He tried to push it out of his mind.

'You'll be begging to go back to your warm bed before the night's over,' he predicted.

'We'll see,' she challenged. 'I'm tougher than you think. Where are we going?'

'It's a surprise.'

'I really don't care. I just want to be with you, Matt. You do believe that, don't you?'

'Yes. Are you sure it's a good idea, letting your father take Will to New York?'

'I'm sure they'll have a good time. I just hope Father doesn't overdo it. I don't want Will to grow up believing money is the key to happiness. I think this is just my father's way of trying to make peace with both of us.'

After what Sam had told him, Matt found it hard to accept that William Ross's motives concerning anything were less than self-serving. But he kept silent.

'Let's not talk about your father or my family tonight, OK?' he asked.

'All right.' She reached out and stroked his whiskered jaw.

Matt smiled. He brought the pickup to a halt. 'Here we are.'

'In total darkness. Where are we?'

He jumped out of the truck. 'On Sam's place. Come on.'

He rounded the cab and helped her down.

'I hear water,' she noted, her eyes rounding. 'We're near the creek, aren't we, Matt?'

'I have a flashlight,' he said, digging through the gear stowed in the pickup's bed. 'Here.'

He clicked it on, swinging the beam to reveal a domed tent set up a few feet away.

'When did you do that?' she asked, amazed.

'This afternoon. Come on.'

She approached the entrance, grinning as she made out the small pine wreath adorning the flap.

'Hold up,' he cautioned as she moved to push aside the flap.

Stunned, she dropped it.

'Is something going to jump out at me?' she inquired.

Catching her off-guard, he scooped her up in his arms. She squealed with delight.

'This is our place. I want to do things right,' he said.

Sierra studied his handsome features. Grasping the back of his neck, she raised forward to press her slightly parted lips to his. Matt drank in the warm, rich taste of her. His muscles tensed with longing.

She drew back. 'Why the wreath?' she asked.

'Because tonight I feel like it's Christmas,' he said. He took her inside, setting her on her feet and turning on the lantern set in one corner.

As the soft light illuminated the tent's compact interior, Sierra inspected her lodgings. The furnishings were simple – two sleeping bags rolled out side-by-side, a cooler set opposite them with a Thermos jug beside it, a pile of folded blankets in the corner.

Her glance fixed on the blankets. 'You thought of everything, didn't you?' she asked.

He had to duck his head to stand up in here. 'There's no heat. I didn't want to give you an excuse to leave.'

She smiled up at him. 'I've no intention of letting you out of my sight until Sunday.'

Reaching out, he gathered a handful of her silky hair in his hand.

'Really?' he asked.

'Actually, I don't imagine we'll be keeping track of the time. Do you?'

'Wasn't planning on it. There's never been anyone makes me feel the way you do, Sierra,' he said. And the words spilled out of him. 'I love you. No matter what happens, I want you to know that.'

She drew in a sharp breath. 'Really, Matt? After everything I've . . .'

He silenced her with a finger across her lips. 'Tonight, there is no past for us. Only now.'

'Only now,' she repeated.

His eyes locked with hers, he stroked the smooth skin of her cheek with the back of his hand. She shuddered slightly beneath his touch.

The canvas rumbled as the wind struck it.

He slid to his knees before her, and she felt his swift, steady hands, unclasping her jeans.

She drew in a deep breath as his warm fingers skimmed her bared hips. With a single tug, he pushed her jeans down, and pulled her to him, burying his face against her belly.

'Oh, Matt,' she whispered. 'It's always been you. And it always will be.'

His lips grazed her tummy, his hands caressing her sleek curves. As his fingertips came between her skin and the narrow elastic band of her panties, he smelled the perfume of her arousal. He slipped the panties lower, revealing the silky triangle of her womanhood.

'Sierra,' he whispered, as sharp longing stabbed him.

He touched her lightly beneath the feathery patch, a moan escaping from the back of his throat as her nectar dampened his fingertip. Gently, he traced the inside of her thighs, until she stood with her legs parted for him.

Firmly, he clasped her round buttocks, pulling her to him and then bowing to bestow a kiss that rushed to the core of her.

Sierra's world went blissfully black, and she cried out as the maddening pleasure shot though her.

If Matt had wanted to remove her from the rest of universe tonight, he certainly had succeeded.

* * *

Matt held Sierra close against his bare chest. For a long moment, the only sound she heard was the beating of his heart and the wind whipping against the tent.

'Sierra, darlin',' he said finally. 'I've been wondering. Do you think you could see fit to give me a second chance?'

Her head popped up, She stared at him incredulously, tears flooding her eyes.

Alarm registered in Matt's expression. 'What did I do?' he asked.

She shook her head, tears flowing freely. 'No, you don't understand. I'm the one who should be asking for a second chance.'

'No. I should have talked to you instead of running off like a wounded lion. I should have gone to your father and stood up to him.'

'I should have stood up to him. I should have refused to marry Ben, refused to let him threaten me. If I'd called his bluff, he wouldn't have carried out his threats.'

He squeezed her shoulders. 'I want to get over the past. I'm tired of running from it, Sierra. But it's not easy. Let's face things and get on with our lives.'

'I want to let go of it all too.'

'Sierra, you have told me everything about what happened, about why you married Ben, haven't you?'

'What else do you want to know?'

Matt felt her holding her breath, tensing in his arms.

'Whatever you want to tell me,' he said, skating his fingers across her shoulder.

Sierra was sure Matt must be close to guessing the truth. But she couldn't bring herself to confess now and ruin everything. She kept feeling time was running out for them as it was.

She buried her damp face in his chest. 'No,' she lied. 'There's nothing else.'

Matt suspected she was holding something back. Lord, but he wanted to trust her. He told himself his funny feelings stemmed from his own inability to trust anyone.

'I'm glad we came out here,' he said.

She rolled over on her back. 'God, I love you.'

His hand grazed her bare breast. 'I plan to spend the rest of the weekend erasing any doubts you might have as to how I feel about you. You might be begging to go home soon.'

Smiling through her tears, she slipped her hand inside the sleeping bag, clasping him and evoking a groan.

'I'm in for the duration, Rollins. Get used to it.'

New desire awoke inside him as she slid over him.

Later, he left her sleeping. Slipping on his jeans and a jacket with no shirt, he left the tent to grab a smoke. An unsettled feeling inside him disturbed the contentment he should have derived from some of the finest lovemaking he'd ever experienced. It wouldn't let him fall asleep. And in the open air, he normally would have been dozing as soon as he closed his eyes.

The sky was clear, stars twinkling like the tiny white Christmas lights the rich folks put on their shrubs. He stood smoking and staring up, wondering if he could make a fresh start here, if it was worth trying. He'd always believed he held no particular affection for Winter, but he'd forgotten all the good things about it.

Suddenly, a trail of sparks illuminated the sky. Matt blinked, and it was gone. Another shooting star. That made two he'd seen since he'd come home. Was the universe in some kind of upheaval? He couldn't remember ever having seen two within a few weeks, and he spent more time outside than most folks.

What did it mean? Probably just that he'd been staring at the sky more than usual. But he couldn't help remembering his mother recovering from childbirth to rush and look up when the sun rose, his sister accusing him of seeing signs and ignoring them.

Signs of what?

He tossed the cigarette on the ground and mashed it out. Signs he needed some sleep, most likely.

He thought of Sierra inside the tent and wondered how deeply asleep she might be. He decided he'd better get back in with her. He didn't want her to wake up and feel cold.

CHAPTER 13

When Matt kissed her outside her front door and said he was going to check on the horses, Sierra caught him by the hand and couldn't let go.

'What's wrong, darlin'?' he asked, smiling inquisitively. She looked into the dear, handsome face she held ever so close to her heart. How could she explain the sudden panic that gripped her?

'I don't want to be away from you,' she offered helplessly. 'I just had this sudden feeling we don't have much time left.'

'No,' he coaxed. 'Everything's only beginning. I promise. I need you in my life, Sierra. It's not like it was before.'

'A promise, Matt?'

'Nothing good in life comes easy. Maybe it took Sam losing everything to make me see that. I'd walk into hell for you, Sierra.'

'I'd sooner die than let you.'

Reaching out, he stroked her cheek. 'What would you think, darlin', about the three of us going away, making a fresh start someplace new?'

Her mouth dropped open. 'Leaving?' she asked.

His expression dropped. 'This place reeks of the past, all the things that have kept us apart.'

'Matt, I want to be with you, but I can't leave Winter.'

'Putting some distance between you and your daddy might do you some good.'

'It has nothing to do with him. I could live in Alaska's interior and he'd charter a plane and drop in for dinner if he wanted to. This sorry little town means something to me, Matt. I know the people here, and I feel welcome. And I want Will to know where his roots are. Growing up without my mother, I always had this emptiness inside. Maybe that just makes having a place where I belong more important to me.'

Matt nodded slowly. 'I don't know if I could tolerate staying.'

She smiled sadly. 'I know. But don't you think if there were someplace better, you would have found it by now?'

'Go on inside and do what you need to. As soon as I'm satisfied the horses have been tended properly, I'll be in.'

He gave her a kiss, then headed off towards the barn.

Sierra watched him, admiring his straight, proud stance, until he was out of sight. After spending two nights and an entire day in his arms, she should have felt full of him, and still she felt herself yearning for his touch. Still, she felt a peace in her heart she'd never known. Maybe she was afraid to be too happy.

If he left again, her heart would shatter. At least he was considering staying here. If he really loved her . . . Dared she hope they could be together?

A distressing thought flashed through her mind. Matt deserved to know the truth about Will. Yet she couldn't spoil things by telling him. Matt already loved Will as though he were his own son. Not knowing the truth left him free to love the boy. Would it be so awful if they were together and he had his son with him without knowing it? She was tired of living a lie, and Matt was the one person she didn't want to withhold anything from. But she couldn't bring herself to think about telling him now. Besides, at this point, her confession would seem like blackmail to hold him here.

With a long sigh, she headed to her room. The weekend had passed like a wonderful dream. No one in the world but her and Matt, nothing between them. They'd teased and played and made love time and time again. Each time was different and new and exciting. Her heart raced at the memory. She and Matt had been born to different circumstances, but born for each other nonetheless.

Leaving the front door unlocked for Matt, she put on a pot of coffee and popped a couple of frozen pot pies in the oven, craving hot food. Reality encroached now. Gathering clothes from her dresser, she retrieved her white terry cloth robe from the closet. She ran a hot bath, shedding her clothes and soaking in the steaming water laced with fragrant bath oil. Stretching out in the tub, she luxuriated in the warm, fresh feeling ebbing through her. After her near sleepless weekend, she succumbed to a drowsy relaxation.

Closing her eyes, she entertained delicious memories of the way Matt played her body so expertly. She'd never felt so totally feminine as she did in his hands. All her life, people had told her she was beautiful. Sometimes, she wondered if anyone ever saw past the way she looked, if anyone really knew her. Ben hadn't. She saw now she'd been just another toy in his collection. But Matt saw her for herself. He made her believe she was beautiful inside, he'd drawn out her ability to love and find joy in life.

Oh, yes, it was Christmas time. And she wanted everyone around her to find happiness.

As the water cooled, she reluctantly pulled the plug and drained the tub. She got out quickly, towelling herself dry.

Excited at the prospect of seeing Matt again, she hurried to comb her hair, damp from being washed, and don her underwear and robe. Her father wasn't due to bring Will home for several hours, and maybe she could persuade Matt to stay for a while. Maybe they'd make love again.

Guiltily, she realized she'd taken him away from Leeann and her family all weekend. But things were going better for them, she understood. Matt had said Jerry was coming home soon.

Tying the robe's belt loosely around her waist and stuffing her feet into a pair of scuffs, she went to the living room. Matt hadn't come in yet. She worried there might be a problem with the horses.

Although it wasn't that cold, she started a fire in the fireplace, then went to the kitchen to check on the pies in the oven. She poured herself a mug of coffee. She wished Matt would hurry and come in to have some with her. Not having got any more sleep than she had, he must be feeling like a zombie.

A knock at the door startled her.

Just like Matt. She'd have to flat-out tell him he didn't have to knock.

'It's open. Come on in,' she called.

The door swung open, and, expecting Matt, she smiled welcomingly.

As she recognized her father's formidable frame filling the doorframe, she nearly dropped the coffee mug.

'Father,' she gasped.

He strolled into the house as Will shot past him, his arms laden with packages.

'Slight change of plan,' William Ross explained. 'I have to leave for Albuquerque tonight. We took an earlier flight back.'

'You should have called.'

'Lord, girl, I left a message Friday night. Don't you check your machine?'

Sierra reflected guiltily that she hadn't thought to check it. But she wasn't going to admit that this was the first half-hour she'd spent at home all weekend.

Will rushed up to her. 'We went shopping. Look what Grandfather got me!'

She nodded distractedly as he waved a boxed CD-ROM.

William Ross gloated. 'No protest, Sierra? I'm surprised.'

'We got you something too, Mom,' Will announced. 'Can I give it to her, Grandfather?'

William Ross nodded. Sierra didn't like the way he was looking at her, like he was trying to discern what was different. Her heart was whirling, anticipating the explosion sure to come if Matt accidentally entered the house now. She tried to calm herself by telling herself he wouldn't. Surely he would see her father's car? And he'd already agreed to give her time to prepare Father for his sudden reappearance in their lives.

She realized her father was talking to her. 'I know how you've always loved cashmere.'

Reluctantly she took the box her son handed her. Opening it, she found an expensive imported mint-green cashmere sweater.

'You shouldn't have,' she protested.

'You don't have to deny yourself nice things, Sierra. Why don't you stop this nonsense and come home? You weren't meant to live like this.'

Sierra turned to her son. 'Why don't you go put your new things in your room, son?' she suggested. She waited until he had scampered away before she returned her attention to her father. 'Please don't start, Father, not today. I'm not in any mood to argue with you.'

The door burst open. Matt, his expression grim, entered the living room.

He glanced briefly at William Ross, then shifted his attention to Sierra as though no one in particular was standing there.

Sierra's heart stopped. She shot Matt a beseeching look, but he either didn't read it or was ignoring it.

'I had to give the horses some more water, but other than that, they're all right,' he reported.

Sierra's father, his complexion an ever-deepening purple, looked disdainfully from his daughter to the man who had just strutted into her house, then back again.

'Thank you, Matt,' she said. Her shaking hands curled into fists. In his rumpled clothes and shaggy whiskers, Matt couldn't have appeared more like a bum to her father if he'd tried.

William Ross stood speechless. A heavy silence inflated the room. Sierra thought she could hear her own heart slamming against the walls of her chest.

How could Matt have done this to her? He must have seen the Lincoln before he came in. He hadn't stumbled in here by accident.

She tried to think how to avert the impending battle hanging over them like a storm cloud about to burst.

Her father eyed Matt as though he'd encountered the devil himself. 'What are you doing here?' he sputtered.

'Reckon I have as much right to live in this town as you or anyone else,' Matt countered calmly.

'We'll just see about that,' Ross replied in a threatening tone.

Matt looked him in the eye. 'I'm not afraid of you, Mr Ross.'

Sierra knew she couldn't let them keep arguing.

'This is my house, and Matt's welcome here,' she declared.

Her father's eyes blazed as he gaped at her. For the first time, seemed to notice her scant attire. 'You whore!' he accused.

She reeled as though he'd struck her, tears flooding her eyes. How could he take the most beautiful thing she'd ever found and make it sound dirty?

Matt started towards him incredulously. 'How dare you talk to your own daughter that way?' he demanded. 'Sierra's not the one who has anything to be ashamed of.'

Ross ignored him, focusing his wrath on Sierra. 'You're no better than your mother.'

Sierra's mouth dropped open. 'What do you mean?'

His color deepened. 'I'll tell you what I mean . . .' he shouted.

All at once he went white. His face contorted, and he clutched his chest. He gasped for breath.

'Father!' Sierra cried.

He crumpled to his knees, falling to the floor. Sierra rushed to him, kneeling frantically beside him. William Ross lay pale and still, groaning softly.

She turned to find Matt. 'Matt, please,' she began. But she didn't have to instruct him to call an ambulance. He was already on the phone.

Sierra lost all track of time as she sat alone in the hospital waiting room, twisting a tissue in her hands and staring at the floor tiles. She ignored the people who shuffled past, the mocking Christmas garlands coiled around the pillars, the constantly chirping phones.

The past hours blurred in her mind – the ambulance arriving, the paramedics working over her father's still body, the rush to get dressed, the drive here. In her haste, she'd donned a pair of ripped jeans and the new ridiculously expensive sweater. Maybe if she wore her father's gift it would somehow reverse everything that had happened.

She'd been too young to remember losing her mother. Foolishly, she'd assumed her father would always be here. He seemed to be made of stone, and stones didn't die. William Ross was a difficult man, but he was the only parent she had.

She wished Matt were here so she'd at least have a comforting hand to hold on to. She had to tell him she didn't blame him for confronting her father. This was her fault. She should have told him Matt was back.

As the ambulance had raced away, Matt had merely told her to go ahead and be careful not to drive so fast she killed herself, assuring her he'd see about Will.

Amidst all the commotion, she'd nearly forgotten about her son. She told herself he should have been her first concern. He'd come rushing downstairs at the noise, and seeing his grandfather lying there on the floor must have conjured up terrible images about Ben for him. What would she have done if Matt hadn't been there? But then, if he hadn't . . .

No, she couldn't blame him for this. He didn't have to hide from her father or anyone else. Her father had over-reacted, brought this upon himself. She still stung from his calling her a whore. Matt was the only real man she'd ever slept with. The only man she'd ever slept with by her own choice.

If anyone had ever made her feel cheapened, it had been Ben. His frustration over his failure to please her had stemmed not from her lack of response, but his failure. Perhaps if he'd touched her with less precision and some degree of caring . . .

She understood love now, and she was determined to love Matt and Will *and* her father. But her father was going to have to resign himself to her finally living her life on her own terms. Was he punishing her the only way he could now? By threatening to leave her?

At least she knew Will was in the best possible hands: his father's. Over the past weeks, she'd seen the bond between them sealing. At times, feeling left out, she'd been almost jealous. She supposed mothers experienced that kind of mystical connection with their daughters. But she'd never had a mother to share it with. Maybe some day she'd have a little girl.

She pushed the thought away. If having Matt meant giving up her dreams of having more children, she was willing to make the sacrifice. After all, she already had Will.

Didn't Will have a right to understand his true relationship with Matt? She didn't want him to grow up fighting the gnawing emptiness she'd known. Ben had had his own reasons for marrying her, not all of them selfless. How much did she really owe to his memory? Nothing would diminish Will's love for him, she realized.

Right now, she couldn't think too much about the future. Without being told, she knew her father had suffered a heart attack. And she was aware the next few hours would be crucial for him.

Exhausted, she propped an elbow on the plastic chair's narrow armrest. Her forehead dropped into her palm.

When she looked up, Matt was standing over her.

'Oh, God, Matt, I'm so glad you're here.' She stood, then fell into his strong arms. He held her tightly, then eased her back into her chair.

'Any word yet?' he asked.

She shook her head.

'Do you want something to drink or eat? I know you haven't eaten.'

'I don't think I could.'

He dropped into the chair beside her. 'I couldn't bear the thought of you sitting here alone. I took Will over to Leeann's.'

Alarm ignited in Sierra's eyes.

He gave her a reassuring smile. 'Leeann loves kids. She'll take as good care of him as I would, probably better since she knows how. And he and Sally and Tanner are keeping each other occupied. He can bunk down there for the night, and I'll bring him back to your place with me in the morning.'

'That's right. It's me she hates.'

'It's not that way. She thinks she's upholding my honor by resenting you. If she knew you, things would be different. Just like your father. He took one look at me and all he could see was a man from a lower class defiling his daughter.'

'I'm sorry. I shouldn't condemn Leeann. I didn't mean to speak so harshly. I'm just tired of everyone around us trying to mold our lives when they couldn't possibly know how we feel. Do you think this town will ever change so people can just be free to love each other no matter where they come from? Do you think the world will ever change? Christmases come and go and everyone pops off about peace on earth, and it never comes. By January, they've all forgotten.'

He clasped her hand firmly in his larger one. 'I've never paid that much attention to what people think. Used to be real important to me, whether people liked me. But you know, it's how you feel about yourself when you're all alone that matters.'

He wrapped an arm around her shoulders and drew her over to him. She rested her head against his chest.

'You're dead tired,' he noted. 'Why don't you just close your eyes for a while? I'll wake you if the doctor comes out.'

Her eyes were already closed. 'I'm cold, isn't that funny?'

Her rubbed his hand over her arm. 'Nerves, darlin'.' He wrapped the side of his jacket over her. 'You'll warm up in a minute.'

'Matt?'

'Hmm?'

'This isn't your fault.'

'I kind of believe it is. I charged into the house thinkin' your father and I had a score to settle. After the way things were this weekend, I wanted to get things out in the open and over with. Maybe I overstepped my bounds, but I never imagined just seeing me would infuriate him. I am sorry about that. You said you'd talk to him. I should have held back until then.'

His words sounded far away as Sierra drifted into a restless sleep.

When she awoke, Matt was shaking her gently, and she grew aware of someone standing over them. Realizing it was Dr Abernathy waiting to speak to her, she righted herself, combing her hair with one hand.

'How is my father?' she asked bracing herself for the worst. 'It must be bad if they called you.'

'Your father's had a heart attack, Sierra, and it is serious, but I think he's going to make it. But, as I told him weeks ago, when his heart condition was diagnosed, he's going to have to slow down. He needs surgery, and now he may not have any choice about taking time off to have it.'

'He knew he had a heart condition?'

'Yes. I assumed he would have told you.'

'No, he didn't.'

'He's resting in the CCU. He's been asking for you, and ordinarily I wouldn't allow him to have visitors until morning, but he seems quite anxious about speaking to you. You can go see him, but only for a few minutes.'

She rose, straightening her sweater.

'Thank you,' she said.

'I'll take you to him.'

Taking a last look at Matt, who flashed her a reassuring smile, she accompanied the family doctor down the wide, unfamiliar corridors.

Her father, ashen-faced, was lying in a bed, covered only by a thin white sheet and surrounded by glowing monitors.

Dr Abernathy left her there.

'Sierra?' her father called.

'Yes, it's me, Father. Dr Abernathy says you're going to get better.'

'What does he know? I've never felt so miserable.'

'You've got to take better care of yourself.'

'Sierra, can you ever forgive me?'

'I know you spoke in anger. Seeing Matt must have been a shock. He's a good man. You were wrong about Ben; you could be wrong about him too.'

'I was always so afraid you'd turn out like your mother. I thought I could shield you from it. She was so beautiful. Men were always looking at her.'

'You should have been flattered.'

'No, she flaunted herself, wanting them to look. I gave her everything, Sierra. But she was so much younger than I was. She had a wild streak in her. Once you were born, I thought she might be happier.'

'You don't have to tell me all this. All couples have problems.'

'I do have to tell you this, so listen because they'll kick you out of here soon. And I may not be here in the morning.'

'Father, you are going to live.'

'Whether I do or not, it's time I got this off my chest anyway. I always intended to tell you the truth about your mother one day, but the longer I waited, the harder it got.'

'What truth?'

'I came home early from a business trip and I found her with a younger man, a factory worker, entertaining him in high style right there in my house. I was angry, but I still loved her, Sierra. I knew I stayed away too much, neglecting her. But I was willing to work things out. She told me she was going back to Mexico. I told her if she left it would be without you.'

Sierra clutched fingertips to her throat. 'My mother is alive? She's been alive all this time, and I've never seen her?'

She trembled with anger and betrayal.

'Sierra, I was trying to do the best thing for you. It was her choice. She could have stayed.'

Her fury was too strong for her to speak without aggravating his condition. How unfair of him to confess this when she had no means to retaliate.

'I can't talk about this now,' she said. 'I'll see you tomorrow. And you will be here.'

She walked slowly back towards the waiting room. All her illusions about her father struggling to raise her alone, missing his beloved dead wife, her mother, loving her too much because she was all she had, crumbled. Yes, her mother could have stayed in her husband's house where he'd control her and make her pay over and over for her unfaithfulness. Sierra's knees weakened. How could her own father have betrayed her so?

Reaching the waiting room, she leaned against the wall and looked for Matt. When she couldn't spot him, her heart sank even further. She'd been counting on him to hold her, console her, make love to her until she felt sleepy and tranquilized and everything grew fuzzy in her mind.

But he wasn't here. She realized she'd been depending on him, just as she'd always relied on her father and then Ben to take care of her. And now when she'd allowed herself to need him the most, he wasn't here for her. Wasn't it just like Matt to run off?

Feeling more alone and abandoned than she ever had in her life, she knew she should have expected it.

CHAPTER 14

Leeann met Matt at the front door.

'Sorry I had to call you away from the hospital, Matt,'

Matt dismissed her apology with a quick nod. 'Where is he?'

His sister pointed towards the old oak tree near the fence.

'Thanks.'

In the darkness, he didn't see anyone out here, but he made his way over towards the fence. Finally, he discerned the outline of Will's slim figure propped against the base of the tree-trunk. Matt sat down on the ground beside him.

'I hear you're giving my sister a hard time,' he said.

'No, sir,' the boy replied. 'She's been real nice. I like Sally and Tanner too. I just needed to be by myself for a while.'

'I like to be alone when I've got something on my mind.' Mike pointed up at the expanse of stars overhead. 'There's something about the trees and the stars lets you know there's got to be a plan to things. If you promise not to go anywhere farther than this tree, I'll leave you be.'

'I don't mind if you stay.'

'All right.'

'Do you really think all those stars have something to do with us?'

Matt took a second look, pondering the boy's question. How many times had Ma told him some things in life were determined by the stars and the planets, things beyond his reach? Maybe he didn't believe the stars or the rising sun had anything to do with him, but he'd always carried in his heart the knowledge that she found him special. Without realizing it, he'd held on to that belief through all his father's goading and the town's low esteem of his family.

Her faith had made him believe he could do a good job for Sam, it had sent him to college at night, it had given him the confidence to be able to earn a living wherever he went. He seldom felt lucky, but Ma's love and hope had sent him a long way.

'Well,' he replied. 'Sometimes if you look at them long enough, you understand more about how you feel inside.'

'How long do you have to look at them?'

Matt chuckled. 'Takes some of us longer than

others. Will, the doctor says your grandfather's probably going to be all right.'

'Why was he so mad?'

'He doesn't like the idea of me and your ma being friends.'

'Why? Why doesn't he like you?'

Matt chose his words carefully. 'I guess because my family doesn't have much money. He's afraid your ma will marry someone who can't take care of her properly.'

'Mom says *she's* taking care of us now. Grandfather doesn't approve of that either.'

'That's something the two of them will have to settle between themselves.'

'Grandfather says Mom's being ob-stin-ate. He says she's being stubborn at my expense. I should go back to private school where I can make friends with the right people.'

'Is that what you want?'

'I like living in the country with the horses and playing with Luke. I like my school.'

'Well, your grandfather has a right to his opinions, but it's up to your ma where you go to school.'

'Grandfather wants me to come and live with him. He made me promise not to tell Mom about it.'

Matt's fury rose. Although he was ashamed of being angry with a man who was lying helplessly in a hospital bed, he resented the man's scheme to manipulate the kid, pit him against his mother.

'You know your ma doesn't want to live with him. When people grow up, they get a mind of their own and they need to live their own way.'

'Grandfather wants me to come by myself.'

'Is that what you want?'

'I don't want him to be mad at me. But I can't leave Mom by herself. She's been sad for a long time, since before Dad died. Sometimes I think she didn't like him much. He made her cry a lot. She likes the ranch, especially since you came to help her.'

Sierra tried so hard to see the best in people; she had accepted her father's attempts at reconciliation as a gesture based on love. She needed to be warned what her father was up to, but considering his condition, this was no time to confront her with the ugly truth.

'Can he make me leave Mom?' Will's voice was small in the night.

Matt didn't know what to tell him. He longed to reassure the kid, yet he prided himself on being truthful. William Ross was a powerful man. From what Sam had told him, he'd driven his own wife out of the country. He could afford to hire shrewd lawyers, and Sierra was on shaky financial ground.

'I don't know. But I know your mother would fight to keep you with her.'

Will blinked rapidly. 'I don't want them to fight.

Matt, when I saw Grandfather on the floor, I thought he was dead, and I almost wished . . .'

Matt looped an arm around the boy's shoulders. 'But you know you didn't mean it, and wishes never make anything happen, Will. Your grandfather put you in an uncomfortable situation, and he should have known better. It wasn't your fault. Human beings aren't always programmed to think nice, happy thoughts. It's what you do that counts.'

If Matt had a lump of coal for every time he'd wished his daddy would pull away in the rig and never come back, he'd have enough fuel to heat hell for the rest of eternity, he reflected. His own words haunted him. It's what you do that counts. Were Sam and Sierra right? Was he still acting in response to the old man instead of what he really wanted? Had he denied himself a home, backed off from fighting for the only woman he would ever love because he was still running away?

Being a kid wasn't easy. Matt couldn't help wondering who would be around for Will through the coming difficult years. Sierra couldn't even see her father for what he really was, and William Ross was too concerned with maintaining his family image to consider anyone's best interests but his own.

He rubbed his whiskers, suddenly craving a cigarette. But he declined giving in to it.

'Come on,' he prompted the boy gently. 'Let's

turn in. You'll have to get up early so you can ride home with me when I go to work in the morning.'

Sierra slept little that night. Bone-tired, she lay in her bed, her eyes wide open. She tried to push from her mind the memory of Matt's having been here with her, the joy of their uninhibited lovemaking. She couldn't think of him now, but he seemed to have left an indelible impression between the sheets.

She beat on her pillow with a fist, as if to drive him away. With Will gone, the house felt strangely quiet and empty. All her life, she'd never doubted her father loved her, no matter what he did. She'd always been precocious enough to understand that he had to be away on business trips for weeks at a time, leaving her with a housekeeper. She viewed him as an important man with serious work to do. And he never forgot to bring back something nice for her.

Now, she knew he had entrusted her to the care of paid strangers at the same time as he'd deprived her of the real and special care of her own mother.

When she was little, she had enviously watched other girls at school with their mothers fussing over them, straightening their dress collars and braiding their hair. Left to the impersonal ministrations of the hired help, she'd tried to pretend she had a mother of her own, but it wasn't the same.

Maybe that was why she'd always ached to have

children of her own. To know at least one side of the relationship she'd missed.

'Damn it,' she said aloud, bolting up suddenly and punching the pillow.

Seeing what her father had done to her, resenting him for going too far in controlling her life, loomed too uncomfortably like looking in a mirror. How could she condemn her father for doing something to her he'd told himself was in her best interests when she was doing the exact same thing to her own son?

Could the mistakes of her life ever be untangled? In her heart, she admitted Ben had wanted to marry her because his parents approved of her family, because being seen with her boosted his shaky ego. That was why he'd been willing to overlook the fact that she was pregnant. Because he knew she wouldn't have married him if she hadn't seen pressed by circumstances. And she'd handed him the means to hold her to him. Ben had loved Will because he was still a child himself. He'd lacked the strength to be a real father, to place the boy's welfare above his own interests.

Ben's parents had always treated Will with a reserved detachment. Mrs Davenport had made thinly veiled comments about her newlywed son rushing immediately into parenthood. From the moment will was born, Mrs Davenport had always appraised Will as though searching for something, some sign of her son in him. No, the Davenports had always been skeptical about Will, never embracing him as a grandson even though he was the only one they'd ever have.

She didn't owe it to anyone to perpetuate her lie. Matt and Will both deserved the truth.

She recalled how Matt had disappeared tonight when she'd been counting on running into his arms. Matt had a history of turning tail when things got tight. First, she'd have to endure his anger over her lie. She anticipated the depth of his disappointment and accepted it. She was feeling the same thing now.

And then Matt would have to deal with the reality of having a son he'd never wanted. Will looked up to Matt, so she hoped Matt wouldn't react by shutting him out.

Her skin broke out in a cold sweat. She dreaded the inevitability of telling him the truth. Yet she looked forward to freeing herself from the lie she had locked herself into out of fear and intimidation so many years ago.

'What in the world . . .?' Sierra mused as the bleating of a strange sounding horn sounded out front. Sounded more like a bicycle horn than a car horn. Curious, she set down the flour canister and measuring cup, pausing in her half-hearted attempt to bake Christmas cookies.

Racing to the front door, she swung it open to

find Matt, clean-shaven except for a mustache and dressed in a top hat and tails, perched atop a pretty white carriage shining like new from fresh paint.

She rushed outside. Grinning, Matt tipped his hat.

'Matt . . . it's wonderful. You look wonderful.'

Matt's heart twisted at the sight of Sierra's face lighting up. This was the first time in days that he'd seen her smile. Ever since her father was hospitalized, she'd been sullen and distracted. Now, she glowed through the flour-smudges on her nose and cheeks.

'Your carriage awaits, ma'am,' he invited with a tip of his hat.

Incredulously she ran her hand along the rim of the carriage. The edges were trimmed with a line of gold paint.

'This is the old carriage Sam had in his barn?'

'I fixed it up some.'

No wonder she'd scarcely seen him the past few days. He must have been working at Sam's every waking hour he wasn't with the horses.

'Where'd you find that get-up?'

'Duncan.'

'But these aren't my horses,' she noted, inspecting the team. The quarterhorses' bridles were trimmed in evergreen garlands.

'Sam's letting us borrow them. They're trained to

harness. Next year, we'll get an earlier start. It'll give me time to train yours.'

Next year? she thought. Would he still be here next Christmas?

'You look absolutely dashing,' she said. 'I can't say I miss the beard.'

'I can't say I do, either. Hop up, Sierra. Might be your only chance between now and Christmas.'

She hesitated. 'I have cookies in the oven.'

'Turn them off.'

'All right. I'll be right back.'

She disappeared into the house and returned quickly, this time wearing her denim jacket. She climbed up beside him.

Matt gave her a long, appreciative look. Reaching up, he swiped flour from her face with his thumb. His touch sent warm familiar ripplings through her.

Aching, she turned her eyes away. She loved him so much she thought her heart would burst. Too much for her own good, she thought. She wanted him in her arms, in her bed. But she was too deeply ashamed of her deception to feel worthy of his lovemaking. Each time she was with him and didn't reveal the truth, she realized, she drove her lie deeper.

Matt wondered what he had done to make her so edgy and withdrawn around him. Naturally, she was worried about her father, but he'd hoped she'd come to him, allow him to comfort her as best he could. Once her father was recovered, he was going to have to tell her what he was up to and what Sam had said about her mother possibly being alive. He was a reluctant messenger, afraid once again that Sierra's loyalty to her father would override her judgment, that she would refuse to believe him.

But he loved her and Will both too much to not at least try to warn her.

'How's your father doing?' he asked as the horses set the carriage in motion.

'Splendid. He's too cantankerous to remain imprisoned in a hospital for long. Dr Abernathy says he'll probably be back home for Christmas.'

Everyone wanted to be back home for Christmas, Matt reflected. Big deal. He'd never had a home to try to get back to.

'Where are we going?' she asked.

'To my house,' he replied.

She raised her dark eyebrows in surprise.

'It's really not very far from here.'

'Your old house?' she asked.

He nodded. 'I don't even know what happened to it after Ma died. Probably some other family living in it. I ran off and I never looked back. Maybe it's time I did. You don't mind going there, do you?'

'I'd like to see it. It's part of you.'

Matt laughed lightly. 'Whether I like it or not? Just like my family?'

Sierra cast him an encouraging smile. 'You never forgive anyone who hurts you, do you?'

'I've been trying, Sierra. Sam's made me see I've got to. We've been talking a bit while we worked on the carriage. I'm beginning to think it's just too hard. This is the first time I've really tried to let go of it, but things keep coming back and leaving a bitter taste.'

Sierra thought of her own father. She recognized even now that only forgiveness would free her, yet a cold and cheated part of her shut out her ability to feel affection or even sympathy for him. He'd gone beyond his rights in keeping her and mother apart. In keeping her and Matt apart.

'What about me, Matt? How much can you forgive me for?'

'I believe you never intentionally wronged me, darlin'. It's different.'

Sierra closed her eyes. Would he still feel that way when he knew the rest?

'Matt?'

'Hmm?'

'Do me a favor?'

'What?'

'Don't call me darlin' any more.'

He eyed her quizzically. Strange request, but he figured maybe Sierra had some notion the endearment encroached on her independence. Woman had some funny ideas these days.

'All right,' he consented.

Surprised and relieved when he didn't ask why,

Sierra couldn't bring herself to explain she always wondered how many other woman over the years he'd referred to by this casual endearment. She couldn't tolerate being just any woman to him.

Matt guided the horses down the gravel road that had always seemed so much longer, the road that always shook under the weight of Daddy's rig.

He brought the horses to a stop in front of what was now no more than a concrete foundation.

'I'll be damned!' he exclaimed.

Sierra silently appraised the remains of the house where he'd grown up. She studied his drawn expression and wondered what was going through his mind.

Reaching out, she covered his hand with her own. 'I'm sorry, Matt. Do you want to get out?' she asked softly.

'No,' he replied. He let out a deep breath. 'I'm glad it's gone, that no one has to live there now.'

'You don't have to live there any more either,' she reminded him.

'I wish I didn't. You know the land on Sam's place where we went camping?'

'The land by the creek.'

'Sam insists he's leaving it to me.'

'I'm not surprised. Sam's always thought very highly of you.'

'I thought I didn't want the responsibility, but

now it's kind of comforting, the idea of having something of Sam's.'

'I have something back at the house I want you to have. I meant to save it for Christmas, but I'd like to give it to you now.'

'Sierra, I didn't get you anything. I . . .'

'Matt, I don't expect a gift from you. I know what you're doing for Leeann's family. We should go.'

He leveled his gaze on her.

'I thought we'd head down Main Street.'

Shock registered in her eyes. 'I'm not dressed for . . .'

'You look terrific. But if you'd rather not . . .'

'No. Let's go. I can't wait to see everyone's face when they see this carriage.'

But she knew people would be looking at more than the carriage. This would be the first time she and Matt would be seen in town together. She couldn't have been prouder.

'Hold on,' he said.

Half an hour later, she was laughing uncontrollably as he drew the horses to a halt at her place. The carriage had turned so many heads, Sierra had felt she was in a parade. Leaning over, she planted a kiss on Matt's smooth cheek, loving the feel of his hot cheek against the cool air.

His eyes caught hers, and the yearning inside her intensified. But she didn't have the right . . .

'Come on inside for a minute,' she invited.

He followed her into the house and sampled one of her cookies while she went to retrieve the gift she had for him.

'I haven't had a chance to wrap it properly,' she apologized, handing him the flat package wrapped in brown paper.

Matt began tearing the wrapping off. The phone rang, and Sierra went to answer it.

He heard the distant sound of her voice as he uncovered the oil painting, a portrait of Sam in his younger, vibrant days, the glory of Texas's vast blue sky and open spaces in the background.

Staring at it, he swallowed a thick lump in his throat. His normally steady hands were shaking.

Sierra returned. 'That was someone wanting to rent the carriage for a party tomorrow night,' she reported brightly. As she glimpsed his solemn expression, her tone dropped. 'Like it? The newspaper had an old photo of Sam on file and let me borrow it. It's the first thing I've done in a long time, and I'm afraid it's not my best work.'

'It's fine, Sierra. Real fine. Thank you. I didn't think there was anything I wanted for Christmas until I saw this. I love it. When did you start working on it? This must have taken you a long time.'

'After I heard you were back in town. I thought it was for me, you know. I worked on it in secret because I wasn't sure how it would turn out. It was meant for you all along, Matt. I gradually realized that.'

Staring at it, he shook his head. 'No one's ever given me anything this special. I don't know if I can let Sam go, Sierra.'

A tug in her heart sent her across the room to him. 'The portrait's to remind you you don't have to.'

He looked up at her, his eyes tinged with a mixture of happiness and sadness.

Hooking his free hand around her shoulders, he drew her close, kissing her with an exquisite, bittersweet tenderness that made her tremble inside. Fierce longing gripped her.

He pulled back, his eyes piercing as they probed hers.

'I know I've never given you any reason to believe in me. I want to be someone you can count on, always.'

The phone was ringing again. Sierra looked towards the kitchen. Propping her chin in one hand, he forced her eyes back to meet his.

'Don't answer it,' he urged. 'What's wrong, Sierra? Have I done something?'

'I've been concerned about my father,' she said. 'That might be about him, Matt. I'd really better answer it.'

Matt wasn't convinced her father was the only thing worrying her. He watched her go to answer the phone.

'I'll be in the barn,' he said and walked out the door.

The scent of pine hit him as soon as he walked through Leeann's front door. A huge, symmetrical tree took up about half of the living room, its branches dripping with lights, ornaments and tinsel.

'We got a Christmas tree,' Tanner announced proudly.

'And Mama says Uncle Dylan's coming,' Sally told him. 'Whoever he is.'

Matt turned to his sister, who was standing in the kitchen doorway, beaming.

'Where'd the tree come from?' he asked.

'Your friend Sierra sent it over. She called and said she wanted us to have it for taking care of Will the other night. I couldn't very well turn her down.'

'Dylan's coming?' he asked.

She pushed a handful of her hair back. 'He called and said he'd try to make it. He wasn't sure he could get away. He's running a marina down on the coast and said something about fishing charters. I can't imagine anyone wanting to spend Christmas Day fishing.'

'I can.'

'That's all of 'em, Matt. They're all coming.'

'I'm glad, Leeann. I know how much you want this.'

'You'll be glad too, Matt, when they get here.'

'I don't know. I have this bad feeling about it I can't shake . . .'

Matt walked into the diner, scanning the booths and tables until he spotted his mother behind the counter, refilling the plastic ketchup containers. Her white uniform bore fresh coffee stains, and wisps of her hair had escaped from her tightly coiled blonde hair. She looked thin and tired. Still, she managed a smile when looked up and saw her son approaching.

'Shouldn't you be out at Sam's place?' she asked.

Matt slipped on to a stool at the counter. 'I already talked to Sam. I'm leavin', Ma.'

She kind of froze for a split-second, then continued her work. She sighed heavily. 'I knew this was comin'. I thought it would have been sooner.'

'I think it will be easier for you, with me out of the way. Daddy won't be so mad all the time.'

'He's never done right by you. But it's not his fault, Matt. It's mine.'

'It couldn't be.'

Her face softened. She suddenly looked younger, and a dreamy look came into her eyes. Matt realized how much Lester Rollins had stolen from her. 'I wish you could have seen your Daddy when I first met him. He was handsome and funny and teasing. Oh, he was a smooth talker, all these big dreams he had. Somewhere along the line, those dreams died. He worked and worked and one day he realized that was all there was. You think you love someone, and one day you wake up and you don't even know him any more, but there's nowhere else to go. What I'm trying to tell you, Matt, is, as much as I wanted to, I couldn't make him do differently.'

'It's not your fault. But there's nothing here for me any more.'

'Where will you go?'

'I haven't decided.'

She got her pocketbook from under the counter, carefully opening the zipper compartment of her cracked plastic wallet and extracting a sheaf of bills so thick Matt's eyes widened in amazement.

She handed the pile to him. 'Take this. It will help you make a start somewhere.'

'I can't take your savings, Ma.'

'I've been stashing it for you. It's precious little to give ya'. Please take it so I won't worry so much about you.'

Reluctantly, he accepted the money. 'I'll pay this back,' he promised.

'You can if you like, but you don't have to.' She smiled sadly. 'You're going to be rich and successful one day, you know.'

'Ma . . .'

'It's in the cards. Your Daddy's always sensed it, and he's jealous of it instead of being happy for you like he should be. Matt, he sees in you everything he never was. Do you understand that?'

'No.'

'Well, think on it while you're away. You'll be happy one day if you let yourself. I'm sorry for both of you. Don't be like him Matt. Don't build a wall between yourself and the rest of the world.'

'Will you be all right, Ma?'

'Yes, son, thank you. I know you're never comin' back. I don't expect you to. Do what you have to do. I just want you to be happy.'

Matt gave her a hug. Within months, he'd sent money back to repay her. But that was the last time he saw his mother.

CHAPTER 15

The night was frozen and still, pale moonlight illuminating the landscape, stars dotting a pure black canvas overhead.

Matt had spent a long night ferrying holiday revelers around in the carriage. His muscles ached and a dull exhaustion was beginning to set in. Still, as he was putting the horses up, he felt good. The cash was pouring in – his money and Sierra's. He was even going to be able to pick up a couple of presents for Tanner and Sally. Leeann had been worried about their not having anything this year, and she'd die before she'd accept charity.

Sierra appeared in the barn like a ghost emerging from the shadows. She was wearing jeans and a fleece poncho that draped her like a heavy veil.

At first, he didn't notice her. When he spotted her, his body jerked in surprise.

'You shouldn't go sneaking up on people, Sierra,' he chided, resuming his work. 'Why are you wandering around here so late?'

'I couldn't sleep.'

'Worrying about your father?'

'He'll be home soon. It wasn't him I was thinking about. It was you.'

'I'm nearly done here. I've missed you, Sierra.'

'You've been working so hard. I hardly see you any more. I've missed you too, Matt. The happiest moments of my life are the ones we've spent together.'

'Sierra, I want us to be together for the rest of our lives.'

'Don't say it, Matt.'

'Something's changed for you, hasn't it? Since your father got sick.'

'It's not what you think. I found out my father's deceived me through my entire life.'

'About your mother?'

She nodded. 'How did you know?'

'He was saying things about her when he had his attack, remember?'

'The other night, I guess he thought he was going to die. He told me my mother isn't dead. They had an argument and she went back to Mexico. He used his influence to see she never had any contact with me. Somehow, he managed to have their marriage annulled. Which makes me illegitimate, I guess.'

'Sierra,' He started towards her, but she waved him off, folding her hands across her chest.

'I'm not trying to evoke your sympathy.'

'But if you think past what he's done, you'll see what the truth has brought you. You can find your mother now, now that you know to look for her.'

She shook her head back. 'I wonder if it isn't too late. For the past thirty years I've been raised as an Anglo, to believe that's what I am. My father didn't just deny me my mother, he denied me my heritage. I have no concept of being Hispanic. I never thought of myself as being like any of the Mexican people I've known. Being half Mexican was like an amusing novelty, like a birthmark or a dimple. If I ever did locate my family, I probably wouldn't fit in with them.'

'You won't know that unless you try. I'll help you look for her.'

She shook her head. 'If I do it, I'll do it on my own. I've been going to the hospital every day out of duty. My father did raise me. But there's an emptiness where I used to feel love for him.'

'I don't know if you can really love someone you can't trust. He betrayed you. Deception is a hard thing to get over.'

She sighed heavily, the vapor from her breath puffing into a small cloud over her mouth. 'I don't want you ever to feel that way about me.'

Matt tensed. Suddenly, he sensed what was coming, something he'd guessed and stubbornly lied to himself about for a few weeks now. He'd refused to believe Sierra capable of such enormous treachery unless he heard her confess to it.

'Why should I?' he asked. His heart was pounding like a tom-tom.

She plucked a piece of hay out of a bale. 'You were the last person on earth I ever wanted to hurt. When I told my father the truth about us, I knew he'd find a way to destroy you if I didn't do what he wanted me to. And I couldn't see any other way.'

'I think we've been through this before,' he replied impatiently. 'It's late, and I'm very tired. You don't have to explain again why you married Ben. Unless there's more to the story than you've already told me.'

She dropped her eyes. 'I married Ben because I was pregnant with Will. With your son.'

The shadows played in his eyes. Sierra stepped back.

'I had a right to know,' he said evenly.

'You never wanted children.'

'At that point, what I wanted was past being a consideration, wasn't it? God damn it, Sierra, the decision wasn't yours alone, any more than your father had the right to take you away from your mother.'

'I know that now. I made a terrible mistake.'

She was crying. But her tears didn't soften Matt's stunned, mounting anger.

'I defended you. Leeann guessed the truth, but I

said no, you would have told me if I'd gotten you pregnant. Maybe I could buy that you were scared and believe you needed your father and Ben back then. But even now, with Ben dead, you waited to tell me the truth. You let me make love to you and couldn't even acknowledge the truth. You let me get close to the boy thinking he was Ben's son.'

Whirling, he slammed his fist against the barn wall so hard that the barn shook. Sierra gasped and jumped back. The horses neighed in protest.

'Would I ever have learned the truth if I hadn't come back here?'

She faltered. 'No.'

'That's what I thought. I'm through here. Goodnight.'

'Your hand,' she said. His knuckles were raw and bleeding.

'It'll heal,' he assured her. Quickly, he raced past her and disappeared into the night. She heard his pickup roar to life and stood alone to face the bleakest moment of her entire life. Only a miracle would ever bring him back to her.

Matt mashed down on the gas pedal, his tires spewing gravel as he drove through the night, his head pounding. He cursed himself for ever coming back, for allowing himself to get involved with Sierra again. When it came to manipulating people, she was just like her father. All this time, she'd known the truth and kept it from him. Just when he'd dared to believe he'd found someone he could trust . . .

By instinct, he found himself at the creek. He parked the pickup off the road and got out, making his way down the banks in the darkness – he knew the path by heart. It was one of those things he'd never forget.

He sat alone in the dirt near the spot where he'd first claimed Sierra, discovered the love he'd believed was his alone. Everything had gone so miserably wrong.

Through the collage of bare branches overhead, he could see a scattering of stars. Taking a deep breath, he heard the creek's rushing water.

Damn it, he should have guessed. Sierra had been wrong, but he knew this was his fault as well. And he couldn't blame this one on his father. He'd been too quick to believe Sierra had been trifling with him, when he'd known in his heart she loved him. Instead of uncovering the reason behind her hasty marriage to Ben, he'd run off.

He cradled his forehead in his palm. The air here smelled of the woods, and it was a scent he would always associate with Sierra's body and the sweetness of making love to her.

Shifting, he raked a hand through the soil. Here he was, thirty-two years old, and nothing belonged to him. He should have made something of himself by now instead of drifting from town to town, never building anything or forming any ties. Sam had started out with little education and no money and built an empire by devoting himself to a place.

Thirty-two years and he had nothing to show for it, except the money he'd saved. Living as he did, his expenses were minimal, so he'd had a broker invest his extra money for him. He wasn't even sure how much there was. He'd have to check. Maybe enough to start some kind of business somewhere.

He thought of the thin, dark-haired little boy he'd grown so fond of. The boy who thought Ben Davenport was his father. That hurt.

He didn't know what kind of father he would be. But he knew he loved the boy too much to ever treat him with the indifferent contempt his father had lavished upon him. Would Sierra tell him the truth? If she did, would Will be disappointed, horrified, repulsed?

Or would Sierra let Will continue living a lie, just as her father had let her live one? Knowing now how far she was capable of carrying her deception, he wondered whether he should leave deciding what to tell Will up to her.

Maybe his Ma had been right. Fate was mapped out on some celestial chart, a plan in which he and Sierra were destined to live apart forever. He didn't think he could ever look at her again without seeing the phony she was.

Leeann's living room smelled of furniture polish, pine, fresh baked cookies, and the bayberry-scented candle a friend had given her as a Christmas gift. The floors were scrubbed and the furniture vacuumed. Still, Leeann was fluttering from one room to another, straightening things here and there, wiping away imaginary dust.

'Take it easy, Lee. This place looks good enough to entertain royalty,' Jerry Wilton cautioned his over-anxious wife. He was sitting in a rented wheelchair in one corner of the living room, a cane propped against the wall close by his side. A handmade quilt was tossed over his legs.

Although he was still pale from his ordeal, Jerry was a handsome, vital man, with broad shoulders on a medium frame and short clipped dark brown hair. He had a quick smile and sparkling hazel eyes that lit up each time he looked at his wife.

'I want everything to be just right,' Leeann told him. 'I'm so excited. I can't believe this is really happening.'

'You'll wear yourself out too much to enjoy seeing your family. Please stop, baby. Watching you makes me feel worse that I can't help you.'

'Jerry Wilton, I want you to know havin' you home is everything I need right now. I mean it, even if none of 'em shows up. And I don't think I'm ever gonna let you out of my sight again.'

Jerry laughed. Whatever Leeann did or felt, she went to the farthest extreme.

She crossed the room, leaning down to embrace him, resting her head across his chest. 'This isn't too much for you, is it, baby? I mean you just got home and maybe you'd rather have peace and quiet inside of my whole family flockin' in here.'

He smoothed her hair back with one hand. 'I've had more peace and quiet than I can stand. And I've always wanted to meet your family. Especially if they're like Matt. I don't know how I can ever thank him for lookin' after you and the kids.'

She shook her head. 'We'll find a way. But don't go makin' a big deal over it or you'll embarrass him. Anyway, I'm kind of worried about him.'

The front door slammed and Matt came in with Sally and Tanner, all three red-faced and breathless from playing kickball.

'Worried about who?' Matt asked as he stepped inside.

Leeann turned. 'You, big brother.'

'What's to worry about?' he asked. 'I told you I'm all right with this reunion. I just hope you're not going to be disappointed. Has Dylan called back again?'

'No. I'm just keepin' my fingers crossed about him. But Darcy and Gage will be here for sure.'

'Matt, what's wrong? You're as restless a bobcat. And you quit workin' for Sierra just when the two of you were making so much money with that carriage . . .'

'Sierra will just have to look out for herself. That's what she says she wants to do anyway, so I'm giving her the chance.'

Little lines creased Leeann's brow. 'That doesn't even sound like you. Did something happen?'

'I don't want to talk about it.' His glance swept through the room. 'This place looks great. Is there anything I can do to help?'

'Just make sure you're not trackin' dirt in.'

The phone rang. Leeann raced for the kitchen. 'I bet that's Dylan now,' she said.

'I guess I'd better go get cleaned up,' Matt mused aloud. 'Can I get you anything before I jump in the shower, Jerry?'

'No, thanks. Leeann's been waiting on me hand and foot. She's about to wear herself out.'

Matt nodded. 'She's got a heap of energy, especially when it comes to taking care of people she loves. She gets it from our ma.'

'Your mother was a good woman. I'm glad I had the chance to know her before she died.'

Leeann's head popped around the kitchen door frame. 'Matt,' she said. 'Phone's for you. It's Jamie Burke.'

Foreboding shot through Matt, his heart waning

as he moved towards the kitchen. He could think of only one reason Sam's granddaughter-in-law might be calling him. And it wasn't good.

His normally steady hand was shaking as he lifted the receiver.

'Matt, I know it's Christmas Eve. I wouldn't take you away from your family if this could wait. Sam's been in the hospital a few days now, and he wouldn't let us tell anybody. It doesn't look like he's going to make it home again. He wants to say goodbye to you. Can you come down here tonight?'

Matt knew the woman on the other end of the line was crying.

'But he was just . . . I'll be right there,' he said.

Replacing the receiver, he hung his head. To see Sam for the last time would be the hardest thing he'd ever done. He hadn't stopped to realize it would come down to this. Despite the grim picture Sam had painted, he'd never stopped hoping. Now, reality washed over him. Time had played out and hope was gone.

Leeann came up quietly behind him. 'Are you all right, Matt?' she asked.

'No,' he answered, raising his head. 'But there's nothing anyone can do about it. Listen, Leeann, I hate to run out on you with everyone coming, but I've got to go. Sam's dying.'

Leeann's eyes flared. She twisted her hands and bit her bottom lip. 'Oh, Matt. I'm so sorry,' she said.

'Yeah, so am I.'

'Go on. I know ya gotta.'

Matt didn't even stop to get his jacket as he raced out to the truck. Knowing Sam, he'd held out requesting his presence until the last possible minute. He'd never forgive himself if he didn't arrive in time.

As he drove, tears wetted his face. He was oblivious to the soft Christmas carols playing on the radio. Damn Sam for dying. Damn Sam for making him do this. Maybe they weren't kin by blood, but Sam had been more to him than the man who sired him.

He ran fingers across his cheeks. Sam would feel real bad if he saw Matt crying like a baby. And Matt refused to do that to him.

'Silent Night' was playing on the radio. Matt grew aware of the song and heard the words, 'Sleep in heavenly peace.'

Heavenly peace. It was the best he could wish for for Sam now. For the first time he realized that, like his mother, he had believed all along that there was more to life than the dirt beneath his boots and things he could reach out and touch. Forces beyond human understanding moved people.

And he tried to console himself with the knowledge that Sam and his Annie would be together for Christmas.

The winter cold settled into his marrow, despite

the truck's heater blasting. Matt felt lost, alone, and tired of wandering. God help him, he wanted Sierra.

'Will?' Sierra called as she came in from the barn. It was getting colder outside, and she'd had to use the bottoms of the metal feed buckets to break the coating of ice forming over the horses' water.

'I'm here, Mom,' Will called from his room.

Pulling off her gloves, she walked down the hall and stood in the doorframe. Will was sitting at his computer, the monitor glowing before his face.

'You'd better start getting ready if we're going to go over to your grandfather's.'

'I don't want to go,' Will complained.

She folded her arms across her chest. 'Why not, honey? It's Christmas Eve. I'm sure your grandfather has lots of presents for you.'

'I don't care. Mom, why did Matt leave?'

Sierra studied the floorboards. For the past few days, she'd been struggling to not think about Matt.

'He decided he wasn't happy working for us any more. Did you need him for something?'

'I need to talk to him.'

'Well, I don't think he's coming back. You know you can talk to me about anything.'

Will's face creased with worry. 'No, not about this. I have to talk to Matt. Did I do something to make him mad?'

'No, I'm afraid I did.'

'What?'

'It's a grown-up thing I can't explain.'

'You treat me like a little kid. Matt doesn't.'

Sierra took a deep breath. 'Sometimes people start caring about each other a lot. But then they find they have differences and don't really love each other.'

'Like you and Dad?' he asked.

Sierra blanched. What did she expect? The lack of love in their house in the years before Ben's death had been nearly solid enough to touch.

'Oh, Will. We tried very hard to give you a good home.'

'You should marry Matt. He's crazy about you.'

'Being crazy about somebody is not enough reason to marry them.'

'You've always said if people have differences they should talk and work them out. That's what you said when I got in trouble at school.'

'Well, you can't punch other boys out just because they tease you about being in a play.'

'Matt said I should stick up for myself.'

'Matt doesn't go around hitting people.'

'Don't you miss him, Mom?'

She clutched her stomach. She missed him so much she felt ill. Never would she love another man the way she loved Matt Rollins. Never would she experience such joy in a man's arms as she did in his.

But she knew he'd never forgive her.

She felt tired and worn down. Maybe she should just put the place up for sale and let her father support them. Everything she did was wrong. Maybe she just didn't have it in her to give her son the kind of life she wanted for him. Like Ben, she'd been pampered all her life. If she'd been stronger, she could have helped him save himself. She wouldn't have sat back and watched him destroy himself. Maybe she didn't know how to accomplish anything on her own.

The phone rang.

'Go take a bath, Will. Your grandfather just got out of the hospital, and he shouldn't have to spend Christmas Eve alone.'

She went to the kitchen to answer the phone.

'Hello?'

'Sierra?'

Immediately, Sierra recognized Leeann's drawl. For Leeann to call her, something awful must have happened.

'Yes, Leeann. How are you?'

'Look, I'm sorry to bother you with the holiday and all. I've only got an inkling of what's been goin' on between you and my brother all these years, and I know y'all haven't been gettin' along like you were these past few days. But I know my brother, and I know he loves you beyond all caution.'

'Leeann, I know you don't like me, and I appreciate what you're trying to do, but Matt and I have problems a rush of sentimental holiday cheer won't solve.'

'I don't really know ya' enough to dislike ya', Sierra. Under different circumstances, we might like each other. The thing is, all my life I've watched my brother get kicked around, and I've been amazed at how he's always bounced back. He deserves someone who'd be real good to him. But he's always wanted you.'

'He doesn't now. Put your mind at ease.'

'He needs you, even if he's too mule-headed to admit it. I owe him, and that's why I'm callin' you, because I know his pride will keep him for doin' it himself. Whatever's happened, I hope maybe you can put it aside for a while. Matt's goin' through somethin' real bad right now.'

'What is it, Leeann?' she asked with alarm.

'He's at the hospital with Sam.'

'Oh, God. Thank you, Leeann. Thank you.'

She replaced the receiver.

She doubted Matt would ever want to see her again. Yet he needed someone tonight. She couldn't leave him alone to face losing his mentor. Even if it meant risking anger and rejection, she had to be there for him.

'Will,' she called. 'Hurry, son. Don't worry about your bath. I'm going to have to drop you at your grandfather's while I take care of some business.'

CHAPTER 16

The acrid smells of the hospital burned in Matt's nostrils. He looked down on Sam, small and shrunken in the bed, plugged into monitors and bottles. Pain was etched in the old rancher's weathered face despite the barrage of drugs intended to mask it.

'I knew you'd come,' Sam said, his voice barely audible, fading out.

'You should have let them call me sooner, Sam. I wanted to be here.'

'I don't want a lot of moanin' and cryin'. I had a good life, Matt.'

'I don't know where I would have been without you.'

'Thank you for bein' a part of it. I want ya' to know you've never let me down.'

'Yeah, I did, Sam. I stayed gone so long . . .'

'Don't make no difference. You're here now. Matt, I lied when I told ya I didn't care what ya do with that land. You take it and make yourself a home. Show this town what you're made of.'

'Sam, I don't know . . .'

'I won't make you promise. Wouldn't be fair. I've always believed in you, Matt. Enjoyed watching you grow into a man. But I'm gonna have to give it up now. Time for you to start believin' in yourself.'

With tremendous effort, he raised a gnarled hand from beneath the sheets.

Matt took hold of it. Sam's grasp was cold and weak, but nevertheless, Matt drew strength from it.

'Ya better go now,' Sam said. 'We've always understood each other, and neither one of us likes scenes.'

'Goodbye, Sam. I love you.'

'I'll be watchin'. Take good care of yourself, son.'

Dazed, Matt staggered out of the room. Duncan and his wife and parents rushed passed him to be with Sam.

As the corridor cleared, Matt saw Sierra standing before him, materializing like a dark-haired angel in her fuzzy white sweater. At first he thought he'd merely conjured her image.

'Sierra?' he asked.

'Leeann told me about Sam. I'm sorry, Matt.'

Matt stepped forward, reaching out and folding her into his arms. For the moment his bitterness evaporated. He had to hold on to something real right now, and that she was here was all that mattered. She held him close for several minutes, feeling his pain and wishing she could ease it somehow.

Finally he drew back, gazing into her eyes.

'You're so beautiful,' he said. 'You looked like an angel standing there in the hallway.'

'But I'm not an angel. I'm just a human being, flawed like everybody else.'

His arms were still around her.

'Sierra, I don't think anything on this earth could ever make me stop loving you.'

'Then don't. Please, don't.'

He shook his head sadly. 'I can't get past it. God help me, I have tried, and I can't.'

Sierra closed her eyes. 'I did it to spare you, Matt. That's the only reason. I've paid for what I did. All those years with Ben . . .'

'It's not you. It's me. I know why you did it. Only there's a part of me holding back from you now, and I don't think it's going away. Having reasons doesn't always make things right. Tell me, does Will know?'

'No.'

'Are you going to tell him?'

'I don't know.'

'I want him to know, but I reckon raising him alone all these years gives you the right to decide about that. No reason why I should suddenly start interfering now, after you worked so hard to keep me out of his life. Were you afraid, Sierra, that I'd be the same kind of father my old man was?'

'No, Matt.'

He nodded. 'Well, considering everything, there's no reason for me to stay on here. I've got some money saved, and I've got a call in to my broker to find out if I have enough to keep Jerry and Leeann going until he can get back to work. I'll be moving on. I'll contact a lawyer about arranging support for Will.'

'You have no legal obligation.'

'I'm not talking about the law. I'm talking about what's right.'

'If you want to do what's right, you'll stay nearby. Will needs you. Even tonight, he was asking for you. He said there was something he wanted to discuss that he couldn't confide in me about.'

Matt released her, his expression darkening. He had to tell her. 'Your father is trying to take the boy away from you, Sierra.'

'What!'

'When they were in New York, he told Will he could come and live with him even if you insisted on staying on the ranch. Will is terrified he'll have to leave you, and the old man made him swear not to tell you.'

'You've known this and didn't tell me?'

'It was the night your father had his heart attack. Will was real upset and Leeann couldn't get through to him. That's why I had to leave you at the hospital alone. Will was worried he'd caused his grandfather to get sick because he was wishing something would happen to keep him from making him go live with him. At the time, I didn't want to give you another thing to worry about. Besides, you've always sided with your father at my expense. I didn't even know if you'd believe me.'

Her hands rested on her hips. 'You knew about my mother too. I don't know how, but when I told you about it, you knew what I was going to tell you.'

'She came around trying to see you when you were a baby. Sam mentioned it the other day. That was the first I knew she might be alive.'

'You knew how much that would mean to me, yet you neglected to tell me that?'

'I couldn't see the point in giving you false hope. Besides, that was all I knew of the story. I didn't think telling you was the best thing for you.'

Her eyes blazed with black fire. 'Well, you're just as much of a damn liar as I am. We're quite a pair, aren't we? Just go, Matt. Run as far as your truck can take you. You can send all the money you like, but I'll just send it back. Will and I aren't taking anything from you.'

He gave her a long, accusing look. He wanted to feel her against him again, tell her he was sorry. But there was no point in it.

Turning, he was out the door and headed into the dark, cold night. A shooting star arched across the sky. Matt stopped his march towards his car.

He stared up at the sky incredulously. Everything was as still as if the sudden brilliant light had never appeared. That made three.

'Ma?' The word fell from his lips. His eyes stung. He'd lost everyone who'd ever believed in him.

Nature's fireworks made a fitting farewell tribute to his old friend, he reflected. He took his hat off.

'Goodbye, Sam,' he said into the silent night.

Matt fished in his glove compartment for the pack of cigarettes he'd stashed there. Taking one out, he lit it and smoked thoughtfully as he headed back to Leeann's. He felt numb inside. Although he knew Sam was gone or soon would be, he'd never felt the rancher's influence as strongly as he did now. A man who lived by his own standards had an essence, a dignity to him no circumstances could strip away. Sam would always be with him, and Matt intended to hold on to that for the rest of his life.

By the time he'd reached Leeann's house, he'd nearly forgotten about the reunion until he saw all the cars parked outside. A late model white Cadillac stood out among the rest. Which one of his siblings did that belong to? he wondered.

Before getting out of the pickup, he considered driving around until they all left. Then he thought of Sam and he remembered his advice about facing the past head-on. This would be a start. Besides, he didn't want to disappoint Leeann.

As he approached the front door, his sister sprang out like a jack-in-the box clown before he could open it, pushing him back with a hand against his chest.

'What the . . .?' he muttered before she shut the door. 'It's cold out here, Leeann.'

She looked at him oddly. 'First time I ever heard you complain about the cold.'

'Is everybody here? Let me in. I want to see them, really.'

'Wait, Matt, listen,' She stood between him and the door. 'This didn't work out exactly as we'd planned. Matt, Gage never understood how things were . . .' she babbled. 'He didn't mean any harm.'

'What's going on?'

'Daddy's inside.'

She stepped aside. Matt looked incredulously from her to the door, then back again.

'Gage knew where he was and called him. He wanted to surprise us.'

Matt gave her a low look. His first impulse was to turn and walk away, as he always had when he'd been on his way home and seen the rig out front.

But something raised his hand to the doorknob. Maybe it was Sam. He didn't know.

He opened the door. Daddy was sitting at Leeann's dining room table. Matt couldn't have said whether he was more surprised by actually seeing him again or by what he was wearing – a gaudy plaid suit and thick gold jewelry dripping from his fingers, his wrist, his neck. A belt buckle as big as Texas adorned his gut.

Daddy's mouth was twisted in the same sneer Matt remembered, but tonight it didn't bother him. He was too drained to raise his defenses.

No one in the room seemed to be breathing. Matt swept his gaze to the corner where Gage and Darcy stood, looking more like strangers than the kids he grown up with. Behind them was a herd of people he didn't know – Gage and Darcy's families, he suspected.

Eyeing his brother and sister, he cracked a grin. 'You two are a sight,' he said.

Darcy, looking prim and more graceful than he recalled, ran to him first, sweeping him into a warm hug, laughing and crying at the same time. Matt turned to his little brother.

He reached out to shake hands, then, muttering, 'Aw, hell,' he swept the kid into a hug.

Suddenly, everyone was talking at once, Gage introducing his girlfriend who come with him from Austin, where he was a clown on a cable television show. Darcy'd brought her husband, an architect she'd met working her way through graduate school, and their three children – three-year-old twin boys and a ten-month-old daughter.

Lester Rollins sat quietly at the dinner table, sipping his beer. Matt knew he'd have to speak to him, but he wasn't in any rush to do it.

Suddenly, he looked around. 'Where's Dylan?' he asked.

Leeann shrugged. 'I haven't heard from him.'

Matt saw a shadow cross his father's expression and he knew why the old man was here. He hadn't changed and the way things were hadn't changed. They never would. But Matt was different. It didn't matter too much now how his Daddy was.

'Well, let's go ahead and eat without him,' Gage suggested. 'I'm starved.'

Gage and Darcy had added food they brought to everything Leeann had cooked, and there was a staggering spread on the table. Matt hadn't realized how hungry he was until he started eating, washing his food down with a cold beer. He entertained the thought of getting good and drunk tonight, but he didn't want to defile Sam's memory that way. And the blissful anesthesia of tonight's high would wear into tomorrow's hangover.

Gage drew him aside. 'Matt, I'm sorry,' he said. 'I didn't stop to realize Daddy bein' here might make you uncomfortable. He lives in some little town the other side of Lake Travis. Since he saw me on television, he's started dropping by the apartment from time to time.'

'What's he doing watching kiddie shows?'

'He's married again, got a young wife with a couple of kids from another marriage.'

Matt shook his head. 'Seems like he should be home with them tonight.'

'I figured he'd bring them.'

'Maybe he didn't want his new wife to find out how good he is at raising kids.' He looked at Gage. 'Sorry, Gage. I know he was a little better with you and Leeann. What's with all the gold?'

'He won the lottery last year. A couple of million at least.'

At the irony of that, it was all Matt could do to break out laughing. He raised his long neck in the air. 'Merry Christmas, little brother. Let's do this again next year.'

'Are you serious, Matt?'

'Sure. Why not?'

'I didn't think you and Dylan wanted anything to do with any of us.'

'I can't speak for Dylan, but I'm glad to see you again. One of these days, we'll have a long talk about why I left.'

Matt finished his dinner and took in the scene. He wanted another cigarette, so he stepped outside, heading for his usual smoking place beside the fence.

Just as he took in the first drag, looking out over the fields and letting himself relax, his father came up behind him.

The sound of his voice startled him. 'I've brought you a gift, Matt,' he said.

Turning, Matt stared down at the envelope the old man held out to him.

'Go on, take it. It's not a trick.'

Matt clasped his hands over the paper. Tearing open the seal, he extracted a check for a thousand dollars.

He laughed. In a heartbeat he would have traded this for a football jersey nineteen Christmases ago.

'Thanks,' he said. 'I didn't get you anything. I didn't know you were coming.' He saw the old man's eyes watching the road.

'Gage wanted it to be a surprise.'

Matt realized it hadn't occurred to the old man he might not want to see him. He didn't even know what he was . . .

'Gave every one of you kids a check just like this,' he boasted.

Conscience payments, Matt reflected bitterly. 'Too bad Leeann didn't know she was getting this weeks ago when she was worrying over medical bills and how she was going to give her kids a Christmas.'

'I lost touch . . . I didn't know.'

The old man was still watching the road, waiting to see Dylan, the son he adored. The son who wasn't coming. How many times had they watched up the road for *him*, when Mama ran out of money and didn't know when he was coming back? Matt looked at the man who'd once towered over him and the hatred he'd harbored so long melted into pity.

'You were never in touch with any of us. We were like little toys you played with when you were at home. I don't think we were ever a part of your life,' Matt said, tossing his cigarette to the ground and crushing it out with his boot heel. 'All I ever wanted to do was be able to love you, and you gave me reason after reason not to. Well, yes, you won. I don't love you. God knows why, but Ma did. All I can do is believe there was something good in that.'

'Things were tough when you kids were growin' up, Matt. There's things you can't understand.

'No. The problem is, I always understood too much.'

Lester pulled a box of cigarettes out of his shirt pocket. He flipped it open, offering one to Matt. Matt shook his head. 'Lost my taste for 'em. Do you have a pen? I want to go ahead and sign this check over to Leeann so I can leave first thing in the morning.' He glanced at his father's face and saw nothing of himself in it. 'You should be with your family tonight. If you'd asked me, I could have told you Dylan wouldn't come.'

A light dusting of snow covered the ground the next morning. The crisp, cold air smelled of it.

'I'll be,' Matt mused as he stepped outside with a coffee mug in one hand. White Christmases were nearly unheard of here. His Ma might have said it was a sign, but Matt's heart was too heavy to dwell on the past. Leeann and Jerry and the kids would be all right. Sam was gone, and Sierra and Will were lost to him forever. Christmas or no, it was time to move on.

He set the coffee mug on the porch and collected his two duffel bags and Sierra's portrait of Sam. As usual, he was traveling light.

He stowed the bags in the back of the truck, throwing a tarp over them in case of rain or more snow.

When he turned, Leeann was standing on the porch in her pyjamas, robe and slippers. She was leaning against the house with her arms folded.

'Tryin' to sneak off without sayin' goodbye?' she asked.

Matt reddened guiltily and feigned innocence. 'Just getting an early start. I didn't mean to wake anyone.'

'The kids will be up in a minute. You've got a phone call, Matt. It's Sierra, and I think you'd better talk to her. She sounds scared.'

Matt's features tightened as he zipped into the house and grabbed the telephone in the kitchen.

'Sierra?' he asked.

'Oh, Matt, I'm so glad you're there. I was afraid you'd gone. I don't know what to do, and there's no one else I can call. Will's gone.'

'Gone?' he asked.

'I woke up, and he wasn't in his bed. I've

searched all around the place. I know he's left because Thunder's not here either. I'm afraid my father may have taken him. Last night, I told him I knew he was trying to take Will and I'd never let him do it. We argued.'

'Sierra, your father's still weak from a heart attack. And Will knows better than to take off with him without telling you.'

'What should I do?'

'I'll be right over. We'll keep searching the place. He couldn't have gone far. Have you checked Luke's house?'

'Luke's family hasn't seen him either.'

'Hold on, Sierra.'

'Thank you, Matt.'

Puzzled, Matt hung up. It didn't make sense for Ross to steal the boy now when he possessed the means of taking him legally. And Ross would have at least told Sierra where Will was so she wouldn't worry herself senseless.

Fear jabbed his gut. If anything had happened to Will . . . No, he refused to lose anything more. He tried to imagine himself ten years old again. What would possess a boy to run away Christmas morning when there were cookies in the house and presents to open? A disappointment so bitter none of that mattered? Something more must have happened last night that Sierra either didn't know about or wasn't telling him about.

Where would he go? Matt would have hung out in the woods, or gone someplace he knew he'd be safe, a place like Sam's. But Will didn't have a Sam.

He set the phone down and spun to find Leeann standing anxiously behind him. She had dressed hastily in jeans, a sweatshirt, and tennis shoes.

'What's wrong?' she asked, trying to read her brother's face.

'Will's missing. I'm going over to Sierra's to help her look for him.'

'I'm going with you.'

'Leeann, you need to be here with your kids.'

'Jerry's here. They'll be fine until I get back.'

Matt didn't have time to argue. And maybe one more person combing the woods would help.

'Come on.'

He cranked the pickup and headed up the road.

Leeann, in the passenger seat, turned to look behind them. 'Where'd that old dog come from?' she asked.

Matt glanced in the rear-view mirror. When he saw the mutt chasing the truck, he stepped on the brakes.

'What's wrong?' Leeann asked.

'That's Thunder, Will's dog.'

He got out of the truck, stooping and calling the animal to him.

When the dog came, wagging its tail, he straightened, scanning the surrounding area.

'Beats me – I don't see him.'

Leeann turned her attention to the back of the pickup, raising a corner of the tarp Matt had thrown over his bags.

'Matt, I think you'd better come look.'

Matt looked down. Will blinked up at him like a caged rabbit.

'What in the devil are you doing in there?' he demanded. 'Your mama's half crazy wondering where you've gone. You can't just take off whenever you get the notion to.'

Will threw the tarp back. 'You do,' he countered evenly.

'There's a difference between you and me. Your running off would break your mama's heart. Have you been outside all night?' He took his jacket off and threw it over Will's shoulders.

'And it's all right if you leave and break her heart? She was crying last night when she told me you were leaving.'

'Will, there's a lot you don't understand here. I don't fit in here, and I never will.'

'Then I guess I don't either.'

'Why is that?'

'I heard Grandfather talking to Mom last night. He didn't know I was listening. I was hiding in the kitchen because he and Mom were arguing. Mom said she was going to tell me you're really my dad, and Grandfather got real mad.'

'Oh, boy,' Matt said, drawing in a deep breath. He felt Leeann's eyes on him, but he couldn't look at her.

'When we were going home, I asked Mom if that was true. She said yes, a long time ago she was in love with you but Grandfather wanted her to marry my other dad, and you were sad and didn't know about me, so you went away.'

Matt's chest constricted. 'That's how it was, Will. Your ma told you the truth.'

The boy's eyes flooded with tears. 'But now you know about me, and Mom loves you. So why are you leaving us?'

Matt searched his face. 'I don't know,' he said quietly.

'Is it because you don't want to be my dad?'

'Will, this doesn't have anything to do with you and me.'

'But you're leaving me too.'

Leeann reached out and touched Matt's sleeve. 'I'll walk back to the house and call Sierra,' she volunteered. 'Why don't you take your son home?'

Matt nodded. 'Come on, Will,' he said, helping him out of the pickup. 'You and me and your ma have some serious talking to do. And don't you ever run off like that again, you understand?'

'Yes, sir.'

Sierra was sitting on the porch step waiting when they drove up. As Will ran out of the pickup, he raced into her outstretched arms.

'Why did you run off?' she asked him, her face tear-stained.

'So Matt would have to bring me back,' he replied.

Matt gasped. The little con-artist.

'Go on in the house. Your breakfast is on the table. Matt and I need to talk.'

Will took a look back at Matt.

'I'll still be here when you get through,' Matt promised him.

Will disappeared into the house, leaving the two of them alone. Matt's eyes were dark, his expression rigid.

'What's wrong, Matt?' she asked quietly.

'No one's ever tried to stop me from leavin' a place before.'

'I would have, if I'd thought of a way how. My son's just smarter than I am. Our son.'

Matt reached out, cradling her soft, damp cheek in one large hand.

'I saw my daddy last night,' he told her.

'Was it awful for you?' she asked, clasping the hand he held over her face in her own.

'Not as much as I thought. He kept watching for Dylan, and Dylan never showed. I felt sorry for him was all. I guess I just let the rest go. There's no point in it anymore. Staying bitter, well, I just do to myself what he always did to me.'

'I'm glad for you, Matt.'

'You did the right thing, telling the boy the truth.'

'I'm not sure he totally comprehends it.'

'He knows enough.'

'When I found Will hiding in the back of my truck this morning, I realized I didn't know where I was headed or why. This is where I want to stay. With you, with Will. I want to be there for him the way Sam always was for me. Hard as it is to stay, going away would be harder. All Will did was bring me back a little faster than I would have come on my own. Sierra, I love you with all my heart, and nothing can ever change that. You're right, I thought I was protecting you when I kept the truth from you, so I can understand how you thought you were shielding me. I was wrong last night, when I said I could never get past what you did. If I could feel sympathy for my old man, I know I love you enough to work through the past. If you're willing. I know I've acted like a damn fool, and I have no more to offer you now than I did ten years ago. I can't give you any more kids or a fancy house or a lot of money.'

She looked into his eyes. 'You can give me everything that matters, Matt.'

'You never give up on anyone, do you? I want you with me all the time. I want to hold you every night, wake up making love to you.'

Sierra gave him a crooked smile. 'Is this a proposition or a proposal, Matt?'

Leaning forward, he cupped her face in both hands, drawing her up to meet his lips. His mouth fell over hers like a sunburst melting the snow.

Slowly, he drew back, still cradling her face. 'Marry me, *amada*,' he asked, his voice low.

A lone tear trickled down Sierra's cheek. 'I thought you'd forgotten you always called me that.'

'No, I've never forgotten. You never stopped being my beloved. But until now, calling you that hurt too much. Can you forgive me? I guess the only way to go home is to remember who you really are and who's important to you.'

'I'd be honored to be your wife, Matt.' Her tears came full force now, but they were tears of joy.

He put an arm around her shoulders. 'Let's go tell Will. Or would you rather tell him by yourself?'

'No way. We'll tell him together. Then we'll go tell our families.'

'Sierra?'

'Hmm?'

'Merry Christmas.'

'It's only the beginning, Matt.'

EPILOGUE

The gently sloping countryside was ablaze with bluebonnets beneath the April sun. Matt had never seen so many people gathered on Sam's place before. His place now. The only sore spot in his heart this morning was the rancher's absence.

He tugged at the rounded collar of his white shirt, scanning the crowd for the one face he needed to see. He was hardly listening to the man standing before him. 'Don't you ever read those quarterly reports I send you?' Matt's former college friend and broker Jeff Culpepper was asking incredulously. 'Of course sending them to you the way you move around has always been hit and miss. Don't you look at your tax return?'

Matt returned his attention to his old buddy. 'I never paid any mind,' Matt admitted. 'Didn't need the money for anything. Just thought I'd let it sit till I needed it. Is there a problem?'

'You told me to put all your dividends back into

investments,' Jeff reminded him. 'So that's what I've been doing.'

'I've got faith in you,' Matt assured him distractedly.

'You should, after all the money I made for you. I can't believe you've been working at odd jobs when for the past two years when you didn't need to be working at all.'

'Money does funny things to people,' Matt said, craning his neck to see William Ross appear over the horizon. The color had returned to his complexion, and he was looking well, now that Sierra had finally convinced him to slow down and stop trying to rule the world – herself and Matt and Will included. His future father-in-law had gone so far as to be coolly polite to Matt, but, as Sierra kept saying, he was coming around.

He turned back to Jeff. 'You're not kidding? Are we talking enough to build, say, a lodge, over there?' He pointed to the edge of the property.

Shaking his head, Jeff patted his shoulder. 'Look at your mail from now on, Matt. You might set your sights a little higher.'

Matt swept his blue gaze across the landscape, the rows of rapidly filling folding chairs. Leeann was sitting beside her husband, the cane he now walked with propped against his folding chair. Tanner and Sally sat beside them, looking terribly cherubic with their hands folded in their laps. Behind them sat

Darcy and her family, Gage and his girlfriend. Lester Rollins had sent his regrets and a fat check that Matt had shredded.

He waved at Sierra's mother, seated among a throng of newfound relatives who'd accompanied her from Mexico. Pride swelled inside him at the sight of Will in a western-cut suit and black cowboy hat, talking to his grandmother and trying to learn Spanish. The son he'd always wanted without knowing it. That he and Sierra had conceived a child who would link them forever was no accident, but fate, he believed.

Somehow, he was going to find a way to give Sierra the other children she desired, because he wanted that too. But he was waiting until the doctor told him something definite. He didn't want to give Sierra false hope. She'd shown him how to love, taught him how good it could be. God, she wanted him even knowing he'd probably never give her the children she longed for. Matt was so grateful he'd come back, that he'd dared to let her touch his heart again.

A firm hand clasped his shoulder. 'It's time, Matt.'

He turned and looked into his older brother's face. 'Thanks for coming, Dylan,' he said. 'I'm glad you're here.'

'I wouldn't have missed the chance to be your best man for the world, Matt. Listen, let's stay in touch, OK? I didn't think I could face everybody after running out on all of you.'

Matt gave a low laugh. 'We all ran, as fast and as far as we could. Now we've circled around and found each other again.'

As he looked over the horizon, he saw what he'd been searching for. His eyes feasted on the welcome sight. His dark-haired angel in white. She wore a fringed blouse above a long skirt teasing the tops of her knee-high boots. A net veil cascaded from the back of her broad-brimmed hat. She'd insisted on defying convention. Widow or no, nothing but white would do on their wedding day. Let people talk if they wanted.

His heart lightened as she graced him with a shy smile. He broke into a grin, and her own smile grew bolder.

'See,' Alison, trailing behind her friend, whispered. 'Remember, I told you he looked good.'

'Yes, he does,' Sierra told her matron of honor over her shoulder. She saw and heard only the man she would love fully for the rest of her life. A black cowboy hat topped his matching tails and printed silk vest. Although the beard had never come back, the mustache remained, and his brown hair still trailed over his collar. He looked perfect. Strong and tall and proud. Just as she'd always seen him.

Impatience surged through her. Dropping her

bouquet of yellow roses and baby's breath, she bolted.

'Sierra, where are you going?' a bewildered Alison demanded. 'You're not supposed to go to him now. It's bad luck.'

'Don't believe in it,' she shot back.

Racing towards, Matt, she whooped as he grabbed her by the waist and dangled her in mid-air.

'You are wild,' he said, laughing with her as he set her on her feet and kissed her soundly.

'I couldn't wait, Matt. We've waited an eternity already. I've never felt so free,' she told him. 'Free inside myself.'

He took her hand. 'Come on, the preacher's waiting. And we've got a busy night ahead of us.'

Matt scarcely heard the words of the ceremony. They sounded foreign and faraway as he got caught up looking at the woman whose face he'd never tire of seeing. The words were for the others. He and Sierra had already committed their souls to one another. Now, all the world would know. Forever.

The gentle Texas breeze played over them, and in it Matt felt Sam's presence, like a quilt covering his heart. He knew his old friend would always be with him in spirit. Just as Ma was. Maybe there was something to be said for being born with the rising sun. Today, Matt felt destined for a future nothing less than glorious. Sierra had resigned herself to a life of hard work and limited means. He wondered how she was going to react when he told her she was going to have to get used to being rich again.

Plenty of time now, to hold her close and tell her so much. As Sam had said, all things come in their own time, and this was theirs. As Matt leaned forward to kiss his waiting bride, he knew he'd at last returned to the place where he truly belonged. Leaving had taught him to appreciate coming home, and he reckoned he'd be staying for a long, long spell.

THE EXCITING NEW NAME IN WOMEN'S FICTION!

PLEASE HELP ME TO HELP YOU!

Dear *Scarlet* Reader,

As Editor of *Scarlet* Books I want to make sure that the books I offer you every month are up to the high standards *Scarlet* readers expect. And to do that I need to know a little more about you and your reading likes and dislikes. So please spare a few minutes to fill in the short questionnaire on the following pages and send it to me. I'll send *you* a surprise gift as a thank you!*

Looking forward to hearing from you,

Sally Cooper

Editor-in-Chief, *Scarlet*

*Offer applies only in the UK, only one offer per household.

Note: Further offers which might be of interest may be sent to you by other, carefully selected, companies. If you do not want to receive them, please write to Robinson Publishing Ltd, 7 Kensington Church Court, London W8 4SP, UK.

QUESTIONNAIRE

Please tick the appropriate boxes to indicate your answers

1 Where did you get this Scarlet title?
Bought in supermarket ☐
Bought at my local bookstore ☐ Bought at chain bookstore ☐
Bought at book exchange or used bookstore ☐
Borrowed from a friend ☐
Other (please indicate) ____________________

2 Did you enjoy reading it?
A lot ☐ A little ☐ Not at all ☐

3 What did you particularly like about this book?
Believable characters ☐ Easy to read ☐
Good value for money ☐ Enjoyable locations ☐
Interesting story ☐ Modern setting ☐
Other ____________________

4 What did you particularly dislike about this book?
____

5 Would you buy another Scarlet book?
Yes ☐ No ☐

6 What other kinds of book do you enjoy reading?
Horror ☐ Puzzle books ☐ Historical fiction ☐
General fiction ☐ Crime/Detective ☐ Cookery ☐
Other (please indicate) ____________________

7 Which magazines do you enjoy reading?
1. ____________________
2. ____________________
3. ____________________

And now a little about you –

8 How old are you?
Under 25 ☐ 25–34 ☐ 35–44 ☐
45–54 ☐ 55–64 ☐ over 65 ☐

cont.

9 What is your marital status?
Single ☐ Married/living with partner ☐
Widowed ☐ Separated/divorced ☐

10 What is your current occupation?
Employed full-time ☐ Employed part-time ☐
Student ☐ Housewife full-time ☐
Unemployed ☐ Retired ☐

11 Do you have children? If so, how many and how old are they?
____
____

12 What is your annual household income?

under $15,000	☐	or	£10,000	☐
$15–25,000	☐	or	£10–20,000	☐
$25–35,000	☐	or	£20–30,000	☐
$35–50,000	☐	or	£30–40,000	☐
over $50,000	☐	or	£40,000	☐

Miss/Mrs/Ms ________________________
Address __________________________
____
____

Thank you for completing this questionnaire. Now tear it out – put it in an envelope and send it before 30 June, 1997, to:

Sally Cooper, Editor-in-Chief

USA/Can. address
SCARLET c/o London Bridge
85 River Rock Drive
Suite 202
Buffalo
NY 14207
USA

UK address/No stamp required
SCARLET
FREEPOST LON 3335
LONDON W8 4BR
Please use block capitals for address

COHOM/12/96